The Nightwood Song

A NOVEL BY

KEVIN FLANDERS

For Sherri,
Thanks so
much for
your support,

KEVIN FLANDERS

THE NIGHTWOOD SONG

Chapter 1

"I am not worthy of Heaven!" Grandpa shouted.

A tenth of a mile behind the pale blue station wagon driven by Evelyn Winters, St. John's Congregational Church had already been swallowed in a sea of fog. Glancing in the mirror, Evvie couldn't even see the steeple, the road ahead barely visible around an approaching bend.

Not five minutes ago, Evvie and her family had bid farewell to their fellow parishioners and stepped out into the gloom, Pastor Mahone's sermon having delivered the brightest light of the morning.

But now that light was quickly fading.

In the passenger seat, Grandpa gritted his teeth and cracked his knuckles. "I am weak," he said through trembling lips. "I have always been weak."

In the back seat, Sonny and Tobias Winters exchanged nervous glances. Something wasn't right with Grandpa. He'd been acting strange for several months – and sleepwalking almost every night this week. Just before dawn on Friday, heading downstairs for a glass of water, Sonny had bumped into his grandfather in the kitchen, his eyes glassy and faraway like those of Mama's dolls. Grandpa had muttered something about music, and yesterday morning Mama had found him in the dirt driveway, kneeling in a puddle and shivering and staring into the foggy woods.

This morning, after a lengthy search, Mama had discovered Grandpa at the edge of the woods, wearing only his long johns and a pair of worn slippers. He'd mumbled again about hearing music – carnival music in the woods.

And now this.

Mama whispered something to Grandpa, but he wouldn't listen, shaking his head adamantly.

"I am not worthy of Heaven," he quietly repeated. "Not until I confront my fears. Not until I–"

"God loves you," Mama blurted. "The Lord is merciful. Let us say no more."

"We love you, too, Grandpa," Toby added.

Nudging his little brother's leg, Sonny shook his head in warning. When Mama or anyone else spoke of God, you listened. It was better for everyone that way.

Fog-cloaked roads showed the way home in small increments. Their house was sequestered in the deep woods off Purgatory Road, accessible by a tire-beaten path that became a muddy bog in the springtime. During the rainiest stretches, Mama parked the wagon at the end of the driveway and they all piled into Grandpa's doorless pickup truck, which plowed through the mud like an old bull and jolted creakily over potholes.

Today the dirt tracks were frozen solid in the November gloom. Arriving home, the brothers wasted no time in getting changed for chores, Sonny removing his Sunday Best and hanging everything in the closet, then pulling a pair of patched, faded overalls atop his long johns.

"Don't forget to hang your suit," Sonny reminded, helping Toby undo his tie and shirt buttons.

"Uh-huh," Toby mumbled.

Sonny fetched his favorite flannel jacket from his side of the closet. Five years ago, when Papa had given him the jacket for his birthday, it had been far too big, the red and black checkers much brighter then, Mama calling it a foolish purchase, Papa, with a smile and a pat on Sonny's head, saying he would grow into it.

Now Papa was dead – and Sonny easily slid into the jacket, no longer needing to roll up the sleeves for comfort. It fit almost as good as his own skin, weathered by the seasons and the work, every scratch and hole telling a story. Sonny couldn't recall most of those stories, days moving quickly once the chores began.

Toby was struggling to work his suit jacket and shirt onto a hanger, Sonny helping him.

"Hand me your trousers."

Toby fetched the bundled trousers from the floor and tossed them to Sonny, who folded them precisely across the hanger.

"See, they go like this. The whole thing gets hung together."

Toby nodded like he'd done last week and last month.

"Don't forget your jacket. It's cold out there." Sonny ruffled his brother's wavy hair. "And your gloves, too."

The gloves in fact belonged to Sonny, Toby having lost his pair in the springtime. They'd been raking leaves still laced with ice and scooping them into wheelbarrows, each load hauled across the stream into the woods, Toby returning at the end of a run without his gloves, complaining that his hands had gotten too sweaty. The gloves had not been seen since that spring day, an extended search of the leaf piles in the shallow woods turning up nothing.

"Mama, we'll be in the woods fetching kindling," Sonny announced at the base of the stairs.

"Do you boys have your jackets on?" Mama called from the living room down the hall.

"Yes, Mama. Back in half an hour."

She didn't respond. A muffled series of moans escaped the living room, Sonny imagining Grandpa in his rocking chair in the far corner, his eyes glazed and distant. In recent months it had taken a while to get his attention sometimes, whereupon he'd blinked repeatedly and groaned as if awakening.

"Run along. I'll be out in a second," Sonny whispered to his brother, pointing to the front door.

THE NIGHTWOOD SONG

"But–"

"Go fetch the kindling box. Meet me in the driveway."

"I wanna stay with you."

Sonny yanked open the door. "Go, or she'll fix us both with whoopins."

Toby shrank away through the door, looking back once with nervous curiosity and then hurrying off to the shed.

Easing the door shut, Sonny turned back toward the living room, where Mama had taken a scolding tone with Grandpa.

"You need to stop this. You're scaring the boys."

"Stop *what?*" Grandpa said with exasperation. "I'm just telling you what happened, is all."

"Nothing happened. You were sleepwalking again – nothing more."

Sonny crept a little closer to the partially opened door, mindful of each step.

"I know what happened. I was wide awake," Grandpa maintained. "They challenged me, and I was too afraid."

"Who challenged you? What are you saying?"

"The woods. They–"

The living room door snapped shut, preventing Sonny from hearing more without venturing closer. He took a step and then another, but the thought of the belt stung him backward. Slowly, he receded down the entry hall and creaked open the heavy front door, then slipped onto the porch and clicked the oak door shut behind him.

"What were they saying? What were they saying?" Toby practically shouted as he scampered up to the porch, carrying the green plastic bin they used for gathering kindling.

"Quiet! Jeez, do you want the belt or what?"

"Sorry. Could you hear them?"

"Not really. Go on now, let's get after it."

"Can you carry the box? It's heavy."

Sonny accepted the empty bin, his brother jogging out ahead of him and scooping up pebbles. One by one he chucked them against trees as they crossed the driveway, then spanned the stream single file along the footbridge Sonny had rebuilt last year. Five hundred feet to the north, the larger bridge Papa and Grandpa had built for the dump truck was still standing strong, even after the bad flood two springs prior.

Later, Sonny would take the truck across the bridge to the woodyard, where Grandpa's stacks of logs towered eight feet tall in some places. Grandpa had shown Sonny how to work the chainsaw and the splitting maul when he was nine; last year, Mama had finally allowed him to learn the skidder, splitter, trucks, and loader, Grandpa acquainting him quickly with each rig. Some Saturdays they went dawn till dusk, only a few water breaks and lunch in between, and the pillow was always softest after those days on the skid road.

But now everything was different. Grandpa hadn't been out to the woods to help Sonny in almost a week, although it felt more like a month with all the jobs piling up.

"Remember," Sonny told his brother, snapping twigs off a low branch, "no pines. Pine don't burn for shit."

Toby scooped up a pair of fallen branches. "These ones are pine, right?"

"Yeah, stay away from the ones with the needles."

"Why don't pine burn?"

"It just don't."

"Is Grandpa coming out to help us?"

"I reckon not."

"Why?"

"Just mind your work."

With a huff, Toby cracked and crunched his way deeper into the fog. For many minutes their work was marked only by the incessant snap of twigs and hustle of kindling into the bin, tendrils of cool mist sidling along their faces. Sonny nearly fixed his brother with a reminder to keep the twigs straight in the bin – it always filled up too fast when he tossed them in haphazardly – but instead he straightened the kindling himself. Toby tended to get overwhelmed by too many reminders, better to have him remember a few things than nothing at all.

"What's wrong with Grandpa?" Toby said when they came together over the bin a while later, each boy with two fistfuls of kindling.

"He's just tired. He hasn't been sleeping well."

"Because of the sleepwalking?"

Sonny nodded, his brother dropping trousers and leaking against a tree.

"Why's he sleepwalking?"

"Don't know. It happens sometimes to people. He'll get through it."

"Why's he going outside when he sleepwalks?"

Sonny shrugged.

"Why'd he say he ain't worthy of Heaven?"

"Enough questions. Let's get back to work."

THE NIGHTWOOD SONG

Without providing sufficient time to drip-dry, Toby dampened his trousers and pulled his gloves back on. "I'm cold."

"Just a little while longer." Sonny wiped blood on his overalls from a nicked finger. "We're almost done."

"How much longer?"

Even the ravens grew weary of Toby's questions, an ominous duo lifting from a near branch and squawking off to the north, disappearing within a weft of fog.

After another round of questions, Sonny permitted his little brother to cut out early. But even though Toby hurried back toward the house, he didn't bring the litany of questions with him. They lingered around Sonny like the fog, no good answers to send them away, more and more questions creeping into form.

Why didn't Grandpa ask Sonny to play chess anymore?

Why hadn't Grandpa taken the brothers down to the pond for fishing since the summer?

Why had Grandpa said he wasn't worthy of Heaven?

"He hasn't been the same since Grandma died," Sonny murmured, but he knew this answer was no good. They'd buried Grandma over two years ago, and although the light had been stolen from Grandpa's eyes, he hadn't been frequently confused. He hadn't been taken by bouts of shouting and frustration. He hadn't abandoned his passions and his work. He hadn't sleepwalked.

But now Grandpa mostly sat in his rocker before the hearth and sipped from his thermos, Toby always asking why he drank coffee all day and night. Toby asked plenty of questions, Sonny providing the answers his brother needed, even if he wasn't sure of them himself.

Chapter 2

After filling Mama's kindling bag and heading inside, Sonny stoked the fire and got Toby fixed up with a hot chocolate.

"Are you boys hungry for lunch?" Mama called.

"Maybe later, Ma." Sonny crossed off a pair of items from the calendar tacked to the dining room wall. "I gotta fill that load for Mr. Foote."

"Is that a shipment or a pickup?" Grandpa said, squinting from the doorway.

"Shipment," Sonny read from the calendar.

"I'll help ya," Grandpa winced, pulling a jacket over his thick shoulders.

A smile glowed along Mama's lips. "Have fun, boys. Lunch'll be waiting in the fridge."

Even though Sonny had completed three wood shipments on his own that week, he instinctively allowed his grandfather to lead the way, watching as Grandpa awakened Big Bertha with a thunderous roar. Sonny couldn't help but smile each time the 1950 GMC dump truck growled to life, but this time his smile was a little wider.

No one knew why Grandpa called the truck Big Bertha. And no one ever seemed to get around to asking, not even Toby.

Across the bridge, in the woodyard, the fog was so thick that Sonny, working beside the shed, could hardly see Grandpa fifty feet away in the loader. An hour later, with Grandpa working the chainsaw and Sonny handling the splitter, they were almost ready to finish up the load for transport. There was great comfort to be found in the rhythm of the process, Sonny rediscovering the easy cohesion he'd always known with his grandfather, and in those perfect moments there was nothing wrong, no questions looming in the fog, no fears.

Resting briefly, Sonny felt a fleeting chill pass along his nape when he remembered being out here alone in the fog. It had been just him and the woods, wondering and worrying, no one to talk with and smell the resin with, no one to join him in the exhausted acknowledgement of a finished job.

"Are you okay, Grandpa?" Sonny managed once they'd loaded a cord of wood into the truck for Mr. Foote, who lived across town on Bradbury Lane, where the fog clotted even heavier in the state forest.

There had been panic in Sonny's question, as though he'd been choking on the words and could only breathe normally again if they were released. He didn't want to hurt Grandpa, didn't want to burden him, but he couldn't leave his fears unspoken.

"I'm right as rain, Sonny boy," Grandpa nodded from Bertha's torn, stained driver's seat, turning and patting Sonny on the shoulder. "Don't mind my little outbursts lately. Bad dreams, is all – you know how they can linger."

Sonny found himself nodding as well in the passenger seat; he wanted to say more, but those questions wouldn't map themselves out in his head. Anyway, Bertha was grumbling, impatient to shed her load at Mr. Foote's place. Then they had to get back and put a dent into the next load, less work tomorrow if you started on it today, Grandpa always said.

With creaky jerks and spasms, the truck trundled down the driveway and, brakes groaning, swung out onto Purgatory Road. The fog had thickened as the afternoon wore along, promising another moonless, starless night. Sonny dug into his mind but couldn't scoop out his last memory of the sun, a week of drizzle and fog and clouds having rushed them even closer to Thanksgiving.

"How's school goin', kiddo?" Grandpa asked a mile down the road. Sometimes he put on the radio – he enjoyed listening to ballgames and country music – but today he stared into the fog with an arm draped loosely over the wheel, looking as though he might nod off.

"Pretty swell," Sonny answered, searching for the road through the gathering gloom. "It's hard for Toby, though. They pick on him pretty good, make fun of how he talks."

"It can be tough, that age."

"Yeah, I keep saying he's gotta stand up for himself, but he don't. It ain't his nature."

"He'll find his way – and he'll be tougher for it."

Sonny nodded. They were passing the new road under construction, Route 31, which Sonny and Toby sometimes toured on their way home from school. The work crews had carved out another few miles of forest since Halloween, a swarm of machinery replacing tree stumps with freshly graded dirt each day, dump trucks lining up by the dozen to haul away the detritus. It was eerie going down that road some afternoons, with the road knifing deep into the foggy forest and eventually reaching a terminus of tall pines, as though the rest of the path had been swallowed by the woods and maybe you'd get gobbled up, too, if you ventured much farther.

"What do they need that road for?" Sonny asked his grandfather. Everyone at school had a conflicting theory, it seemed, even the teachers.

"New neighborhood, I suppose, just like the subdivision they put in a few years back in Engelhard."

"Are you sure it's not gonna be a mall…or maybe a drive-in?"

Grandpa chuckled. "They'd need people to drive fifty miles in order to have enough to fill up a mall. Out here, we barely have enough folks to fill the church."

"Did you always live out here?" Sonny said, surprising himself with the question. He and Grandpa talked all the time during chess and fishing, but somehow they'd skipped over some of the most basic facts.

"Moved up here from Frisco a few years after I met your grandmother. She thought we should stay in the city, but I was bent on following the logging boom up the rails. Pay was good for the time, and Grammy came to love it up here." His laughter rattled along with a stubborn cough that flared up in the mornings and at night. "Her parents, on the other hand – they hated this place. Grammy's mother called it *bucolic*, and I suppose that's the kindest term she could muster for these woods."

"What's bucolic?"

Grandpa waved a hand. "I forget – something to do with the countryside, I think. After a while, the mind needs to trash useless information in order to free up space. Lord willing, I'll forget that woman's name before long."

Their laughter rolled like the fog, and soon they were on the other side of the state forest, paralleling the railroad tracks on their way to Bradbury Street.

Randall Foote, a wisp of a man who walked with the assistance of two canes, hobbled down the porch to meet them. By the time he made it down the steps, Grandpa was already lifting the dumper and spilling the wood in the same clearing where they'd unloaded last year and the year before last. Long before Sonny joined the operation, back when it had been Papa in the passenger seat, Mr. Foote's biannual cord of wood had probably been dumped in this exact spot.

Even older than Grandpa, Mr. Foote was surrounded by his sons and grandsons, though he shook them away like puppies when they tried to guide him.

"Much thanks, as always, Mr. Winters." With a near toothless grin, Mr. Foote shook Grandpa's hand and passed him an envelope labeled: **CORD WOOD MONEY**, then fixed his smile upon Sonny. "And aren't you growing up quick, ya little whippersnapper. How old are ya, son?"

"Twelve, sir. Almost thirteen."

"Ha! You could've fooled me for fifteen, no doubt. I betcha all the gals at school would like a dance with ya." With a shaky hand, he reached into his coat pocket and handed Sonny a pair of quarters. "Keep up the good work, son."

"Thank you, sir."

The others were milling around and rearranging dirt with their worn soles, a pebble or two kicked about.

"You having yourself an early Thanksgiving, Mr. Foote?" Grandpa said, spreading an arm to regard the group.

"Wouldn't be a bad idea, but no, we brought the clan out today to search for a lost mutt," Foote answered. "Found the old mongrel not an hour ago, halfway to the Nightwood, I swear it."

A collective shudder seemed to whisk through the others, their relief palpable.

"Good on you," Grandpa congratulated. "Had that pup gone into the Nightwood with this fog, he never would've found his way out."

"Damn right about that." Foote blew into his craggy hands. "We've already lost two mutts to the forest, and about six cats."

"Ten cats," a heavily pimpled teenager corrected.

Foote nodded blandly. "You lose count after a while. Fog comes in 'specially heavy some mornings, and the cats don't never come back from critter-catchin'. No sen'sa direction for half of 'em, and the others get gobbled up by yotes and fishers."

"We put up a cross for all of 'em," a boy about Sonny's age added, pointing to the woods.

"Indeed," Foote nodded. "We got more crosses in them woods than our family plot at the ceme-tree."

Sonny glanced about. Fog-skirted and hilly, the property was an island peeking out from an ocean of redwoods and sugar pines. In the northwest, where the Nightwood lay, an even deeper fog poured over the hills, obscuring all but the tip-tops of the distant trees.

"Well, it was nice seeing you folks again," Grandpa said, shaking Foote's hand. "We best be getting back to finish up before supper."

"Always a pleasure, Mr. Winters." Foote nodded at Sonny. "And the young Mr. Winters as well. You boys stay warm now. Ms. Thiele up the road at Cedar Grove Farm says it's gonna be a real doozy of a winter – and she's never wrong."

After washing up before bed, Sonny helped Toby with his math homework and then finished his own assignments. Sliding into a pair of hole-torn long johns fresh off the line, he made his bed and redid Toby's sheets.

"Did Grandpa tell you more about the music?" Toby asked.

"What music?"

Toby was struggling to case his pillow. "The carnival music he heard in the woods this morning. He said the music's been calling him – and he needs to answer it."

"When did he say that?"

"While you were finishing with the kindling."

"He's been having bad dreams, is all. Just forget about it."

"But–"

"Here, toss me the pillow."

Toby chucked the pillow to him, the case sliding off midair and whispering to the floor. As Sonny fitted the case, Toby tugged on a pair of wool socks and pulled the blankets up snug.

THE NIGHTWOOD SONG

"There we are." Sonny placed the pillow beneath his brother's head and adjusted it just right. "Comfy?"

Toby nodded.

"Is your homework all packed?"

"Uh-huh."

"Want another blanket?"

Nods.

Sonny grabbed a blanket from his own bed and spread it over his little brother. "There. Warm?"

"Uh-huh."

Sonny patted his shoulder. "Love you, brother. Goodnight."

"Tell me a story," Toby requested per usual, Sonny clicking off the lamp and sliding into his bed across the room.

Outside, trails of mist pressed up against the window and then receded, not a light to be seen out there, nothing to disturb the expanse of fog-caped blackness.

"I want a scary story," Toby implored after Sonny began a tale about gold rushers and big dreams in the city.

"You'll have nightmares again."

"No, I won't."

"You will."

"I won't, I promise."

"Fine, then." Sonny tried to abscond with a tepid story of Bigfoot in suburbia, but it wasn't long before Toby called him on it.

"That's kid stuff. I want a real scary story."

Sonny knew he would regret it later, but he had a science exam tomorrow and couldn't waste precious hours telling one boring story after another. The first thing that came into his head was the thought of the myriad Foote family pets lost to the woods…and the crosses they made for each one…and the idea of those pets being chased down by coyotes in the Nightwood…coyotes with fangs as sharp as knives and eyes like–

"Did you hear that?" Toby blurted, Sonny knowing his story had done its job.

"Hear what?"

"Outside the door. It sounded like scratching."

"See? Now you're gonna have nightmares."

"No, I won't. I'm not scared!" Toby protested. "I really heard it. Go check."

"No. I'm comfy."

THE NIGHTWOOD SONG

"Please."

"Fine."

Sonny switched on the lamp and opened the bedroom door. "See? Nothing. Nothing at–"

Sonny feigned a yelp, pretending his arm had been grabbed, Toby screaming.

"I'm only faking. I'm fine. Toby, I'm fine."

Toby peeked out from the covers, looking as if he would cry. "That wasn't nice, Sonny. Wasn't nice at all."

"Boys, go to bed!" Mama shouted from the first floor. "I won't tell you twice!"

"Do you think a few of their dogs and cats got away from the coyotes?" Toby whispered a while later in the darkness.

"Probably. Now go to sleep before we both get whooped."

Sonny assumed he would be woken by Toby after a nightmare, but instead, coming awake just before dawn with a mean urge to piss, Sonny clicked the lamp and eyed his brother's empty bed.

Not bothering to put on his slippers, Sonny hurried barefoot down the cold hall, checking the bathroom and the guest room where Grandpa slept, even risking a peek into Mama's room, but he couldn't find his brother.

"Toby? Toby, where are you?" he whispered.

The stairs creaked noisily beneath him, as though every last tread were determined to see Mama's belt reacquaint itself with his backside.

"Toby? Are you down here?"

The first floor was dark and cold, Sonny flipping on a few lights and then a few more, but none of them revealed his brother. It wasn't until Sonny stepped onto the porch, shivering and scanning the quilt of fog, that he spotted Toby on the front walkway, barely visible thirty feet away…and only because of the candle he held.

"Toby, what are you doing?"

His brother didn't respond, didn't even move, just stared into the woods, eldritch shadows creeping over him in the candlelight.

"Toby, wake up. Come back inside."

Nothing, Toby's eyes open but unseeing.

Finally, when Sonny gently squeezed his brother's shoulder, Toby dropped the candle, the flame dying instantly in the mist.

"Can you hear it?" Toby murmured.

"Hear what?" For the first time, Sonny became aware of the chill seeping through his feet.

"The *music.*"

Even in the foggy gloom, Sonny was sure he could see his brother's eyes widening as he continued to stare into the woods.

"What music?"

"Listen," Toby urged. "There's a lady singing. Can't you hear her?"

Sonny held his brother by the shoulders. "You had a nightmare. Let's get you inside."

"No, I can still hear her. Listen!"

Sonny obliged, but all he could hear were the clandestine clanks and squeals of a distant train hauling timber to Truckee or Sacramento or Stockton, a train to be heard only by the earliest risers and a handful of insomniacs.

Sonny yawned and sighed out his frustration. Taking a lengthy piss into the front bushes, he tried to remember the periodic table symbols he'd spent an hour studying after dinner last night, but they were all scrambled up now, as nebulous as the predawn dark. Perhaps he was going to flunk this exam, and then he would have no one to blame but himself when the whoopin' came.

"I can't hear her anymore," Toby announced as Sonny dripped dry. "I think she's gone."

"Come on, let's get you back to bed. If Mama catches us out here, we won't be able to sit for a week."

Toby required no further coaxing, hurrying back into the house without looking back, Sonny grabbing the candle and easing the door shut behind him.

"I'm scared, Sonny. It was really scary," Toby whispered, pulling up the blanket tight.

"It was only a nightmare – and then an extension of the nightmare. The mind plays tricks when it's coming out of sleep."

"No, it was real. She was real!"

"Keep your voice down, will you?"

Toby got riled up again when Sonny tried to turn off the lamp.

"Fine, fine, I'll leave it on. Just go to sleep – please."

Toby was off to sleep again in ten minutes, breathing softly, but Sonny lied awake, rolling this way and that, sweating despite the cold, brooding about Grandpa's sleepwalking and now Toby's sleepwalking, both of them reporting music in the woods.

But neither Grandpa nor Toby had ever sleepwalked before. And no one had ever mentioned music in the woods.

THE NIGHTWOOD SONG

Abandoning hope for another hour of sleep, Sonny squinted into his textbook until the troublesome chemical symbols stayed with him. He'd breezed through them last night, but now, with tiredness and nerves, the process verged on physical exertion. For some reason the noble gases were especially pesky this morning, only six of them to remember, but Sonny kept forgetting one each time in spite of the mnemonic his teacher had shown.

The dull nausea in his gut didn't help, sharpened with each memory of Grandpa's words and now Toby's words. He wondered if he should tell Mama about this; no, that would be foolish. Mama would find out about him frightening Toby with the story, and then he'd have to bend over and face the belt.

When Toby woke up, he was groggy but still convinced that the softly-singing woman in the woods had not been a dream.

"Please don't tell Mama," Sonny said.

"Why not?"

"It'll upset her, and she'll whoop me for scaring you with the story."

"But it had nothing to do with your story. It wasn't a nightmare."

"I know," Sonny conceded, "but let's keep this between us, okay? I'll give you the first shower for a week. Sound good?"

Toby grinned. "Deal!"

Sonny shivered through the dreaded second shower, which was always cold by the time Mama, Grandpa, and the first brother finished up. Sonny and Toby alternated diligently, and Sonny had been looking forward to some hot water ahead of the big test.

But it wasn't to be, Sonny still shivering as he wrapped a towel around his waist and then returned to bed, swaddling himself with blankets.

"You look like an Eskimo," Toby teased.

Sonny hurled a pillow at him. "Come here and say that."

Toby went to the closet and arranged clothes for Sonny on the bed, finishing with his favorite flannel jacket atop the pile. "Get dressed. You'll be warm once you get your clothes on."

"Thanks, little bro."

"Don't mention it."

"Hey, Toby, wait up," Sonny called, his brother stopping in the doorway. "If you hear that music again, get me up, okay?"

Toby nodded, then shut the door behind him and thudded down the stairs.

Chapter 3

"Tell me what happened, from the beginning," Sonny said on their walk to school. He knew he should have been reciting chemical symbols again while Toby chucked stones off trees, but this was more important. Far more important.

"What do you mean?"

"The lady singing. When did you first hear her?"

"Around midnight. I could hear her even with the window shut." He let a handful of pebbles drop to the road. "I fell back asleep pretty quick, but I woke up outside. And I could still hear her after you woke me."

Pangs of guilt rattled through Sonny's veins. All of the talk about Grandpa's sleepwalking and nightmares, combined with last night's story, had infected Toby through some strange form of osmosis. Sonny had learned about osmosis last year in biology class, but he hadn't heard of anything quite like this. Perhaps he, himself, would be sleepwalking before long.

"What did she sound like?" Sonny said.

"She had a really high voice. Soft. Kind of pretty, but more scary, like she knew I was there. Like she was calling me."

"How far into the woods was she?"

"I dunno. It sounded like her voice was coming from everywhere."

They were passing the road under construction, soon to be called Route 31, a dump truck churning up dust in the distance, chainsaws and a chorus of other machinery buzzing and grinding out of sight. Route 31 marked the halfway point between home and school, still another mile to go. In two years, Sonny would have to take the bus to high school, Toby to walk alone because he was terrified of riding the bus and getting tormented long before the first bell rang.

"You know you don't got nothing to be afraid of, right?" Sonny said, wrapping an arm around his brother's shoulders. "I've got your back. Always."

"I ain't afraid."

"Has that Staley kid bothered you lately?"

"Not since you tuned him up at the Strawberry Festival," Toby grinned.

Sonny still felt sort of queasy at the memory of beating up a kid two years his junior, but he'd given Roger Staley fair warning to leave Toby alone. When Toby had left school with a bloody nose and a fat lip on the last day of classes before summer, Sonny had taken a name and sought out Staley at the Fourth of July Strawberry Festival, ambushing him behind the vendors' row when fireworks began to color the sky.

Four months later, Sonny couldn't tell which brought greater remorse, the actual beatdown or his subsequent threat to Staley: *If you tell anyone or hurt my brother again, I'll burn your fucking house down.* A few kids still picked on Toby pretty hard, but since the summer their attacks had been limited to words, Staley unable to look Sonny in the eyes anymore.

Before long, Toby was back to chucking rocks at trees and skipping them along the road, Sonny going through the noble gases and the alkaline earth metals again. He kept getting beryllium and barium goofed up, but everything else was ironed out okay by the time they arrived at school, the fog soon to burn off but not Sonny's unease.

He dreaded the night and what it might bring when the fog was thickest. Although he kept telling his brother to stand unafraid, Sonny was helpless against the fear rising in his own heart, gathering like a wave, threatening to wallop him.

Chapter 4

"How'd your chem test go?" Toby asked on the walk home.

"Good...I hope," Sonny smiled, feeling like a new man since the morning, confidence having spread through him with the sunshine.

"I knew you'd do great." Toby threw a rock at a distant pine, missing badly. "But I'm afraid of taking Mr. Incobrasa's chem class – we all are."

"It's not so bad."

"Is it true he gives detention for being a second late?"

"You bet."

"And he makes kids stand in corners all class for wearing hats?"

"Yup."

"And he calls kids Mr. and Ms., not by their first names?"

"Yup." Sonny ruffled his brother's hair. "Just be polite and on time. You'll be fine."

A convoy of dump trucks passed them in the opposite direction, each one filled with stumps and brush and rocks.

THE NIGHTWOOD SONG

"Let's go down the new road, see what they're doing," Toby said.

"Maybe tomorrow."

"Come on, Sonny."

"Nah, I'm hungry for a snack."

In truth, Sonny didn't have much of an appetite. The closer they got to home, the stronger his disquiet became as the woods deepened around them. He found himself frequently glancing back down Purgatory Road and searching the woods, bothered by a nagging feeling that they were being watched.

Past Route 31 now, Toby kept up his pouty silence a while longer, sailing rocks down the road.

"You're no fun," he said at last.

"Oh, cut the gas already."

Toby tossed a pebble off Sonny's leg, Sonny responding with a light shove. A minute later, they were rolling around beside the road, kicking up a little cloud of dust, Sonny letting his brother pin his arms down like always.

"Say uncle," Toby panted.

"Uncle, uncle! Please, just don't break my arms."

For a while they stayed on their backs, watching the dust clear away, staring at a blue sky slowly giving way to gray.

Eventually Sonny grabbed up his book bag and put his flannel jacket back on. He made sure to take it off each time before their horseplay, and Toby always made sure to keep the pebbles low to Sonny's legs when he pestered him into a scuffle, never wanting to risk harming the jacket.

Almost home, they bought a few snacks at Sal's General Store, no time to waste at the soda fountain this afternoon, for light was tight this time of year and Grandpa needed Sonny manning the loader to prep the next delivery.

As he'd done last week and the week before last, Toby beseeched Sonny to buy him the latest PEZ dispenser, this one featuring Goofy's face. But unlike the previous visits, they weren't there that afternoon in search of items to cross off from Mama's list – and Sonny had two extra quarters in his pocket from Mr. Foote.

Toby's eyes expanded to match the size of those quarters when Sonny told him to put the PEZ dispenser on the counter along with the other goods.

"And what about that one there, the creepy old witch?" Sonny pointed. "I didn't see that one here last time."

"Yeah. Maybe for my birthday," Toby smiled.

"Well, consider it an early birthday. Go on, put it up there, and an extra pack of candies, too."

"Really?"

"Don't give me time to change my mind."

After Toby wrapped both arms tightly around him, Sonny set down the second quarter and selected this week's Life Magazine for Mama and a pack of Wrigley's spearmint gum for Grandpa.

Back home, Toby hurried upstairs to sneak candy into his dispensers' gullets and hide them away. In the dining room, Sonny set the magazine on the table for Mama and hastened through a bowl of cereal.

"Ready to head out?" Grandpa said, ambling in with his cherrywood pipe. "We should have about an hour of good light, I figure."

Sonny downed the rest of the cereal straight from the bowl. "Ready. Sorry we took so long – we stopped by Sal's General." He handed off the pack of gum, bringing a smile to Grandpa's lips that glinted in the late afternoon light.

"You're too kind, Sonny boy."

He pulled Sonny into an embrace, their rush briefly delayed. With his head tucked into Grandpa's sweater and a pair of big hands on his back and the scent of tobacco wisping through the room, Sonny would have gladly let more light drain from the day. There was relief and strength offered in that moment, as though

things would continue to be as they'd always been,
Grandpa keeping him safe, Sonny keeping Toby safe,
days and nights holding firm to their schedules.

But the moment and the day were fading alike,
Grandpa pulling away. "Let's see how big a dent we
can make before supper."

THE NIGHTWOOD SONG

Chapter 5

That night, with Mama's apple pie resting warmly in their bellies, everyone went to their respective corners, Mama washing the dishes and fixing up the kitchen, Grandpa tending to the schedule and turning the rotary dial to confirm next week's deliveries.

Sonny and Toby were in their room, the younger boy flipping through an action comic on his bed, the elder toiling through his latest chemistry assignment at the desk, both brothers turning in occasional acknowledgement of a heavy wind that had poured in from the west.

Sonny was so engrossed by his battle with compounds and molecules that he didn't even notice Toby leave the room. Half an hour later, he was stunned when his brother snapped open the door.

"Sonny, come quick!"

"Not now. Can't you see I'm busy flunking my homework?"

"The music's back!"

Sonny's pencil fell to the floor as he pushed the chair back, Toby leading him toward Grandpa's room. By now, Mama was probably finished up with the kitchen work, a book or a magazine in hand as she rocked before the hearth, its pages turning quickly. Grandpa usually joined her in the living room before bed; he used to invite the brothers down for chess but not lately.

"Have you been messing around in Grandpa's–?"
Sonny was stunned to find Grandpa standing by the
far window, his ear tilted toward it.

"Listen to the music, Sonny boy. It's louder than ever."

"I...I don't hear anything," Sonny said moments later.

On either side of him, Grandpa and Toby fixed him
with baffled expressions, as though he'd suggested
they all head to church in their underwear next
Sunday.

"You really don't hear it?" Grandpa said, his jaw
falling.

Toby shook his head. "How can you not hear it?"

Sonny lifted the window a little higher and strained his
ears. He could hear the wind and even the distant
hum of a motor, but nothing more.

"It's the carnival music again," Toby nodded.

"Sure is," Grandpa said. "Would you listen to that
beautiful calliope? It's as if the circus has set up shop
in those woods. Come on, boys, I've got to know
who's doing this."

"Wait, please, I don't hear anything," Sonny
shuddered, but then he could feel his face flushing.
"Are you playing a trick on me?"

"No, I swear it," Toby said.

"Listen to it!" Grandpa barked, his eyes bluer than Sonny could ever remember, wild with curiosity. "There's something mighty wrong with your hearing if you can't hear *that*."

Sonny thought about fetching Mama and asking if she could hear it, but the thought of disturbing her reading kept him glued to the window, listening.

"I still don't hear anything, only wind. I'm sorry, I just don't hear it."

"It's fading," Grandpa nodded. "It sounds like it's moving off to the west."

"Slipping away," Toby agreed, patting Sonny's back. "Don't worry, you must not hear faraway things as good, that's all."

Grandpa grabbed his coat and drew it over his thick shoulders. "Stay here, boys. I'm gonna head out for a quick walk, see if I can tell which way it's going."

"Grandpa, don't go, please," Sonny blurted, suddenly feeling small and weak. "Just stay here."

"Nonsense, Sonny. Someone's been fooling around in our woods – I'm gonna get to the bottom of this."

Grandpa was gone for over ten minutes, Sonny repeatedly holding his brother back. "If you don't stay still, I'll fetch the belt and whoop you myself."

"But Grandpa needs our help. What if he gets lost out there?"

"He knows these woods better than the trees. He'll be back any minute."

Just when Sonny worried he wouldn't be able to keep his brother at bay any longer without hurting him, they heard Grandpa creaking up the stairs.

"Couldn't track it down," Grandpa groaned, sighing as he removed his coat and shoes. "It got all muddled up with the wind, and then it was just...gone."

Sonny's stomach was sick with worry and confusion, Mama's apple pie turning heavily. Why couldn't he hear the music? Why was he the only one who couldn't hear it?

Again the thought of a trick crept into his mind – a mean, nasty trick – but they wouldn't go this long at his expense. Plus, neither of them would have been able to keep up the act without giggling.

"What do we do?" Toby asked.

"Nothing to do," Sonny hissed with irritation. "We can't run around the woods chasing music all night. Let's just go to bed."

Sonny hurried back to his bedroom, leaving Grandpa and Toby to their murmurings. For once, he was glad when Mama came upstairs twenty minutes later and herded them to the bathroom to wash up.

"I can't believe you didn't hear it," Toby said after Sonny clicked off the lamp.

"Yeah, me neither."

"What's a calliope?"

"It's like an organ. It plays the carnival music…carnival music I can't seem to hear."

"You will. It'll come back, I just know it."

This time, it was Sonny who needed the lamplight on, though he was too embarrassed to admit it, waiting until Toby fell asleep to illuminate the room again.

On either side of midnight, Sonny rolled around with his questions but squeezed no answers from them. He tried to count sheep but wound up counting protons and neutrons, an atomic nucleus glowing and throbbing in his head. An hour later, sweating and cursing, he removed his clothes and lied naked in the damp sheets, pressing pillows against his head, bleary-eyed and bothered by the beginnings of a cough.

"You don't look so good," Toby said at daybreak, waking him for school.

"I don't feel so good."

"You forgot to set the clock. Lucky I woke up."

"Yup."

"Why are you nudey?"

"Cuz I couldn't stop sweating."

"Are you sweating cuz you're sick?"

"Probably."

"Are you mad cuz you couldn't hear the music?"

"A little."

"You'll hear it."

"Maybe. Now go shower up already – and save me some warm water."

"You go first," Toby offered.

"Really?"

"Yeah, you should be warm. You're sick."

"Thanks a million, Toby."

"Uh-huh."

Sonny hurried through his shower to conserve the warmth, Toby waiting outside the stall in his towel so as not to waste even a few seconds. The walk to school was miserable, Sonny's cough worsening by the step, Toby reminding him every other minute that he should have stayed home.

"I'm sure Mr. Incobrasa wouldn't give you detention. You're sick."

"I'll be fine. It's nothing."

THE NIGHTWOOD SONG

Toby didn't fire many rocks this time, his worried expression locked on Sonny.

"Want my gloves? *Your* gloves?"

"Nah, I'm good."

"Take them."

"Thanks," Sonny shivered.

The morning was sunlit and cold, the repeated glints off the grills of approaching dump trucks giving Sonny a headache to go along with his gut ache. He wondered if he would manage to get through first period without rushing to the bathroom to puke.

Almost to school, he realized he hadn't finished his chemistry homework, which added another stone in the nauseous stream wending through his stomach. Yet he found after a while that his homework was a small concern compared to the others. The music. He couldn't stop thinking about the music which came to Toby and Grandpa from the woods, but not to him, never to him.

Who was responsible for the music? And why? There was nothing but acres of wilderness out there, no roads and only a handful of trails, Grandpa had said. And none of the trails were large enough or flat enough to fit a vehicle.

"Thousands of acres," Sonny murmured as they stepped through the school doors and went down their respective halls. "Thousands and thousands of acres."

Chapter 6

Somehow Sonny survived the day without puking or retreating to the nurse's office. A pair of teachers suggested he see the nurse, but he battled through it, feeling halfway normal by the time the final bell sounded.

"You're walking slow," Toby said, glancing back at Sonny on Purgatory Road. "Are you still sick?"

"I'm all right, just weighed down by fifty more pounds of homework from Mr. Incobrasa."

"I hope he retires by the time I'm your age…or dies."

"Don't say that."

"It's true. I don't want fifty pounds of homework a day."

"Maybe he'll ease up by then and give you only five pounds."

At home, Mama prepared a bowl of chicken noodle soup and set it before Sonny at the dinner table.

"This won't get you out of chores, young man. If you can walk to school and back, you can do the work," Mama said after Sonny finished the soup.

"Yes, ma'am."

"Run along now. And bring your brother with you —
see to it that he's understanding what you're doing,
not just watching."

"Yes, ma'am," Sonny coughed.

"Cover your mouth! Are you trying to infect us all?"

"Sorry, Mama."

Suppressing another round of coughs, Sonny climbed
the stairs and rounded up his brother. "Grab your
jacket and gloves. Meet us in the woodyard."

"Do I hafta?"

"Yes, now get moving."

"But I always get cold cuz I'm not allowed to do
nothing fun."

"That's why you should bundle up."

Toby continued to protest, but Sonny's head wasn't
right for all the questions and back talk. He hoped
Mama's aspirin would kick in soon, his head
becoming foggier than the Nightwood.

In the woodyard, Grandpa was already hustling with
the chainsaw, dicing up logs as though he were in a
competition.

"Splitter's on the fritz again," Grandpa called to
Sonny, pointing to a pile of smaller logs heaped by

the splitting stumps. "We'll have to do it the hard way tonight."

Nodding, well-accustomed to the splitter's frequent malfunctions, Sonny readied a log on the first stump. Soon, Grandpa would haul over another cartload of logs with his rusty grappling tractor, and Sonny would help split them all down to size on the stumps, no help coming from the splitter until Grandpa found the part that needed fixing.

"Toby's coming out soon," Sonny alerted.

"Huh?" Grandpa cranked, setting down the chainsaw and removing his earmuffs.

"I said, Toby's coming out soon."

Grandpa poured his frustration into a sigh. "Maybe another time. We're short on light."

"Mama said so."

Grandpa sighed again, this time with resignation. He glanced toward the house and sighted Toby trudging along the footbridge, gloved hands in his jacket pockets.

"Watch him," Grandpa said. "Make sure he don't go fooling around with the equipment."

"Yes, sir."

Sometimes, in moments of exasperation with his pupils, Mr. Incobrasa would toss his dwindling stick of chalk against the tray and throw his hands up. Scanning the rows of confused faces, rubbing his thick mustache, he would say, "It's like bashing my head against the wall."

The feeling was foreign to most of the other pupils, but Sonny knew it well. He'd known it from an early age, Mama always ordering him to watch Toby and teach him and show him the way. *Your brother's not slow, he's just uncomfortable around people*, Mama had said following Sonny's first report of students and teachers alike calling Toby slow. A year later, after Toby was briefly lost in the woods: *You can't let him out of your sight, Sonny! He's your responsibility! We don't have time to watch you boys and mind the work.* This had followed a brutal belting, Sonny trembling against the wall, and it had only stopped on Grandpa's account, begging Mama to let Sonny go.

Now, as then, Sonny endured the weight of his responsibility, glancing often at his little brother.

"Make yourself useful and pile up those logs," Sonny said after ramming down the maul and busting through a log.

"Why aren't you using the splitter?"

"It's broken again."

"How do you swing that devil so darn hard?"

"Lots of practice."

"But I've practiced, too, and I can't do it like you."
Toby tried to heft a large pre-split log but dropped it
on his foot and yowled.

"How many times do I gotta say it? You only pile the
ones I split," Sonny growled, coughing and spitting.

"But I thought—"

"Did you see me split that one?"

"No."

"Right, then. Pay attention."

Shaking his head, Sonny imagined himself with Mr.
Incobrasa's mustache and angry stare, his maul
momentarily becoming a stick of chalk, unavailing in
its quest to impart knowledge. The image softened
him up, and he set down the maul.

"How's your foot?"

"Hurts."

"We'll be in soon for dinner."

"Can I try the maul?"

Sonny eyed his grandfather, who was turned away
from them, sending up a spray of woodchips that
smelled sweeter than pie. "Make it quick," he waved,
setting a smaller log on the stump and handing Toby
the maul.

"Like this?" Toby said, mimicking a swing but struggling to wield the maul.

"Yup, just like that. And put your back into it."

Toby took a few swings, but he would've been hard-pressed to cut a birthday cake. Sonny, taking up the maul, weakened the log till she was ready to give, then returned the tool to Toby and savored his triumph.

"That was one of the biggest ones I've done!"

"You're getting strong, kid."

"Pretty soon I'll be right beside you."

"No doubt."

Sonny went back to splitting while Toby piled. He wished Grandpa would give Toby the time to work through his failings, but he was too impatient. Had Sonny not been blessed with a quick mind and a strong frame, he knew he would've been piling alongside his little brother, Grandpa doing everything himself.

You'll all absorb this material eventually, even if it takes summer school, Mr. Incobrasa sometimes threatened.

Darkness fell, the moon arriving early and bright. They worked by Bertha's headlights as they often did this time of year, mostly sorting and stacking, Grandpa filling the loader with fuel.

They were almost done with the last pile, only a few logs left to round up, when Grandpa shouted, "Get inside, boys!"

"What? Grandpa—"

"Now! Go, go, go! Inside!"

Thoughts of coyotes flashed into Sonny's head. Momentarily paralyzed, he glanced about but was blinded by the headlights. He didn't even realize he was moving until his arms were on Toby's shoulders, spinning him around. "Go on, move! Get to the house!"

They ripped across the bridge, Grandpa right behind them, Toby tripping up the porch steps and yelping.

"Was it yotes, Grandpa?" Sonny said, helping his brother up.

Panting at the end of the porch, arms stationed at his sides, Grandpa stared into the woods. The only island of light was provided by Bertha's headlights, the rest an evening grave.

"Grandpa? Are you okay?" Sonny's hand on Grandpa's arm went unnoticed. "Grandpa, what's wrong?"

Toby worked himself into a panic and dashed inside, Mama coming out moments later.

"What's all this commotion about? Grandfather, what is the meaning of this?"

THE NIGHTWOOD SONG

She'd always called him Grandfather, nothing else, but it seemed he would respond to no name tonight.

Finally, when Mama shouted in his ear, "Wake up!", he jolted back into awareness, Sonny never to forget the distilled terror in his eyes, nearly strong enough to make them glow.

"Boys, go inside!" Mama pointed.

"But, Mama–" Sonny started.

"Do as I say!"

"Yes, Mama," the brothers answered, closing the door behind them and hurrying to the foyer window overlooking the porch.

"What was it?" Mama was saying. "What did you see?"

"It. *It!*" Grandpa had turned back to face the woods.

"*What?*" Mama pressed.

"Fetch my gun!"

"Grandfather, no, this is madness! Would you listen to yourself?"

"I said, fetch my damn gun! None of us are safe here. None–"

With a choking gasp, Grandpa clutched his chest and fell to his knees, Toby squealing, Sonny running for the phone. Grandpa was loaded into the ambulance fifteen minutes later, Mama scolding the paramedics for not arriving sooner, Sonny, with a tear streaming lengthily down his cheek, staring at the flashing red dome atop the car. He held his brother against him in the driveway, Toby's sobs having diminished to sniffles.

"I'll be just fine, boys. You be good," Grandpa groaned, and then the back doors were snapped shut, the ambulance whispering away, the flashing red light carving through the woods like a campfire ghoul.

Sonny watched that light trail down the driveway, then knife out onto Purgatory Road. Even after Mama and Toby went back inside, Sonny watched the devilish light until it was swallowed by the woods, Grandpa's warnings ringing in his head.

For just a moment, drying his eyes and wiping away the track forged by a single tear, Sonny thought he heard music capering out of the woods, a woman's voice, soft and soothing like a lullaby, calling to him, drawing his feet briefly in the song's direction.

But when the wind gathered and spread its chill about him, he could hear only the hammer of questions in his head.

Chapter 7

"Your grandfather will pull through. It was a minor heart attack, is all —hardly uncommon for older folks," Mama told the boys in the living room after setting down the phone.

Toby sniffled beside Mama on the sofa, Sonny bringing in a bag stuffed with firewood and kindling.

"When can we see him?" Sonny said.

"Soon. He needs his rest." Sighing, Mama ran a hand through her curly hair, her face blanched with fears that didn't arrive in words.

"Tomorrow?" Toby hoped.

"Perhaps. His doctor will let me know." She eyed the clock. "Meanwhile, it's well past your bedtime. Go wash up."

Sonny lingered behind after Toby went up, just in case Mama had anything else to say, but she simply stood and went to the hearth, staring inscrutably into the flames.

"Don't worry, Mama, I can handle tomorrow's delivery." Sonny kissed his mother's cheek and stoked the fire. "And I'll watch Toby while you visit Grandpa."

Mama nodded, her eyes never leaving the flames.

Sonny started toward the door, then stopped. "We heard Grandpa talking about his gun, saying we aren't safe. What do you think he meant by–?"

"He's overtired and overworked," Mama said, still searching into the fire, a kiss of sparks puffing out from a log. She shook her head. "A man his age shouldn't be taxed in such a way, but we've all had to pull extra hard since your father's passing." At last she turned to Sonny. "I know it's been hard on you boys. It's hard on us all, but we have to keep going. The Lord never said it'd be easy."

Nodding, Sonny closed his mouth before more questions could escape.

"Good night, Mama."

"Go wash up," she murmured, turning back to face the hearth. "Tomorrow's a long day."

The boys layered up in extra clothes before bed, but no amount of blankets or layers could keep out the chill of terror.

"Why did Grandpa say we aren't safe?" Toby said in the lamplight.

"He's been tired. Lack of sleep makes you not think straight sometimes."

"But why did he want his gun? Why did he rush us out of the woods? What did he see?"

"I'm not sure he saw anything. He just got scared – maybe he could sense something going wrong inside him."

"But–"

"Just try to rest. I'll leave the lamp on – promise."

"Can I sleep in your bed?" He was already crossing the room, padding softly over creaking floorboards in his wool socks.

Sonny shifted back against the wall and patted the sheets, the bed barely big enough to fit them.

"I'm scared, Sonny."

"Don't be. I've got you."

"What if something comes for us – the thing that makes the music?"

Turning onto his side, Sonny wrapped an arm around his brother and pulled him against his chest. "Nothing's coming for us."

"How do you know?"

"Because I'm your big brother."

"So?"

"Big brothers know things."

"How? How can you know things if I don't?"

"Same reason my eyes are blue and yours brown."

"That don't make no sense."

"Go to sleep, or I'll tickle-torture you."

"Fine." Toby let out a tired sigh. "Can I sleep here all night?"

"As long as you don't ask more questions."

"Promise."

"Good. Now let's say our prayers – and an extra one for Grandpa."

"For Grandpa," Toby repeated, yawning.

Prayers complete, Toby couldn't manage five minutes before whispering, "Do you really think Grandpa will be okay, or is Mama trying not to scare us?"

"He'll be all right. He's resting now – you should, too."

"Right. Sorry."

"I love you, little bro."

"Love you, too, Sonny."

THE NIGHTWOOD SONG

Chapter 8

They weren't allowed to see Grandpa the next day or the day after; doctor's orders, Mama said.

When Friday rolled around, the Winters boys were up early, showered and dressed before Mama woke, hoping for a visit to the hospital before school.

"Maybe tomorrow," Mama yawned in bed. "He's still resting. If he overdoes it, he could put himself at risk."

"Can we at least call him?" Sonny said.

"I'm afraid not. Go on, now, and quit disturbing me."

Toby broke into tears. "It's not fair! I wanna see Grandpa!"

Toby thudded downstairs, Sonny chasing after him and following him onto the porch. The predawn fog was heavy, Sonny glancing at the driveway and remembering the ghostly red light flashing portentously. *I'll be just fine, boys. You be good*, he remembered, praying those wouldn't be the final words Grandpa spoke to them.

They brooded in silence for a while, Sonny feeling marginally better than the previous few days, his cough abating. Yet his physical improvement was made meaningless by thorns of fear sharper than the briar thickets clustering along the stream. Questions never led to answers these days, only more questions – enough questions to drown in.

"There!" Toby blurted, pointing west. "Can you hear it?"

"Hear what?"

"The music!"

"Good Lord, not again with this."

"Cut the gas and listen! It's coming closer!"

Sonny listened for ten seconds as Toby, pointing and nodding, waited expectantly.

"I don't hear anything."

"How?" Toby huffed. "It's right there! Someone's playing the guitar, just like Papa used to."

"I don't–"

Toby took off for the woods, Sonny calling after him but quickly losing his brother in the fog. By the time Sonny crossed the footbridge, his movements were guided by memory alone, the lights of the house fading like harbor lamps behind a departing ship.

"Toby, get back here this instant! Toby!"

Sonny was shouting so desperately that his voice faltered into a cough. "Toby, please come back! We'll look together, I promise!"

THE NIGHTWOOD SONG

Sonny shoved blindly through curtains of mist. Before long, the glow seeping from the house was gone altogether.

"Toby! Toby, where are you?"

Sonny was beyond the woodyard now, tripping and snagging his favorite jacket on branches, pain flaring through his elbow.

"Toby! Follow my—"

"Over here," Toby called.

"Where?"

"I'm next to Big Bertha."

"Stay there. Don't move."

Smacking his way through branches, cutting his hands on briars, tearing his jacket, Sonny at last made it back to the center of the woodyard and pulled his brother into a hug. "Don't ever scare me like that again! What's wrong with you?"

"I can't hear it anymore," Toby said, baffled, his face expressionless in the foggy darkness, his body nothing more than a shape. "As soon as I chased after it, it moved deeper."

"Come on." Sonny took his brother's hand and led him back over the bridge.

"I don't understand," Toby said once they were inside, Sonny fetching a pair of bowls from the cabinet and pouring cereal. "It was so close, right on the other side of the driveway."

Sonny clinked spoons into the bowls and set them down on the table. "Say nothing of this to Mama. Got it?"

"But the music—"

"She's got enough to worry about already."

"Why don't you believe me?"

"I do believe you. I just don't get what's happening!" Sonny fought to lower his voice. "This whole thing, it just…it gives me the creeps. I don't have any answers, okay?" He checked the stairs, then brought his voice down to a whisper. "One thing's for sure – you need to stay the hell out of the woods. You scared the tar out of me."

Toby went to the dining room window, pulling the curtains back and searching the fog.

"Come eat," Sonny said, jingling his bowl with a spoon.

Instead, Toby lifted the window a few inches and listened. "I don't hear it."

"Maybe it's some kind of illusion or something," Sonny pondered aloud, swirling cereal about his bowl but never lifting the spoon.

"What do you mean?"

"I don't know, maybe the music's coming from much farther off than we realize, like Sal's General or something."

"But that's way up the road. You wouldn't be able to hear a gunshot that far."

"You're probably right," Sonny admitted. "Maybe it's coming from a house."

"But we're the only house around."

"Kids partying in the woods, maybe. High school kids."

"Kids don't sound like that lady who was singing the other day," Toby said dreamily. "She sounded like an angel."

Sonny remembered the ephemeral song he'd heard after Grandpa was hauled away in the ambulance – the only trace of music that had visited him. There hadn't even been enough time for him to confirm it wasn't an imaginary creation.

But now, hearing his brother…*an angel…*

The voice had indeed been ethereal, alluring, tantalizing, but it had cut out as quickly as it arrived, leaving Sonny to wonder whether he'd imagined the whole thing.

Sonny considered telling his brother about it, then reconsidered. He saw no way to help matters by recounting the incident, only a path to more confusion and fear.

"Sonny, you made coffee!" Mama smiled fifteen minutes later. "You're so good to me."

"Glad to help, Mama." Sonny was standing before the calendar, crossing off items from the schedule. "We've got a delivery for the Ahearns lined up today. Bertha's all loaded – I'll swing by after school."

Mama turned him and pecked his forehead. "Look at you. You're becoming a man before my eyes – your Papa would be so proud."

"Grandpa, too," Toby said, cereal milk having dried on his chin.

"Wipe your face, Toby." Mama went to the coffee pot and prepared a mug. "And clear your dishes proper. I'm not here to pick up after you all day."

Toby obeyed, setting his bowl in the sink.

"Drain the milk first, please," Mama reminded. "Otherwise it sours."

"Yes, Mama."

"By the way, I need to stop into town after work. I won't be back until later."

"Yes, Mama," the brothers said in unison.

THE NIGHTWOOD SONG

Sonny recorded the names and phone numbers underlined on the schedule. "Should I call the people needing confirmation, or can Grandpa do it from the hospital?"

"Call them tonight," Mama instructed. "Your grandfather needs his rest."

"When can we see him?" Toby bothered.

"I don't answer questions twice, young man, never mind three or four times."

"But–"

"Mind your manners, Toby, before I see fit to add more chores to your ledger tonight."

Working swiftly and precisely, everything in its place, no wasted time or energy, Mama fixed her breakfast and spread out yesterday's paper on the table. Sonny continued with the schedule and then proceeded to the invoice books, making sure to write out everything in detail so Grandpa could follow it. Lionel Singletary, for example – whose load of wood Sonny had filled the night after Grandpa was carted off to the hospital – had admitted with great sheepishness that he could not afford to pay. *Would your grandfather mind terribly if I paid double next load?* Singletary had asked when Sonny stepped down from Big Bertha, the old man's breath reeking of alcohol, his eyes downcast. Sonny had said it wasn't a problem, Singletary thanking him profusely, then telling him about how a childhood friend named Benny had fought alongside him during the First World War. The story had rambled on for twenty minutes…*And by the way, you sure are a young fella to be hauling that rig around all by your lonesome. You remind me of myself before the war, but my leg's all busted up now, can't seem to find steady work.* Back home, Sonny had been promptly greeted with a scolding from Mama, first for being late, then for allowing a man to go into arrears without paying a cent: *You're twisting up an awful nasty knot for your grandfather to loosen. We don't heat people's homes for free!*

"Can I help?" Toby said, swinging by and scooping up a pair of checks. "What're these?"

"Give 'em here," Sonny said without looking up from the books. "Go make sure your homework's ready."

"But I can–"

"Tobias Winters, if I hear one more word, it's the belt for you," Mama clapped, glowering up from the newspaper. "Let your brother focus."

"Yes, Mama."

Sonny took another ten minutes to get everything squared off, and he could only pray he wouldn't come across another guy who couldn't pay for his cord.

Heading back upstairs with Toby, Sonny unbuttoned his favorite flannel jacket and checked for further damage, snarling at the sight of the tear on the right arm. It wasn't until he had the jacket back on a hanger in the closet (he couldn't bring himself to wear it again without proper mending), that he noticed Toby's absence. The bathroom was empty as well.

"Toby!" he called downstairs. No answer. "Toby, where are you?"

He checked the living room and the kitchen, expecting to find his brother pouting somewhere, but there was no sign of him, the only sounds coming from Mama's turning of newspaper pages.

"Mama, have you seen Toby?"

"I have not." She glanced up with fresh irritation. "Why can you never manage to keep track of your brother?"

"Sorry, Mama. It was only–"

"Don't bother with explanations. Just go find him."

Light was surging into the morning, though it did nothing to eat away at the fog. In fact, it seemed even foggier when Sonny stepped onto the porch, the light somehow thickening the mist into a disorienting clot.

This time, Sonny didn't have to go searching with blind panic into the woods. Toby stood at the end of the porch, hands in his jacket pockets. "I heard it a little, but it was far away. Sounded like Elvis."

"Elvis?"

"I swear it, Sonny."

"So, let me get this straight – somebody with a guitar is gearing up for a concert with Elvis Presley in our woods this morning? I'd say it's time to play hooky!"

"That's not funny. Why won't you believe me?"

"I do. It's just…I don't know. Let's get ready for school."

"Listen! You can kind of hear it again!"

"All I hear is a train."

"Yeah, but listen closer. Over there – can't you hear it?"

"Elvis?"

"No, it's drums now."

"Good Lord."

"Sonny, listen!"

"I am."

It went like that for another half minute, Toby finally becoming so frustrated that tears sprang down his cheeks.

Back in the house, Mama shook her head at Sonny. "I see you've been tormenting your brother again. You're far too old for this."

"I'm sorry, Mama."

"Get to school, the both of you."

"But it's still early," Toby complained.

"Then get there early." Mama shook her head again. "I'm tired of the both of you. I could use a little peace and quiet around here."

A pang of terror lurched through Sonny, bringing a tingle to his spine. The thought of Mama here alone, with the music in the woods and no one here to protect her…

Don't be ridiculous. Someone's playing all this music in the distance, and the sound travels mighty well. Nothing to be afraid of.

Sonny resolved to check Grandpa's maps after school and plot out the nearest homes. If he gathered just enough bravery, maybe he'd see Mr. Incobrasa after class and ask how far sound could travel.

Chapter 9

"Why do you think Mama ain't letting us see Grandpa?" Toby said, casting a stone into the fog. It bounced twice at the edge of Purgatory Road, then disappeared into the drapery of mist; yet the stone hadn't seemed to fade off as an increasingly vague form, instead vanishing as if vaporized.

"He needs his rest," Sonny said, feeling guilty for regurgitating Mama's words. There was something deeply wrong with Grandpa – well beyond his heart attack – and even Toby could detect Mama's omissions.

"Sometimes when people get old, they…their minds change," Sonny added. "They forget things sometimes, and they can be anxious."

Toby clanged a stone against a rusty speed limit sign. "Is it cuz they're afraid of dying?"

"I'm not sure that's it. Their minds, they just change over time and lose their sharpness. Picture it like an axe. After years of use, it ain't as sharp as it once was – perfectly natural."

"Grandpa's mind is changing quick," Toby muttered. "He never used to shout crazy stuff like that. And he was never scared-uh-nothin'."

"Hopefully he'll benefit from rest. It's hard on the mind to constantly be at work."

"Nobody works harder than Grandpa."

"You got that right."

They plodded through the fog, passed up by occasional dump trucks headed for Route 31, their taillights glaring mistily. Because the boys were twenty minutes ahead of schedule, Sonny devised a throwing contest to help take his brother's mind off their troubles. They would each gather ten stones and take aim at the mile marker to their right; loser had to strip down to his skivvies and do jumping jacks when the next car came.

"Better start undressing now," Sonny goaded.

"Cut the gas. You couldn't hit the brown side of a barn."

"It's broad side."

"Right, that's what I said."

"Did not."

"Did, too."

"Just get your rocks, already."

Sonny's aim was much worse than usual, but his three pings off the mile marker were good enough to best Toby's two. And since Toby had demanded to go first, Sonny didn't even require his last ups.

"I don't wanna strip."

"Deal's a deal, bro."

"Your last one barely even hit the thing."

"Don't be a poor loser, kid," Sonny grinned, setting down his book bag to do a triumphant cartwheel.

"Come on, Sonny, don't make me."

"Fine, don't have a cow, Mr. Shy."

"I'm not shy."

"Are, too."

"Am not. You're the shy one!"

"Am not."

They volleyed back and forth like tennis pros until, by some unknown means, Sonny found himself accepting a challenge from Toby to strip and prove he wasn't shy, the occupants of a passing station wagon getting a look at his hole-torn long johns and languid jumping jacks (supposing the boys could be seen at all in the foggy breakdown lane).

"It's really cold," Sonny shivered, dressing quickly once the car disappeared into the mist.

"Nah, you're just a little sally," Toby chirped, pegging him in the ass with a stone.

"Kid, I'm gonna get you, I swear it."

Toby ran down the road, his book bag joggling over a shoulder, Sonny chasing after him, both boys stopping cold when they heard it. Surging from the distant woods to their right, quickly building toward a crescendo, the fury of howls and shrieks cannoned through the fog. Just when the chaos seemed to reach its height, the gruesome sounds rose even higher, the boys huddling together as the yelps faded to death bleats and then silence.

"Ain't never heard a yote attack at this hour," Sonny murmured. "Usually they hunt between sundown and midnight."

No matter how many times you heard them, those murderous paroxysms in the woods were never any easier to endure, Sonny always imagining somebody's lost dog getting torn apart, no help to be had as the yotes converged.

"It'd be an awful bad way to go, wouldn't it?" Toby said, quickening his pace.

Sonny kept an eye toward the foggy woods, briefly thinking he glimpsed a cluster of approaching shadows amid the veil. "Yeah, mighty bad."

"They wouldn't go after us, right, not if we're together?"

"We're fine. Just keep to the road."

Sonny couldn't concentrate at school, his thoughts like pinballs ricocheting about. Except the mental pinball machine didn't rack up points but fears, forcing him to open his notebook and scrawl out a loose timeline. He started with this past Sunday morning, when Grandpa had randomly shouted, "I am not worthy of Heaven!", on the way home from church. Sonny penciled an asterisk next to that date, then plotted out the many occasions on which music had been reported in the woods. He was about to write the date of Grandpa's heart attack, but Mr. Incobrasa, arms crossed, appeared in the row to his left.

"Well, Mr. Winters, do you have the answer?"

"No, sir. I'm sorry."

"Your mind was elsewhere, wasn't it, Mr. Winters?"

"Yes, sir."

Sonny's face burned all the way down to his neck, relief sweeping through him when Mr. Incobrasa moved down the row and scolded a pair of students for whispering and passing notes.

"I know it's the end of the week, but let's all try to stay focused," Mr. Incobrasa scowled, returning to the head of the classroom. "I'm only halfway through grading your periodic table exams, but judging by what I've seen thus far, focus has been an issue in this class."

Sonny swallowed hard, feeling as if a knot had formed in his throat. The class seemed to drag along even slower than usual, Mr. Incobrasa filling up the entire chalkboard with diagrams and equations. This would probably be an especially heavy homework weekend, but Sonny's apprehension had far transcended academics.

After the bell finally sounded to end last period, the knot in Sonny's throat bunched even tighter when Mr. Incobrasa asked him to stay after class, a few kids snickering on the way by, others glancing at Sonny with sympathy.

"I'm sorry I wasn't paying attention, sir. It won't happen–" Sonny started when the classroom emptied, but Incobrasa held up a hand.

"Are you feeling okay, Sonny?" the teacher questioned, Sonny wondering if this was the first time Incobrasa had ever used his first name.

"Yes, sir. I've been a little under the weather this week, but I'm better now."

"Good. Very good." He cleared his throat and went to his desk in the corner. "Now, I don't normally do this, but your hard work is deserving of special commendation. You received a perfect score on your exam, Sonny."

"I did?"

"You most certainly did. As I said before, I'm only halfway through the exams, but thus far the next highest grade is an 86. Congratulations, Mr. Winters. You must have studied very hard."

"Thank you, sir. I did, sir."

The teacher nodded sharply. "Keep up the good work."

"Yes, sir." Sonny gulped, afraid to disturb the most feared teacher in school, who gathered up a stack of assignments and readied his red pen. "Mr. Incobrasa, if you don't mind, I'd like to ask you a question."

"Fire away," the teacher said, scribbling out a few red check marks but mostly exes on the first assignment.

"How far away can sound travel?"

Setting down the pen, Incobrasa clasped his hands behind his head and leaned back in the chair. "It depends on many variables: weather, time of day, altitude, the energy of the sound, competing noise in the area…"

He went on to define longitudinal waves, amplitude, and propagation speed; he even went to the chalkboard and drew up a formula, Sonny beginning to regret asking the question. The lesson carried on so long that Incobrasa discussed how the 1883 eruption of Krakatoa had been heard thousands of miles away in Australia.

Long story short, sound could travel extremely far – especially explosions – but what about music? Sonny almost asked but elected against it; Toby would already be impatient, verging on scared.

"Thank you, Mr. Incobrasa. I appreciate your time."

"Of course, of course," the teacher nodded with a smile. "I always love to see students seek out knowledge. You never stop learning – always something to discover."

Sonny nodded. "Have a good weekend, sir."

"You as well, Mr. Winters."

As predicted, Toby was pacing with his arms crossed in their meeting spot out front, inhaling bus fumes and kicking pebbles.

"What took you so long?"

"Sorry, bro, I stayed after class to ask Mr. Incobrasa some stuff. By the way, you're never gonna believe this, but I aced the exam!"

"Really?"

"Yeah, Incobrasa just told me."

"Congrats, Sonny! I knew you'd do good, but I've never seen nobody ace a test besides Missy Marner. That's amazing."

The morning mist had transitioned into a foggy drizzle nearly cold enough to freeze to surfaces. On Purgatory Road, headlights spilled out an eldritch glow in the distance, and you couldn't tell if the approaching forms were pickup trucks or station wagons until they were right on top of you.

The Route 31 construction zone was a ghost town, the workers always cutting out early on Friday afternoons, not a single dump truck in sight. Sonny expected his brother to petition him for another walk down the new road, Sonny ready with excuses about how muddy it would be, but Toby said nothing as they passed. Ahead, Purgatory Road stretched out secretively into the gloom, visibility less than a tenth of a mile, Sonny imagining all kinds of menaces in the mist, tracking the brothers down the road.

Back home, it was just Sonny and Toby, Mama headed for town after work. Readying logs and kindling in the hearth, Sonny glanced at the lonely chess board and forced back a sudden urge to cry. In the kitchen, the repeated clacks of Toby's PEZ dispenser testified to a glut of candy.

"Hey, take it easy in there. I'll make you a sandwich."

"Yes, Mama."

"You little creep."

"Don't belt me, Mama. Please!"

Once the fire was roaring, Sonny got the wood stove going and then started on Toby's PBJ.

"Make sure you cut off the crusts," Toby reminded, glancing up from his comic book to find Sonny delivering a crust-free sandwich sided with potato chips.

"I'll be out in the woodyard getting ready for Mr. Ahearn's delivery," Sonny said, pouring a glass of milk for Toby.

"Can I go with you?"

THE NIGHTWOOD SONG

Sonny nearly declined, but considering the strange events over the last week, he thought it wise to keep Toby close.

"Do exactly what I tell you, and don't go running off nowhere. I swear, you'll be walking home if you do."

"I won't, I promise."

Sighing lengthily, Sonny peered through the dining room window into the fog. Before long, he was taken with a powerful need to draw the curtains shut and turn away.

Why does it always have to be so darn foggy?

Munching his chips, Toby seemed to also feed on his brother's anxiousness. "What if we get lost?"

"We won't. I've been to Mr. Ahearn's place two or three times with Grandpa. Meet me out in the yard."

Jogging over the driveway toward the bridge, crossing the stream, Sonny couldn't suppress his urges to search the fog and listen. That tingling feeling of being watched quickly returned, Sonny scolding himself for being silly. But with the fog swirling and eddying down by the water – and Grandpa's words echoing in his head – how could he not seek out signs of trouble?

Turning back toward the house, Toby's jogging form gave Sonny a momentary fright. He helped his brother into Bertha's passenger seat, the truck growling to life; she sounded a little angrier than usual this time, as if demanding Grandpa's return.

"Buckle up," Sonny said, then fetched a napkin from the glove compartment and wiped a smudge of peanut butter from Toby's chin. Balling up the napkin and pocketing it, he held out his hand for a high-five. "Ready to roll, partner?"

"Ready," Toby grinned.

With a full load of wood behind them, Sonny depressed the clutch and shifted into gear. He was surprisingly nervous with his brother in the passenger seat, far more nervous than his solo journeys, feeling as though he had a carton of eggs to keep from cracking.

"Wow," Toby said as Bertha knifed through the fog, night making a rapid descent in the surrounding woods. "We're already at Route 31. Imagine how fast we'd get to school if we took Bertha instead of walkin'."

"She hums pretty good once she gets going."

A hot pang of fear jolted through Sonny when a police car appeared in the gloom, parked in the library lot, facing the road. But Grandpa said Chief Clark and his boys mostly napped through traffic details, nothing to worry about from the boys in blue, and sure enough the police car remained where it was, Sonny nervously eyeing the mirrors.

Fifteen minutes later, they were on the northern side of the Nightwood, where the train tracks branched out into two lines and the freighters could hustle up toward Shasta County. The Ahearns' twisting driveway provided a smooth ride over fresh pavement, snakes of mist slithering along the edges, chased out by Bertha's headlights.

"Back it up and dump it over there," Mr. Ahearn pointed after Sonny cranked down the window.

Ahearn's entire family joined him on the porch, three boys and a girl named Mary who was two years older than Sonny. She was so pretty that you started sweating right away, Sonny having met her during the last delivery over the summer, when she'd talked about her nervousness over starting high school. She'd seemed to look at Sonny a certain kind of way, her smile staying on him, the memory lingering warmly, but now she was watching alongside her family in the mist, Sonny hoping not to bump into something and break it, or back over Sophia the family cat.

Carefully, perhaps comedically so, Sonny got Bertha turned around and then dispensed the cord. He sighed and wiped his brow when it was done, then climbed down and accepted payment from Mr. Ahearn.

"A gratuity for your hard work, young man," Ahearn said after following up the payment with a dollar-bill, Sonny wondering for a moment if it was real. "I don't suppose I've ever seen boys so young acquitting themselves this finely. Why don't you stay for supper?"

"Thank you, sir, but we shouldn't impose on your–"

"Nonsense! We're always happy to have company out in these lonely woods."

Mary smiled at Sonny, who could feel the sweat beginning to trickle beneath his johns. He hoped Toby wouldn't say nothing embarrassing, like how Sonny had jumped around in his underwear like an idiot that morning.

After an awkward series of introductions in the foyer, Mr. Ahearn said, "Is your grandfather running another load across town tonight?"

"No, sir, he's been a little under the weather lately."

"I'm sorry to hear that." Ahearn, whose muscles bulged against his suit, crossed a pair of meaty arms. "He's lucky to have some good soldiers to keep the mission going."

"Thank you, sir."

Sonny tried his best to hold Ahearn's gaze, but the intimidation factor made him sweat even more. Like Papa, Ahearn had fought in the Second World War, and sometimes his movements and his stance suggested that he was still very much ready for combat.

"Johnny, show the boys to the washroom," Ahearn told his eldest son. "Supper'll be on in ten."

After everyone washed up, Sonny and Toby were led to a candlelit dining room table. Luckily, Toby kept mostly quiet as he often did when company was around, sitting to Sonny's right, Mary sliding in to his left and lifting the temperature ten degrees. Mrs. Ahearn's spaghetti wafted so deliciously as to be tasted, Sophia scooting beneath the table and nudging Sonny's leg.

The Ahearn boys sat opposite the Winters brothers, folding their hands across the table and staring with the same probing intensity as their father. Sonny felt like he was on the doctor's table, a light to be shined into his eyes, his breathing to be checked, questions to be asked, plenty of questions.

The table was already set, both ends reserved for the parents, who brought in steaming dishes of spaghetti, the Ahearn boys rising dutifully to serve glasses of ice water and lemonade.

"Thank you all for dinner. You're very kind."

"It's our pleasure, Sonny. Any time," Mrs. Ahearn smiled.

Sonny didn't know where to look, sensing that every set of eyes was upon him, and he prayed Toby minded his manners and didn't stick his fingers into the food or start slurping spaghetti.

"If you don't mind me asking, how long have you been driving that truck all by yourself?" Mrs. Ahearn said after a while.

Sonny carefully washed down a bite of spaghetti. "About a year, ma'am. I only drive when Grandpa isn't feeling well."

"So industrious." Mr. Ahearn nodded at his sons. "You boys would do well to take a lesson."

"Do you enjoy that work?" Mary questioned, her voice sending an electric buzz into Sonny's head.

"It's fun working with my grandfather," he said, then quickly added, "And also showing Toby the work."

"I'll be driving Bertha, too!" Toby offered with a mouthful of spaghetti.

"Isn't that lovely." Mrs. Ahearn dabbed her mouth with a napkin. "I bet you all make an excellent team."

A strange tension seemed to exist within the Ahearn family, everyone eyeing each other obliquely and then averting their stares, as though Sonny and Toby had intervened on a quarrel. Sonny spoke only when spoken to, Toby doing the same until he eventually loosened up as dessert was being served. Sonny lightly kicked his ankle, but it did nothing to shut Toby up about the music in the woods and Grandpa's warnings that they weren't safe.

"He's absolutely right," Mr. Ahearn said. "You can get turned around real easy in those woods, especially in the fog. I'd say there's been at least ten people who've gone missing in this area the last few years."

"More than ten," Mrs. Ahearn corrected. "Probably ten hikers and campers alone – and another five or ten runaway kids, elderly folks, and people who just don't wanna be found, I suppose. Chief Clark's always searching for somebody in the Nightwood."

THE NIGHTWOOD SONG

"Be careful in those woods, boys," Ahearn warned, digging into his blueberry pie. "They're awful deep. You could bring fifty people into those woods, and after they went their separate ways, they'd never find each other again."

The conversation circled back to the music, everyone remarking about how strange it was, Sonny doing his best to divert the subject. He asked the Ahearn boys how their classes were, then asked Mary how she was liking freshman year. She looked even prettier than before, with her hair combed down over a blue sweater, her smooth hands gesturing as she spoke, her green eyes lit by some strange incandescence. Sonny's self-consciousness returned after a while, making him unsure where to look. He coached himself against holding Mary's gaze too long, but then it would be rude if he glanced away while she spoke…and under absolutely no circumstance could his eyes drift down to the nascent swells of her chest.

He reached for the glass of water, condensation nearly causing it to slide from his grip. But he held on. He nodded politely. When Mary finished and he could look away, relief jetted through him with the force of a geyser.

Ten minutes later, they were shaking hands and stepping back onto the porch, Bertha almost entirely hidden in the gathering fog. It was full dark now, and cold, their breaths adding more mist to the heavy night.

"Thank you all for dinner," Sonny called, waving, grateful for dodging calamity. Now all that remained was heading back down the driveway without damaging anything. (Where the hell had the damn cat gone after slipping through the door?)

There. Thank God. The cat was in Mary's arms, held against her chest and stroked lovingly, probably purring against the soft, warm fabric, possibly even feeling Mary's heartbeats. Lucky cat.

"So long, everyone," Sonny called after cranking down the window, the Ahearns standing on the porch once more, waving like a bunch of paradegoers on Memorial Day, until at last they faded away in Bertha's mirrors, nothing more than shapes in the fog.

"Can I drive?" Toby asked five minutes into the homebound journey, the only lights in sight belonging to Bertha.

"Absolutely…not."

"Sonny, please."

"No way, bro."

"Why not?"

"Because you're ten."

"You're only twelve."

"Thirteen next month."

"So?"

THE NIGHTWOOD SONG

"So what?"

"If you can do it, so can I."

"Probably, but not tonight."

Toby sulked for a bit, Sonny reducing his speed down to a crawl, the fog sending heavy plumes their way. At one point, rounding a curve, they probably could have gotten out and walked faster than Sonny was driving, Big Bertha growling in annoyance, another driver flashing his lights with far greater irritation.

Sonny pulled over and let the car pass, fog pressing against Bertha from all sides as if threatening to haul her into the woods with chains of mist.

Inexplicably, Sonny made sure the windows were rolled up.

"If you're gonna drive like a sally, let me drive."

"Cut the gas already."

"But I could–"

"Toby, enough. Seriously."

"I'm not a baby, you know."

"Of course I know." He reached across and took Toby's hand, fighting his brother's attempt to pull away. "You'll be driving before you know it, I promise. We'll have more than enough time."

"Really?"

"Really."

"You're not just saying that?"

"Do I ever tell you falsely?"

"Yeah."

"Like when?"

"Like when you and Mama say Grandpa's gonna be fine. If he's fine, why can't we see him? Why can't we even call him?"

"Because he needs to rest."

Sighing, Toby leaned his head against the window, probably with more force than he'd been hoping for, the thud suggesting at least a little pain.

"Tell you what," Sonny blurted a moment later, equally determined to satisfy Toby's urges as his own. "I'll call the hospital when we get home. I'll ask to speak to Grandpa."

"Really?"

"Yup. I don't see the harm in talking for a few seconds, but you can't tell Mama, okay?"

"Okay."

"Promise? If you spill, we'll both be eating the belt till Christmas."

"Promise."

After parking Bertha in the woodyard and guiding Toby back over the bridge, Sonny hastened inside and went straight to the phone, not even bothering to start up the hearth and the stove. By his guess, they probably didn't even have twenty minutes before Mama got home.

"Keep watch," Sonny instructed, shooing his brother away. "If you see headlights coming up the drive, you let me know straight away."

Sonny looked up the hospital number and dialed, a high-voiced receptionist answering after a few rings. Sonny gave his name and Grandpa's name, the receptionist taking a few moments to thumb through records before saying, "Looks like he was transferred a few days ago. Engelhard State—I'm afraid I'm not at liberty to tell you any more without parental consent. Are your parents there?"

With a cold catch in his chest, Sonny let the phone dangle away. Transferred? Why didn't Mama mention anything about Grandpa being transferred? Did that mean he'd gotten worse? Did he need an operation?

Sonny suddenly needed to pee, and badly. Mrs. Ahearn's spaghetti clawed back up his esophagus, his stomach throbbing nauseously. He almost called the hospital again, but there was no sense in that; the receptionist wouldn't say anything else without Mama's consent.

"Well? What'd they say?" Toby asked when Sonny trudged down the hall.

"They said he's sleeping…and to call back tomorrow."

"Why can't they wake him?"

"They just can't, okay? Now go upstairs and find something to do."

"What time can we call tomorrow?"

"Nine," Sonny blurted, hurrying to the bathroom.

Outside, the fog thickened. In the distance, a locomotive's horn cut through the night gloom, a decidedly spectral sound when the house was dim and answers were in short supply.

Chapter 10

That night, sleep might as well have been a thin post hidden in the deep fog, impossible for Sonny to find as he wandered the fields of worry.

His cough started up again and his nose had gotten stuffy. He was sweating heavily again, but this time it was a chilled sweat that made him seek an extra layer. Toby had asked him to keep the lamp on again, which didn't help his quest for sleep.

Transferred, transferred, transferred. The word became a nemesis in his head, not unlike Grandpa's chess knights. Just when you thought you had them figured out, they danced around and confronted you in a new and even more threatening way.

Engelhard State, the receptionist had begun before refusing to say any more without parental consent. Maybe Engelhard State was a much bigger hospital, with doctors who specialized in...what? What was wrong with Grandpa that had required a transfer?

Sonny itched to talk to Mama about it, but her only answer would be supplied by the belt. Instead, suppressing a cough but not a sneeze, he crept downstairs and pulled out the phonebook, quietly riffling through its pages. But the only listing he saw beginning with Engelhard State was:

ENGELHARD STATE ASYLUM

Asylum? As in, nuthouse asylum? Sonny checked again, just to be sure, but there were no other listings.

Closing the book and returning it to the drawer, Sonny paced the lower floor and rubbed his aching head, but nothing would erase Grandpa's words from his mind. No doubt he'd been acting strangely at times, even crazily, but he wasn't crazy like the people in nuthouses. He was just old and tired and a little broken up after Grandma's death, that was it, nothing more, nothing horrible, nothing deserving of an asylum.

Had Mama made him go there? Sonny's throat felt cold and constricted. Surely Mama wouldn't have…but she sometimes threatened to send the boys away to reform school if they didn't behave. What if she'd sent Grandpa away to Engelhard State?

Sonny popped an aspirin and downed it with cold water. He returned to bed and resumed the hunt for sleep, not realizing until he woke up to early light that he'd nodded off.

He was barely awake five seconds before Toby launched across the room. "Come quick, Sonny! You'll never guess what I found!"

"Let me sleep," Sonny groaned.

Toby tore off his blankets. He was already fully dressed, even his coat and hat.

"Did you go outside?"

"Yeah, there's a house! In the woods!"

"*What?* Where?"

THE NIGHTWOOD SONG

Sonny was mad enough to swat his brother, but he didn't have the energy to get out of bed.

"Come on, I'll show you!"

"I'm not going anywhere. Now tell me what happened already."

"I woke up in the middle of the night. The music, I could hear it again, it woke me…and there was this glow in the woods. I went to it, Sonny – I found the house! The Charnelle house!"

"Who?"

"The Charnelles must live there. That's what it said on the sign. Charnelle."

"You had a dream," Sonny realized. "A very vivid dream. You only *thought* you went out to the woods."

"No, Sonny, I found the house, I swear it. I went up to the porch. I rang the doorbell!"

"Why? Why would you go in the woods alone?" Sonny coughed at length, his head aching sharply.

"I had to see where the light was coming from. You gotta believe me. Please believe me!"

"Okay, okay, you went into the woods. Which way?"

"Just past the woodyard. It's right there, Sonny – I can't believe we ain't never seen it before."

"Kid, if you're pulling a trick on me, I swear–"

"It's no trick. I swear on Papa's grave."

They were both silent for a while, staring at each other. "Show me," Sonny finally said, hurrying into his clothes, choosing his favorite flannel jacket by reflex, forgetting the mending that needed to be done.

"Be quiet about it," Sonny whispered as they creaked down the stairs.

It was just after seven o'clock, the early light perfusing through a still heavy pall of fog. Mama wouldn't likely be up for another hour; Saturday was her sleep-in day, and the boys would pay dearly if they woke her, probably a belting and a skipped dinner, Sonny guessed.

It took Sonny a while to get his legs underneath him, and he struggled to keep up with Toby across the driveway and the footbridge.

"Slow down, I just got up!"

"Come on, hurry!" Toby waved, dashing across the woodyard, where Bertha was slumbering along with the tractor and loader. All around them, piles of wood watched from bedsheets of mist, Sonny trailing his brother past a few rusty trucks at the back of the yard. They hadn't worked since last decade, Grandpa said, and he occasionally brought someone out to see if they wanted to buy a little scrap.

"Careful," Sonny called as his brother climbed over a stack of torn-up tires and rusty parts.

"Come on, Sonny, would ya hurry up?"

Sonny coughed and spat his way down a thin, brambly path carving through the fog. Beyond their hasty footsteps and panting breaths, not a sound could be heard, no birds, no distant trains or traffic, no music, nothing.

"I don't get it." They'd arrived at a small clearing, a fog-laced pond in the distance, Toby glancing wildly about. "I'm sure this is the right spot. Yeah, this is definitely it." He pointed to a boulder and then the pond. "I saw all this last night. The house was right there."

"Congratulations," Sonny yawned. "You just forfeited first shower for today *and* tomorrow. And I'm gonna lather myself nice and long till all the hot water's gone."

"Sonny, please, you gotta believe me!" Toby rushed over and squeezed his arm, tears shining in his eyes. "I know what I saw! Please! The sign was slanty, and it said Charnelle, and the moon came out just a crack above me, and I went up the steps! I rang the bell, and a light came on inside. I could see someone coming toward the door, but they didn't answer. They didn't..."

He exploded into tears, Sonny embracing him.

"It was just a really vivid dream that tricked you into thinking it was real."

"No, it was real, I swear it!" Toby pulled away and searched the clearing again, as if this time the house would appear.

"Come on, let's get back inside," Sonny shivered. "You can have first shower, okay? I was only kidding."

Toby didn't seem to hear him, glancing about with disbelief, shaking his head repeatedly.

"Come on, Toby. I'll make you breakfast. Let's just forget all this."

Sonny got eggs and toast ready for everyone, glancing often into the dining room to make sure Toby stayed put. He remained seated before the table, staring out the window into the fog.

"I've had bad dreams all the time since Papa died," Sonny admitted. "Vivid dreams. I think about what it must've been like…you know, with the accident that night. I think about how bad Papa must've been hurt." He rounded the table and held Toby's shoulders. "Sometimes when I wake up, it's still real. Other times I'm crying even before I wake up."

"The house is real," Toby murmured.

"We're all gonna be all right." Sonny kissed the side of his brother's head. "I love you, little bro."

THE NIGHTWOOD SONG

"Love you." Toby's words were softer than a whisper, and farther than the sun.

Sonny spent the day checking items off his ever-expanding to-do list. He started indoors, giving the day a little time to warm up, his first order of business bringing him to the wood stove, the gaskets on its doors in need of replacement. Toby came by on Mama's orders, watching silently from the corner, Sonny offering rudimentary instructions. Next, the boys went down to the basement, Sonny showing Toby how to sharpen Grandpa's chainsaw properly, Toby asking the same questions as last fall when Grandpa had shown him. At least he kept quiet about the Charnelle house; hopefully he'd arrived at the realization that it was all a dream. Yet the look of terrified certainty in his eyes had haunted Sonny, staying with him for most of the day.

Mama made sandwiches for lunch, and then it was back to it. The boys spent an hour in the largest of five woodsheds on the property, sorting and stacking logs, then hustling the driest wood into the trailer. Once it was fully loaded, they hopped into Grandpa's doorless pickup truck whose shifter had snapped in half a few years back. Unbothered, Grandpa had lit up his pipe, disappeared into the garage for a bit, and returned with a pair of vise grips that were now clamped to the base of the broken shifter.

Sonny smiled at the memory as he backed up to the trailer. A minute later they were unloading the seasoned wood in the house shed, where it would continue to dry out until it was summoned in February or March.

Once this chore was complete, they hustled the truck and trailer out to the pre-seasoning sheds in the woodyard, Sonny backing the unit dexterously into the larger of the sheds. Grandpa had plans to level these two dilapidated buildings and replace them with a modern structure, but he'd been mentioning these plans since Papa was alive and trucking. Grandpa and Papa had always set plenty of irons in the fire, Mama often scolding them to stay focused on the task at hand.

As the sorting and loading wore on, Sonny's mind wandered far away and found itself lost in fear and regret, his thoughts centering on things large and small. Scattered among his regrets was the one-dollar bill Mr. Ahearn had given last night as a tip, Sonny wishing he'd kept it for himself rather than add it to the books. But he'd been seeking to make amends since Mama's reproach over letting Mr. Singletary skip his payment, and he hoped the gesture would buy him a little slack.

Before long, Sonny's thoughts circled back to the business of Grandpa's transfer. Engelhard State – what did it mean? And why wouldn't Mama give him the truth? Of course, he knew some things weren't meant for understanding, like how Toby could sleep with his socks on and how Grandpa always found his way to checkmate, but other things he felt he deserved to be let in on. He was mature enough – he could handle it.

But why didn't Mama trust him? Why would she lie to him?

"I'm tired," Toby sighed. "Can I go in?"

"Finish up those last few logs and you can call it quits."

"But my arms hurt."

"Fine," Sonny murmured, distrait, staring through the sliding doors into the unrelenting fog, thinking of what Grandpa might be enduring.

Toby wasted no time in making himself scarce, and now it was just Sonny and Grandpa's purring truck, its doors long ago removed for convenience in tight spots. He breathed in and blew out. Before returning to work, he hurried out of the shed and glanced through the misty woods across the stream, watching until Toby disappeared inside the house.

"You best not get in Mama's way," he muttered, stepping back into the shed and donning the pair of leather chainsaw chaps Grandpa had gotten for him last Christmas. Grandpa's chaps were hung up beside them, and still no one had gotten around to deciding what to do with Papa's chaps. They couldn't bring themselves to throw them out, but wearing them was equally out of the question. That would be—

Sonny spun around at the sound of shuffling footsteps outside the shed.

"Did Mama throw you back out already?" Sonny called.

But Toby didn't answer, the footsteps slowly approaching the shed, still out of sight.

"Toby, get in here and quit wasting time!"

Sonny hustled back out, but no one was there. He searched into the deeper woods past Grandpa's junker trucks, listening as the now distant footsteps casually crunched over leaves and faded into the fog. He could just barely descry a diminishing form at the edge of vision, but it was far too tall for his brother – and it was headed toward the clearing Toby had shown him that morning.

Before today, Sonny hadn't been out that way in years, Grandpa and Papa having felled and harvested almost every tree in the clearing six or seven years back. They'd even taken out the stumps and planted grass, Papa with visions of building a house there for one of the boys to live in one day, and the other boy could live in the next clearing they carved out. They would have all been nearby and happy if Papa's story had played out, but that story had ended in flames south of Salt Lake City.

Knowing he shouldn't do it but helpless to stop himself, Sonny followed this morning's path until he reached the fog-strewn clearing. He scanned the hoary maze, his eyes lingering on the unstill waters of the pond, gentle ripples coming in from the middle. Stepping closer, Toby's words about the Charnelle house whisked through him, the latest additions to a series of bizarre occurrences this week which kept Sonny's stomach roiled and stormy.

THE NIGHTWOOD SONG

Rounding the tiny pond, Sonny briefly thought he heard footsteps trailing deeper into the woods...and a softly played guitar somewhere in the mist.

"Just your imagination, dummy," he scolded. "Get back to work."

Instead, he waited. A minute passed and then another, the silence of a midnight graveyard creeping in. A midwinter's silence. The pond stilled and fresh troops of fog moved in, Sonny leaning against a tree and remembering the morning Mama got them up real early...*It's your father, boys. There's been an accident...*

The good thing about the foggy woods – you could sob till you started retching, and nobody could hear you. And the work would provide ample time for his red eyes and blotchy cheeks to normalize. Nobody had to know and it was best that way; they all had enough burdens without him going around flooding the place with waterworks.

But for now, in the foggy solitude, Sonny cried for Papa and Grandpa. He cried because he was afraid, and he knew Papa wouldn't have been afraid. He would've known what to do; he'd always known how things should be handled.

If Sonny had been so inclined, he could have gone to the northern lot right then and stood in the clearing where Papa had kept his hauling rigs, a pair of Kenworth beauties, one cab blue with gold lettering, the other white with blue lettering. Sonny had loved nothing more than summer hauls with Papa, sometimes headed up to Portland and Seattle, other times trucking down the coast to L.A., then hauling east across the desert on Route 66. Papa had known all the best diners to stop at, and they'd seen things out there in the lonely desert that should have only existed in novels.

Figuring he'd wasted just about enough time with thinking back and wishing things were different, Sonny returned to the woodyard and forced the bad thoughts out of his head. The ones that remained were drowned out by the chainsaw and a spray of woodchips.

By sundown, the next cord was loaded in Bertha's bed, ready for Monday's haul across town. Another half cord was already split and covered in tarps beside the loader, Sonny setting several rocks over the edges of the tarps to keep them in place. When it was all done, he sat with his back against the front tire of the loader, his hands blackened and bloodied from scrapes here or there. When he coughed and spat, a little blood was mixed into his saliva, but overall he felt okay. Probably just another sinus infection like last year.

Hauling himself up, the short walk back to the house felt like a mile. Before getting washed up for dinner, he filled a couple buckets with ashes from the hearth and stove, to be used over the winter to treat the icy driveway.

Mama made chicken and rice for dinner, Sonny's favorite. She'd even cooked the rice in tomato sauce and prepared bread, Sonny's gathering throat ache briefly knocked down by the hot meal and apple pie for dessert.

"Boys, I have news on Grandfather – good news," Mama announced as their pies were whittled down to crumbs, both boys setting down their forks and looking up eagerly.

"He's doing much better." Mama's smile was thin but hopeful. "The doctors say he needs a few more weeks of complete rest. Unfortunately, that means no calls or visitors. *But*," she hastened when the boys began to grumble, "if all goes well, he should be able to come home by Thanksgiving."

Sonny was dangerously close to mentioning the transfer to Engelhard State, the words venturing to the edge of his tongue, but he held them back at the last moment. If Mama hadn't offered the information by now, she wasn't planning to give it up.

"What's the matter, boys? I thought you'd be encouraged by this news."

"I don't wanna wait till Thanksgiving to see Grandpa." Toby's eyes welled with tears, Mama reaching over and patting his arm.

"He needs his rest. He'll be as good as new before long."

Sonny choked his words back as they helped Mama clear the table. Once the fires were freshened in the hearth and stove, Sonny cranking the damper just right and preparing fresh kindling, the boys were permitted to stay up an hour later, so long as their faces were washed, teeth brushed, and Sunday Best ready for church.

Sonny would have preferred to use the hour to catch up on sleep. He was feeling even worse than before dinner, nauseous and achy, but Toby nagged at him to play cards.

"All right, you're on," Sonny said, joining Toby on his bed. They played poker and canasta and pitch, Sonny dominating the latter game as usual, poor Toby always bidding with only an ace or falling for Sonny's lure of game and letting low slip through.

"How do you always win?"

"All skill, bro."

"You're the luckiest person alive."

"You know it."

"But how good are ya at 52-card pickup?"

"Don't do it."

Toby feigned a toss of the deck.

"Don't do it, kid. Big mistake."

Toby did it anyway, Sonny knowing it was coming when the mischievous grin lighted on his brother's lips. They rolled around on the bed for a bit, clapping each other with pillows, both boys scrambling to pick up the cards before Mama came in.

Tucked into bed a while later, Sonny was too spent to even think of a story for Toby. But tonight Toby didn't even ask.

Chapter 11

"Sonny, look! The light's out there in the woods again!"

Sonny winced, his throat blazing with pain, his eyelids feeling as if weights had been set atop them. Turning onto his side, wiping sweat from his brow, he shivered back the nausea and checked the clock. It was just before five, Toby's vague form pressed against the window.

"Sonny, get up and look! The light!"

"Go back to sleep," he mumbled.

Toby continued to urge him, but his words faded away, Sonny feeling like he was falling down a long, dark well. He tried to remain perfectly still and avoid swallowing; only then was the pain manageable.

An hour later, Sonny awoke but refused to lift his eyelids, too achy and nauseous. The only thing that made him feel halfway decent was thinking of Mary Ahearn and reaching beneath the sheet. That chased a little of the nausea back, but the other half of his brain was urging him out of bed to check on Toby.

Cracking an eye open, he switched on the lamp and confirmed his brother's form beneath the blankets. That was good enough, Toby safe in bed, and the questions could come later, Sonny too exhausted to even click off the lamp.

THE NIGHTWOOD SONG

When the clock sounded just after seven, Sonny felt as if he'd been struck by Big Bertha...with a full load of wood adding to her weight out on Purgatory Road.

Drenched in sweat, squinting against the foggy morning light, he padded across the room and stripped off his johns. Wrapping himself in a towel, he called to Toby, "Hit the shower, or it's mine."

No movement from his brother's bed.

"Last chance. Don't pretend you slept through the clock." Toby made not a sound. "Fine. Cold water's all yours."

Sonny knew that would get his brother up quick, but he didn't see Toby's toweled form appear minutes later on the other side of the steamed glass. Oh well, his loss, Sonny lathering extra long and drinking up the warm water. Nonetheless, he shivered and shook and coughed, the blood a little thicker this time as it swirled down the drain.

"Toby, get up already." This time, fresh out of the shower, there was anger in Sonny's voice, for his brother was still tucked away beneath the covers. "You best not make Mama late on Sunday."

No movement. No sounds. Reaching for his brother's shoulder, Sonny instead shoved a pillow hidden beneath the blanket.

Cold with fear, Sonny tossed the covers away and revealed an elaborate heap of pillows gathered from the guest room and living room. Toby had carefully arranged them to model his height, even tapering off with the smaller pillows at the end to give the impression of legs.

For a moment of hot-white terror, Sonny's pain and exhaustion were gone. He flew into his clothes, his Sunday Best forgotten on the hanger.

He raced downstairs, nearly bumping into Mama as she stepped out of the kitchen.

"Sonny, what on earth are you doing?"

"I gotta find Toby!" he called from the doorway, then scrambled down the porch into the fog. "Toby, where are you? Get in here!"

The only answer was supplied by a distant train horn.

"Toby! Toby!"

"Toby, come inside this instant!" Mama screamed from the porch, loud enough to clear a few birds from trees.

No reply.

"Toby, you best take heed of my words this instant!" When there was still no response, Mama turned worriedly to Sonny. "Did he sneak out while you were in the shower?"

"No, he was gone before I got up. He stuffed pillows under his blankets to fool me. He's gone off looking for that house again, I think."

THE NIGHTWOOD SONG

"What house?"

"He told me he found a house in the woods night before last. We went out there, but there was nothing. I kept telling him it was only a dream."

Mama's face was dazed for a moment, and then, orienting her thoughts, she stalked up to Sonny and smacked his cheek. "You didn't see fit to tell me about any of this?"

"I'm sorry, Mama. I told him he was mixing things up with a dream. We didn't wanna wake you."

"Show me this place you went!" she shouted, and Sonny wouldn't have moved quicker if it had been a locomotive bearing down on him.

They shouted Toby's name endlessly into the fog, but, across the bridge now, only the chuckle of the stream answered back. Standing in the misty woodyard in her Sunday dress, hands on her hips, Mama's expression could have sent entire armies fleeing.

By the time they reached the clearing, Mama's threats to Toby were replaced by desperate pleas.

"I won't hurt you, baby, just come back to me! Please, Toby, come back to Mama!"

The clearing was occupied only by fog and grass and that horrible little pond, with its obsidian waters that never seemed to be still. Doubled over, coughing with his hands on his thighs, Sonny was very nearly sick.

"You find my boy!" Mama bellowed, coming up to Sonny's side and shoving him off balance. "You boys have been messing around these woods, and now look what you've gone and done! You've been filling his head with stories and adventures, and now look! My boy's lost out there!"

"I'll find him, Mama. He's probably just around–"

She clapped a hand across his cheek so hard that he could feel something click in his jaw. "You find my boy! Don't come back till you do, you hear?"

She tried to hit him again, but Sonny dodged away, stumbling into the woods, calling blindly for Toby, tears hot on his cheeks. Behind him, Mama's shouts and screams blurred into a hellish cacophony that didn't cease until Sonny was far away, perhaps a mile off, his face and hands cut open by thorns, his jacket and trousers ripped.

He didn't recognize any of these trees, tall and thin, jutting out of the fog like sentries. He wondered if he was still on their property, or if he'd crossed into the state forest, which ran all the way up to the Nightwood and its miles of tall, stately, evenly spaced trees.

"Toby! Toby, where are you?" His shouts only endured another minute before they broke down to hoarse screeches. He spat a thin wad of blood and tried to shout again, but his voice didn't have much strength left.

He staggered down to the icy edge of a pond and cupped water into his mouth, cold enough to stun him and momentarily bring his voice back. He expended his few remaining shouts, but they didn't bring Toby; now, glancing skyward, his eyes stung with tears, all he had were whispers to God.

Almost immediately, his words were answered – but he was sure it wasn't God who did the answering. Distant but unequivocal, a calliope sounded through the fog, sending out a song so joyful as to be taunting, weaving it among the hills and the trees and the mist, proffering it to Sonny's ears. If he'd closed his eyes, he might well have been at the county fair, standing in line for the merry-go-round.

Coughing and spitting more blood, Sonny went in the direction of the music. It became just a little louder as he walked, but then it seemed to be coming from another direction, Sonny banking to the northeast. Before long, the music had him going in circles, sounding as if it were coming from all points on the compass, rising and fading and then rising eerily anew.

By now, with the sun hidden beyond the fog and the trees, Sonny was thoroughly lost. Yet his fear didn't concern his own safety; he would eventually find his way in these woods, but what about Toby? What if he got to panicking and stumbled so deep into the Nightwood that no one could find him? What if he kept on chasing the music which Sonny now ignored?

Although the calliope tantalized him with a seemingly specific origin, Sonny sharpened his focus, using tree moss to hone his navigation. When a train horn sounded, he pieced the clue into place and further defined the map in his head. If he kept plowing east, he'd eventually run into Purgatory Road, not far from the Route 31 entrance.

Occasionally he glanced back, thinking he'd heard footsteps crunching behind him. After a while the calliope faded and drifted away altogether, though Sonny didn't notice right away, the music humming on in his head. Where could it be coming from? And how could it alternate so wildly in direction and volume?

Sonny pictured his brother chasing the music endlessly, until fatigue or injury made him stop and darkness surrounded him. He pictured Mama screaming and sobbing in her Sunday dress, and it was all Sonny's fault. He should've told her about Toby going into the woods, but he'd been too afraid of punishment.

And now Toby was gone, alone in the foggy woods.

Sonny wiped away his tears and told himself to focus. Up ahead, perched on a high branch, a crow peered down at him contemptuously, deciding whether he was worth fleeing over. As Sonny passed beneath the crow's branch, it made a series of baleful caws that tore through the woods like shrapnel. Sonny interpreted these sounds as a warning that he was headed the wrong way, but he stayed true to what Grandpa had taught him about the thickest moss growing on the north sides of trees. Checking trunks wide and thin, he guided himself through pockets of denser fog, the trees becoming so tall that he couldn't see their tops through the mist. They hardly compared to the sequoias of the Nightwood, but the gloom could make even a one-story house seem as though it were a tower, very few truths to be had in these conditions.

Sonny plodded along, topping hills and coming down the other side, coughing the entire way. When he still hadn't reached the road after another half hour, he figured the moss had somehow led him astray.

He took a quick, panicked rest along a stream, his empty stomach roiling, his head throbbing.

How did I get turned around?

He alternated between calling for Toby and croaking his brother's name. His legs began to cramp on the next hill, dampness invading his old shoes and soaking his socks. Knowing this wouldn't do for long, he stripped off his socks and cast them aside, feeling as though he'd given away far more than a pair of socks; in fact, he felt like this was his first defeat conceded to the wilderness, the trees and the fog and the thorny thickets to be emboldened by this observation.

And all the while he wondered how Toby was holding up. Maybe someone had found him by now – a hunter or a hiker – or maybe he'd lucked out and wandered back home. Maybe.

Glancing up into the mist, Sonny tried to estimate the sun's position by seeking out the brightest patch, but there was no way of approximating the time. How far had he walked? Had his guesses at time's passage been excessively high or low? It felt like he'd been going for half a day, but he knew his sickness was throwing things off kilter. He was a little dizzy now, and maybe his stuffy head was to blame for going off track.

"I should be at the road by now," he muttered. "Or the tracks…or somewhere."

Grandpa's instructions flashed in his head – *If you're ever lost in the woods and you don't have a compass, try to find water and stay still* – but Sonny knew he couldn't be still, not with Toby out there on his own and the fog thickening.

Ten minutes or an hour later, drizzle pierced the fog, a thin wind clearing a few patches and allowing Sonny to glimpse into the distance. He huddled against a fallen, badly rotted oak tree, shivering and coughing, chilled so badly that he dug beneath a blanket of leaves and peeked out like a hunted soldier. It felt good to close his eyes and be out of the rain for a bit, and even the guilt of inaction couldn't impel him back to his feet.

Eyes still closed, he listened to the patter of light rain and the lulling whisper of wind. He could feel each cold gust assert its will, chasing out the fog like a cowboy's whip.

Move! he urged. *Toby needs you!*

Sonny thought he heard things in the storm – voices, footsteps, even music – but it was all quickly dispatched by the wind.

Tricks, all of it. Just a bunch of tricks!

THE NIGHTWOOD SONG

The coyote was no trick. Watching him curiously from a ledge fifty feet away, head tilted, the yote appeared no more menacing than a family dog. Slowly, Sonny rose to full height, wanting to ensure he wasn't mistaken for a small animal.

The yote held its position, yellow eyes gleaming, ears pointed, fur matted in the rain. It remained as quiet as the fog, not growling or glaring, not even raising its hackles, just watching Sonny.
A moment later, when a twig snapped loudly not far behind Sonny, then another, the yote whimpered and darted away, a few crows taking flight as well.

Sonny spun around and searched through the moderate rain, but the only movement was supplied by branches in the wind.

Following the yote's lead, Sonny hustled into an achy jog, looking back a time too many, the woods punishing him with a rock hidden in the leaves. He landed hard on his shoulder, and he could hear something pop in his neck.

It hurt for him to look sideways now. He was soaked down to his underwear, panic digging in deeper, and before long he was running again, panting and spitting blood as he climbed yet another hill.

On the downside of that hill, Sonny glimpsed colors in the distance, yellow chief among them. Raincoats. Umbrellas. Staggering closer, he could hear their voices over the rain and wind. They were calling Toby's name.

"Over there!" someone shouted upon seeing Sonny, triggering a rejoicing wave.

But when Sonny reached the group of ten strangers and gave his name, their brief joy was dampened. "That's not the boy we're looking for – it's his older brother," someone murmured.

A tall policeman bent down to wrap an arm around Sonny's soaked shoulders, pain flaring in his neck. "You look like you've been through hell, kid. How long have you been out here?"

"Since before church, sir," Sonny told him with a wince. "Have you heard music out here?"

The policeman eyed him as if he were speaking a foreign language. Nodding at another officer, he said, "Duggan, get this kid to Chief Clark's group. He needs some dry clothes and fast."

As though he were navigating the foglands of a dream, Sonny followed the officer to a narrow path, which led to a slightly larger trail and eventually a clearing where a trio of police cruisers and a school bus were parked.

After sending an update over the radio, the officer wrapped Sonny in a blanket and told him to wait in his cruiser where he could warm up. Ten minutes later, a small group led by a white-haired officer appeared from the gloom. Sonny would eventually learn that Police Chief Jack Clark had been born twelve years after the Civil War ended, the son of carpetbaggers from New Jersey who'd chased the railroad money down to Atlanta.

"H'ya, son. I'm Chief Clark," the man greeted with a gritty southern accent, extending a gnarled hand when Sonny stepped out of the cruiser.

Sonny felt as if his hand might be broken in the old man's grip. "My name's Sonny Winters, sir. Thank you for looking for my little brother."

"Thass m'job," the Chief grunted. "Y'look like ya seen better days, son. You get in a scuffle with somebody in them woods?"

"No, sir, just the thorns and thickets. I lost my way a little."

Clark squinted at his watch. "Well, I best get ya home to thaw out. Come on this way."

Sonny wanted to stay and help them search, but adults weren't meant for arguing with, especially not ones who looked like Chief Clark. Despite his age, he moved swiftly, his muscles bulging beneath his short-sleeved uniform top. When a stiff wind howled and Sonny shivered, the Chief didn't seem to notice it.

"Hop in," the Chief said, opening the passenger door of the cruiser two cars over.

"Thank you, sir." Sonny slid into the seat and buckled up, Clark hurrying around to the driver's door.

"We've covered a lotta ground today, but no sign of your brother. Even the county's best dogs lost the scent." Clark lurched the car into gear and tore through a half-frozen patch of mud, the overgrown trail leading downhill to meet Purgatory Road. "Your mother's searching with Pastor Mahone's group. They won't be back till dark, but I'll let them know you're safe and sound."

"Thank you, sir. For everything."

"Ah, I ain't done nothin' to be thanked for just yet."

The car was redolent with cigar smoke, Chief Clark driving fast through the fog. It amazed Sonny that he'd been lost in the woods for hours, trekking and toiling, yet a three-minute trip in the Chief's cruiser had him home, the fog rolled up much thicker out this way.

"Keep yourself put and wait for your mother," the Chief called through the window after Sonny stepped out. "We're gonna find your brother. It'll just be a little while longer."

"Thank you, sir. Thank you for–"

The car hastened off down the driveway, kicking up mud. At first, Sonny was intent on obeying the Chief and keeping himself planted, but the thought of Toby out there alone brought him upstairs. He gulped down water from the bathroom faucet and popped an aspirin, then changed clothes and bundled up. He fetched Grandpa's knapsack from the guest room closet, loading it with Papa's compass, Grandpa's maps, two flashlights and extra batteries, two extra pairs of johns and socks, a hunting knife, a book of matches, two full canteens, Grandpa's gloves, and a couple snacks. No matter what, he wouldn't be caught unprepared out there again.

Last, he grabbed his flannel jacket from its hanger and buttoned it up, then topped it with a hooded raincoat. On the way out of his bedroom, he passed his fingers over a framed family photo hanging by the light switch, Papa with his arms around the boys, Mama's face lit by a joy that had been five years absent.

Before leaving the house, Sonny Winters left a note for Mama, then went to his knees and prayed aloud.

Chapter 12

Sonny blew out a deep breath before venturing into the woods again, this time doing it properly with the compass and maps in hand, a bag of supplies over his shoulder. He coughed and spat, not wasting time to check for blood; the only thing that mattered was finding Toby.

With warmer attire, a decent stock of supplies, and an aspirin dissolving in his gut, he felt reinvigorated and resolute, as though he could go at it all night if needed.

The maps didn't show another house for a mile in any direction, and Sonny figured the police had already interviewed the nearest neighbors and covered the areas by the roads. That left a diamond-sized chunk of woods where Toby was likely sheltering, surrounded by Purgatory Road on one side, the railroad tracks on another, a river on the third border, and an old logging road on the fourth. Assuming that Toby hadn't crossed any of those boundaries, he had to be somewhere within the diamond of wilderness.

Yet despite its smallness on the map, this diamond represented hundreds of acres, its northern fringes crossing into the Nightwood. But Sonny didn't let that discourage him, checking his compass carefully and penciling notes into Grandpa's map.

The rain and wind had moved on, leaving what remained of the fog to its lonesome. It was already starting to get dark, a train horn echoing in the distance, Sonny confirming the position of the tracks against the compass. Everything checked out, and now Sonny felt strong enough to shout his brother's name again. Maybe he'd fallen and knocked himself out on a rock. Maybe he wasn't half a mile from the house.

"Toby! Toby, can you hear me? Toby! Toby!"

A coughing jag forced him to stop twenty minutes later and briefly consult his first canteen. Water was the least of his concerns; he could always refill at a stream or pond, but light, on the other hand, was in direly short supply. Not knowing how long the batteries would last, he was determined to bleed out as much sunlight as possible before forcing use of the flashlights.

Up ahead, he thought he saw a cluster of deer flash into the fog, his coughs and hacks scaring them off. In the extreme distance, he could hear a group of voices calling Toby's name, possibly the folks with Mama and Pastor Mahone. The thought of everyone hauling through the woods in search of Toby brought a warm solace to Sonny's heart; it made him feel that despite living far off in the middle of the woods, they were never alone.

A new batch of precipitation eventually rolled in, but this one brought a mixture of ice and flakes, Sonny grateful for his extra layers, wool hat, and Grandpa's gloves. He didn't need the gloves just yet; they were tucked away in the knapsack so he could make his markings on the map. But the creep of sleet over his fingers made him long for protection (and it also caused him to wonder how Chief Clark had seemingly been impervious to the cold).

The searching voices grew louder, clearer, the bob of flashlights becoming visible through the fog. Sonny steered clear of them, afraid that Mama or Chief Clark would be there to send him home.

Keeping quiet, he banked northwest and marked the adjustment on Grandpa's map, the flashlights disappearing behind him as if swallowed by the fog.

He made good time over the next hour, hunting for the colors of Toby's jacket and hat in the gloom, checking behind trees and boulders, checking in ruts and patches of brush, dodging thorns and tussling with branches, following a stream for a while. By the time the daylight died and he switched on a flashlight, he figured he was more than halfway to the railroad line.

His legs were ready to collapse like crumbling clay formations. Fire burned freshly in his abraded throat, his head throbbing. His neck strain from the earlier fall was redoubling now that the aspirin had begun to wear off. He'd packed a few more tablets, but he knew he'd be wise to conserve them. This wasn't going to be a short night, after all.

Onward. Deeper. Pushing through branches and brush, becoming so tired that he felt as if the fog were pressing its weight in opposition.

Occasionally he stopped and listened, half-convinced that he would hear distant music, but the night wilderness was silent but for the whispering-ticking song of sleet. He tried not to think too long about the calliope music from earlier, or the coyote that had departed suddenly as if threatened, or Toby's descriptions of the Charnelle house in the clearing just beyond the woodyard, or the strange form he'd glimpsed in the misty woods yesterday. He tried not to let his imagination get to painting devilish illusions in the dark, foggy gaps between trees.

A handful of times, he willed himself into glimpsing Toby sitting against a tree, or lying beside a rock, but the next glance always revealed vacant tides of fog coming and going. When Sonny climbed a slight hill, however, the tall, hooded form standing up ahead was no trick of the fog. The man was facing away from Sonny, standing between a pair of massive black oaks, the orange eye of a cigarette brought to his lips.

Sonny lurched backward and switched off his light, suddenly terrified that someone had abducted Toby...and now Sonny had stumbled across him. A shivery urge told him to turn and run, or at least hide behind a tree, but instead he clicked the light on again, expectations of a gun or a knife causing him to backpedal.

The man had turned around, tossed away his cigarette, and pushed back his hood. Squinting against the light in his face, dressed in a black raincoat and gray wool cap, he wasn't recognizable to Sonny until he spoke.

"I mean no harm. I'm looking for the Winters boys. They've been missing since–"

"Mr. Incobrasa?"

"Sonny, is that you?" He pulled his own flashlight out of a coat pocket and directed it into Sonny's face.

"It's me, Mr. Incobrasa." Sonny turned his light away and moved toward his chemistry teacher, Incobrasa fumbling him into an embrace.

"Thank God you're okay, Sonny! Are you hurt?"

"Mostly just tired, sir. I've been looking for my brother."

"Yes, we all heard about his disappearance this morning – and then *yours*. Principal Moffat managed to organize a few search teams of students and staff. They all headed home at sundown, but I couldn't stop searching." Mr. Incobrasa's voice quavered a little. "The thought of you boys lost out here…thank God you're okay, but your brother…"

"No sign of him all day," Sonny muttered, his eyes adjusting to his teacher's shadowy features.

"We'll keep looking. Together," Incobrasa offered. "Do your parents know where you are?"

"I left a note for my Mama. I've got a compass and maps."

"Good. Very good. Me too. Come along now, we'll go this way and–"

"Mr. Incobrasa, I think it'd be best if we split up. We can cover more ground."

"Heavens, no. I couldn't leave you out here."

Sonny went to his teacher's side and showed him Grandpa's map. "I started at my house and covered this distance. Roughly. What about you?"

Incobrasa took a few moments to acquaint himself with the map. "There," he finally pointed. "Our group began around noon at the Hoosac Lane trailhead. The others went back when it got dark, but I kept moving south. And here we meet."

The precipitation tapered off to a few leftover flakes. All around them, bigleaf maples, Douglas firs, white alders, and ponderosa pines watched apathetically, perhaps more interested in what the weather would ultimately choose to do with itself by dawn, presently undecided between rain, sleet, and snow.

"Would you like some water, sir?" Sonny said, fetching his second canteen. "I brought a few snacks, too, if you're hungry."

"Thank you, but no. I haven't had much of an appetite today."

Sonny handed him the canteen, anyway. "You can get dehydrated real quick out here."

"Yes, you most certainly can." Incobrasa accepted the canteen and drank, then sighed out his frustration.

"There's a lot of people looking for your brother. Someone's going to find him, Sonny."

"Yes, sir. Thank you, Mr. Incobrasa."

"You should go home to your mother. She must be worried sick."

"Yes, sir, but she'd rather have me out searching. She knows I can handle myself, but Toby…he ain't got the wherewithal for being on his own."

Sonny turned away and wiped tears from his cheeks before they could dampen his map. He tried but failed to keep back a new round of coughs.

"Sonny, please, come with me." Incobrasa put an arm around Sonny's shoulders. "I couldn't live with myself if you got lost out here, too."

"I can't leave until I find him, sir. I won't." Sonny was stunned by his defiance. "He needs me, Mr. Incobrasa."

The teacher nodded, a brief silence interrupted by the hoot of a distant owl. "Aren't you afraid out here on your own?" Incobrasa finally said.

"Yes, sir, but not as much as Toby. He's probably scared to death. He's two years younger."

"Yes. Yes, he is." Another sigh, this one conveying helplessness. "Please be careful, Sonny. Show me the route you're planning for the rest of the night. And are you warm enough? It'll be below freezing tonight."

THE NIGHTWOOD SONG

Sonny showed him the map again, but Incobrasa wasn't listening. "What if you fall down and hurt yourself? What if an animal attacks you? There's plenty of bears out here, not to mention mountain lions and coyotes. Is there any way for you to contact the authorities? No, no, I can't let you do this, Sonny. I simply cannot–"

Smothered by all the questions, but mostly by the wasted time, Sonny took off running, weaving between trees and shoving through underbrush.

"Wait, Sonny, please just wait!"

"I'm sorry!" he shouted back, tripping over a fallen branch and skidding along his stomach, pain spiraling through his neck and back. He popped up quickly and continued on, ignoring Mr. Incobrasa's pleas until a resurgent wind drowned him out.

The cold wind brought a nasty squall ten minutes later, but at least it chased off most of the fog. With better visibility once the snow relented – plus the contrast of white terrain against black forest – Sonny was able to improve his speed. He felt horrible for ditching Mr. Incobrasa, who'd dedicated his entire day to finding Toby, but there was no time to waste. Every moment spent staring at a map or checking a compass or drinking water was another moment Toby had to endure on his own.

And it was starting to get mighty cold out here.

Sonny spent the next few minutes praying through the darkness, slipping and tripping along hills laced with powder. Just in case God was plenty busy elsewhere on the planet, Sonny asked Papa to keep Toby safe a little while longer.

"I'll find him before sunup, Papa," he declared, picking up his pace again. "Toby, it's me! Can you hear me? Toby!"

The wind tried to silence him, but Sonny screamed over it and spat blood into the snow – the thickest gob yet. He knew he should eat, but fresh nausea had entrenched itself since the Incobrasa ordeal and he was loath to even drink.

He focused on each word, each syllable. "To-by! Toby, can you hear me?"

His imagination proved to be a challenging foe. He envisioned a pair of brothers in some distant house, one of them asking the other if he could hear shouts in the woods, the second brother saying, *What shouts?* Next, he imagined a house coming aglow – a house with a sign reading *Charnelle*, where a calliope came to life every few hours and attracted all who heard it.

Half an hour later, Sonny was still shouting for his brother while doing battle against his imagination. In the far-reaching distance, nestled in a valley between wooded hills, the headlight of a locomotive gouged the night.

Sonny checked his compass and map. If he kept up a decent pace, he could probably reach the tracks in another hour or two, then move southeast along the border of the woodlands. He would scour the trees abutting the tracks before angling across to the junction with Purgatory Road. It would likely take him till dawn to get back home, but he prayed that when he got there – regardless of whether he was crawling and puking or frozen solid – his little brother would be at his side.

Chapter 13

It was mostly downhill to the rail line, and Sonny's flashlight stayed bright for much of the way. By the time he changed the batteries, he could hear the clanks and squeals of rail cars being shunted onto a siding. He could even hear the purr of the engines, and there couldn't possibly have been a more beautiful sound at this hour, not only signifying his proximity to the tracks but also reinforcing his faith that he wasn't alone out here. Of all people, he'd stumbled into his chemistry teacher in the middle of the wilderness, and he supposed there were quite a few others still out searching through the night, braving the wind and the precipitation and the cold.

Thankfully, nothing had dropped from the sky since the squall. Sonny could even make out a few stars and the edge of the setting moon beyond a bank of thin clouds.

As tempting as it was to pocket the compass and navigate by the sounds of the train, Sonny stayed true to discipline and made repeated confirmations on his bearings. He refused to be deceived again by these woods, which seemingly had more tricks than Houdini – and more miles to boast than Bertha's odometer.

Owls and distant coyotes testified to the deepening night, clouds scudding overhead. Sonny tripped and went down to his hands and knees more times than he could count, strewn branches and hidden declivities promising a spate of bruises in the coming days, but the pain was tempered by desperation. And guilt. He remembered ignoring Toby's reports about the light in the woods. He should have gotten up and joined his brother at the window, but he'd wanted only to drift back to sickened sleep.

Now his sickness was taking its toll, the aspirin continuing to fade, his adrenaline carrying him onward. He suddenly felt exceedingly far from home. Far from warmth. Far from laughter. Out here in the deep woods, Sonny Winters felt as if Halloween with Toby had occurred a year ago, not a few weeks.

"Fuck you!" he screamed after becoming snagged on a branch. "Fucking asshole, get out of my way!"

He flailed and twisted but only managed to get himself caught on more branches, as though the trees were intentionally reaching out to grab him. He snapped off branches and tugged his knapsack free of a young pine's grip.

"Bastard! Fucking b–"

His ankle twisted over a rock and sent him rolling briefly downhill, kicking up an avalanche of leaves. Remarkably, he stood and continued on with no new pains, gathering his flashlight twenty feet away and brushing off his raincoat.

An eerie, protracted ululation in the northern distance spurred him on, less a sound of aggression than careful calculation. But it was a singular sound, no accompanying shrieks of attackers, as though a lone wolf were embarking on a hunt.

The howl resonated in Sonny's bones. He shined his light wildly about, clusters of shadows and wooded phantoms tightening the sickened knot in his gut.

Almost to the rail line, he stooped and retched, but he couldn't get much up, only blood-laced drool and a little bile. He tried to wash the taste out of his mouth, an unavailing waste of water, and now he was carefully stepping along the edge of a swamp bristling with trees.

The black water hugged up against the rail line embankment, Sonny skirting the swale for five hundred feet until it yielded to a boggy stand of sedge. His squishy footsteps became alarmingly faint, as if he were slowly transforming into a ghost, doomed to forever walk these woods and swamps.

Keep going! Almost to the tracks!

Although his shoes were quickly soaked, Sonny thought he could manage to slosh through the ankle-high puddles – until the grass suddenly fell away beneath him like a trapdoor, stealing him neck deep into a muddy morass.

Gasping and kicking, Sonny fought to stay above water, feeling as if he were swimming in a tub of syrup. Somehow maintaining his grip on the flashlight, he used his other hand to cling to a thin, low-hanging branch, then splashed across to another branch. Even as relief blossomed through him when he reached the shallows, new fear swept in with a cold gust.

"This is bad, real bad," he panted, shivering his way up to the rail line and stripping naked, his foot poked by a sharp rock. "I should've brought blankets – and more food! Much more food!"

He pulled open the knapsack, gaping at the sight of mud-spattered supplies and clothes. At least the fresh johns and socks were only partially wet.

Propping two flashlights against opposite rails, he got himself into the new johns and tried to clap mud out of his shoes and gloves. He tossed away the raincoat whose bright yellow hue was now caked with deathly brown. He listened to the night winds haunt along the rails, sharp with disdain and malice, forming trains of shadows and much blacker forms beyond the light's edge.

At last, he grabbed his flannel coat, an unrecognizable mess of mud. He folded it up and stuffed it in the knapsack. Sitting in only his johns on the rails, shivering violently, he tried to brush mud off Grandpa's map, but in the process he caused the wet paper to tear.

"No, please no. Please-God-no."

Wind lashed against his face, a new burst of snow clinging to his numb cheeks. Protected by a hat which hadn't been wet, his head was the only source of warmth on his entire body.

"Toby!" he screamed, blowing into his hands but only making them colder. He tried to put the gloves back on, but they were useless now.

He decided to layer up with the extra johns and socks he'd brought, but it was tantamount to putting on a few more T-shirts before ascending Everest. He was rapidly losing heat, his shivers shaking him off balance, and only when he stumbled and fell onto his side did he catch sight of the headlight in the distance.

The locomotive's horn bit through the night. Two minutes later, Sonny was walking alongside the slow-moving southeasterly freighter, his muddy shoes squelching with every step. He jogged a little to keep pace with a boxcar, first tossing his knapsack and flashlight through the partially opened door and then hauling himself up.

He gathered his flashlight and knapsack and scuttled into a corner, shining the light high and long, the boxcar suddenly seeming as capacious as a ballroom.

Immediately Sonny's shivers stopped. His breaths caught in his throat. He shined the light back into the far left corner, and yes, yes indeed, he was forcing a lanky, heavily bearded man to squint. A man whose prison stripes were balled up beside him, replaced by a brown coat and trousers he'd stolen from some house along the rail line.

"I...I'm sorry, sir...I was just looking to find my brother," he spluttered.

"And I was looking to not be found," the man grunted with a near toothless grin, remaining seated, a bottle of liquor at his side. "If I weren't so damn lazy, I'd toss your ass off this car, kid."

"Please, sir. I fell in the mud. I'll freeze out there."

"Yep, I'd say winter's here, all right."

The man took a swig, the train beginning to pick up speed, snow whirling through the door.

"I've got water, if you're thirsty," Sonny offered. "I brought some snacks, too, but they're all muddy now. The water's in canteens, though. It should be fine."

The man tapped the bottle, his long fingernails making a reverberating clink. "I've got all I need to drink right here, kid. Now get that light out of my eyes before I change my mind about not tossing you."

"Yes, sir. Sorry, sir. I won't tell nobody I saw you, I promise."

The man shrugged. "How long's your brother been missing?"

"Since this morning. He went off into the woods."

"Bad idea." He took another drink. "My brother was always full of bad ideas, too. Best idea he ever got was enlisting and getting the fuck out of this place. He drowned in Normandy."

"I'm very sorry, sir."

"No need. What's done is done. Life goes on."

He spoke impassively, as though he were describing the death of a squirrel beneath someone's tires.

"Your brother was a hero," Sonny said, moving carefully toward the door and peering out, shining his light into the passing woods, knowing he would never spot Toby in such conditions but trying nonetheless.

"Careful, kid, or you'll get your damn head lopped off," the man yawned, sounding even more apathetic than before as Sonny reeled backward, cursing, his forehead gashed by a branch that had snapped out from the woods.

"Jesus, kid, you're bleeding pretty good," the man said, producing a flashlight. "Come here, let me see it closer."

The man reached into his own knapsack, which he'd been using as a pillow. He extracted a rag and tossed it to Sonny. "Keep pressure on it. You'll scar up nice and fine, but it won't need stitches." He held up his bottle. "Go on. Drink. You'll thank me later."

Sonny reluctantly took the bottle and drank, feeling as if he'd consumed the flames from Mama's hearth, coughing and retching as the man laughed.

"You ain't never popped an ounce of liquor, have you?"

"No, sir."

"Well, there's a first for everything. Go on now, let me finish her off."

Still dripping blood when he removed the cloth, Sonny went back to the door and shined his light, figuring the train had to be close to the Purgatory Road crossing. He searched for the signals in the distance, keeping a close watch for looming branches.

Meanwhile, the escaped prisoner lit a cigarette. "Say, kid, you wouldn't happen to have any matches, would you? I'm almost out."

"I do, sir, but they're a little muddy."

The man waved uncaringly. "Mind if I take 'em off you?"

"No, sir." Sonny dried the matchbook along his johns. "Here you go, sir."

"Your daddy in the military? You're mighty polite, kid."

"Yes, sir, he was. He fought in the war."

"Did he make it back?"

"He did, sir, but he passed in a wreck five years back. There was a bad storm in Salt Lake City."

"Jeez, sorry, kid." For the first time there was emotion in the man's voice, and now he was back to drinking, Sonny catching notice of the crossing signals up ahead.

"Good luck, sir. I hope you make it wherever you're going."

"Wait, kid! The train's going too fast!"

The ground seemed much farther away than before, but Sonny knew it was an illusion of speed and darkness. The pain upon landing, however, was unequivocal and unforgiving, the air choked clean out of Sonny's lungs, his hands shredded along the rocks, his knapsack flying away as if taken by a twister.

For a few moments he saw fireflies and colorful orbs flitting through the darkness, his ears ringing sharply. Blood erupted from his hands, and when he wiped his chin he came away with mud and more blood.

"Good Lord! Jesus Almighty!" someone was shouting, but Sonny could see little more than sparks of pink and blue and orange in the distance. He'd landed well short of the crossing, skidding along the rocks and rolling onto his back.

"Good God, do you have a death wish, kid?"

"No, sir, I was just..." Sonny winced from the sharp pain brought by his words. "I need to find my brother."

"Why are you wearing nothing but your underclothes in this cold?"

"I fell in the mud, sir. My clothes were soaked."

Slowly, the man's face took form, illuminated by the headlights of a car stopped at the crossing. Helping Sonny up, the man carried him to the car, set him gently against the tire, and opened the passenger door.

"Please, sir, will you help me find my brother?" Sonny closed his eyes, and when he opened them again, he was in a hot bath, the man from the railroad crossing softly dabbing his face with a cloth and turning the fabric red.

Sonny lurched back, but the man held his shoulders. "Easy now. Easy. You're safe. Just rest."

Sonny blinked away the remnants of a nightmare in which he'd peered out his bedroom window, spotting a light where there shouldn't have been one, just inside the foggy woods. He'd heard soft music, followed it through the fog, chasing down the music and the light, just in time to watch Toby go up the front steps of a small house and ring the bell. Sonny had screamed for his little brother to *Stop/Come back/Get away from there*, but Toby hadn't heard him, drawn to the slowly opening door and through it, wrenched into the black void beyond, the entire house disappearing in his wake…

"You've had yourself quite the adventure, kid." The man shook his head. "You're lucky to be alive."

He was a heavyset man with glasses, a white collar poking up from his green sweater. He'd worn a black fedora back at the crossing, Sonny remembered, but now he smoothed a hand along his bald pate.

Sonny tried to stand, but the man wouldn't have it. "You ought to rest awhile."

"Please, sir, I need to find my brother. He's been missing since this morning. He went into the woods."

"What's your name, kid?"

"Sonny, sir. I'm Sonny Winters. I live on Purgatory Road with my Mama and brother, Toby. He's been missing since this morning. He went off trying to find the Charnelle house in the woods."

"Easy now, take it easy. We'll sort through all of this." He went to the door hook and handed Sonny a towel. "First off, let's see if you can walk all right."

With stinging, burning palms, Sonny wrapped the towel around his waist and, with the man's help, stepped out of the tub onto a pair of towels spread across the floor.

"Careful now, it's slippery. That's it, nice and slow. Does it hurt to walk?"

"No, sir."

The man let go of his wrist. "Follow me, nice and slow, that's it. You're one sturdy boy, you know that?"

He led Sonny to a lamplit bedroom, where several articles of clothing were laid out on a neatly made bed.

"My son's away at school. His clothes will be far too big for you, but they'll do. That's what belts are for, right?"

"Yes, sir," Sonny cringed.

"Go on, now, get dressed in something you like. I'll be back in a bit to get you bandaged up."

The man closed the door behind him, his footsteps tapering down the stairs. Sonny threw on some clothes, taking a moment to identify the shorts as underwear and not swim trunks. The bowling shirt hung off him, the socks going to his knees, and despite the agony in his palms, he had it all belted and buttoned in place by the time the man came knocking.

"You all set, Sonny?"

"Yes, sir. Thank you for everything, sir."

Sonny wiped his chin and came up bloody. "I'm sorry if I soil your son's clothes, sir. I'll pay for–"

"Nonsense," he waved, setting a kit of medical supplies on the nightstand. "Here, let's get you some ointment and a few bandages…Jesus, that's a nasty gash." Gently, he dabbed ointment along Sonny's forehead and adhered the bandage, then tended to his chin and hands.

"I know it hurts – just a little while longer," he consoled when Sonny's grimaces turned into groans. "There, that should do. Now, can you tell me who the President is?"

"President Eisenhower, sir." But panic spread through Sonny when he tried to remember the circumstances leading to his arrival at this man's house, several large blanks in his memory.

"Good. Very good. I'm John Stevens, by the way." He held out his hand, then withdrew it. "I'd say we should probably give your hands a break."

"I need to get back outside to look for my–"

"No, sir-ee, you aren't going nowhere, kid. You can't even close your fists. Come on downstairs and let's grab something warm to eat."

"Yes, sir."

The house smelled strange, Sonny taking a while to pinpoint the source: an absence of woodsmoke. Mr. Stevens must've been heating entirely from a furnace, highly unusual for these parts, almost everybody's chimney billowing nine months out of the year, plus wood stove pipes venting smoke along the sides of houses.

The walls were heavily occupied with family photos, even in the kitchen, where Mr. Stevens prepared soup as Sonny sat before the dinner table and stared at his bandaged hands. He had to get back to the woods and continue looking for Toby, but he knew he wouldn't make it very far with useless hands. He couldn't even grip the spoon when the chicken vegetable soup was on, Mr. Stevens bringing a wooden ladle to his lips each time.

"I sure am sorry, sir. I'm imposing terribly."

"It's no trouble, Sonny. I'm just awful glad I was paying attention when you decided to defenestrate yourself from that carriage." He raised the ladle yet again to Sonny's mouth. "And to think, if I hadn't stayed a little later tonight with Mom, I would've been long gone by the time that train rolled through."

The soup felt good on Sonny's throat, but its warmth also brought a stab of guilt. What if Toby was drowning out there in the mud, screaming for help while Sonny enjoyed steaming chicken vegetable soup?

"I visit Mom almost every night. It's important to stay connected," Mr. Stevens was saying.

"Engelhard," Sonny murmured, twitching with memory. "Mr. Stevens, do you know what Engelhard State is?"

John Stevens rested the ladle in the bowl. "The asylum?"

"I think so. Is there anything else around here that starts with Engelhard State?"

He rubbed his chin. "I don't believe there is. It's up in the northern part of town, well past the mill and the dam. Why do you ask?"

"I think my grandfather was sent there. I don't know why. He's been acting weird lately, and he heard the music. My brother did, too, and then he saw this house in the woods. The Charnelle house. Do you know anyone around here named Charnelle?"

"Can't say I do, son. It sounds like you and your family have been through a hard time. What's your mother's number? I'll call and let her know you're safe."

Sonny gave the number. "You probably won't reach her. I bet she's still out with Pastor Mahone's search team."

"At this hour? No, I don't suppose that's the case, Sonny."

"But my brother – everybody's gotta keep looking!"

"They will. No doubt they'll be back on it at sunrise."

Sunrise? That was still several hours off – far too much time for Toby to be alone in the wilderness. He was probably verging on unconsciousness from the terror alone, not to mention the elements.

Mr. Stevens went to the phone and dialed, Sonny stunned into a coughing spell when he reached Mama.

"...Yes, ma'am, I've got him here at my house on Cedar Ridge. He's a little banged up, but I tended to him...Yes, ma'am, absolutely." Stevens turned around a corner out of sight, walking as far as the line would allow. "He's a good boy, ma'am, he's just desperate to find his brother...Yes, ma'am, I'll have him over right away."

Setting the phone back in its cradle, Stevens returned to the table and took up the ladle.

THE NIGHTWOOD SONG

"Have they made any progress, Mr. Stevens?"

"Not just yet. I'm sure they'll catch some breaks tomorrow. For now, let's finish up this soup. I've got your things in the garage – I managed to wash some of them off a little, but it'll take some doing to get all that mud out."

After taking a few more spoonfuls, Sonny followed Mr. Stevens into the garage, ashamed by the pool of mud encircling his knapsack. He stuffed his possessions into the sack, everything but the flannel jacket, which he neatly folded.

"My father gave this to me just before he passed," he explained after the brief delay. "It's just me, Mama, and Toby now."

He fought to keep the tears from falling, John Stevens setting a hand on his shoulder. "They'll find your brother, Sonny. I know they will."

Back in the car, Sonny was embarrassed by the mud caked onto the seat and floor. "This mess won't do. I'll clean this up. I'll see to it that–"

"A little mud is nothing compared to the nightmare you're facing, son. You leave that to me."

"But Mr. Stevens–"

"No buts. Just focus on recouping – you'll need all your energy tomorrow."

"Yes, sir. I certainly will, sir."

The drive home was long and foreboding, guilt mounting with every mile.

Crossing back over the railroad tracks, Mr. Stevens said, "You know, the more I think about this Charnelle house your brother was talking about, I keep getting this odd little kernel of a thought in my head. Did Toby read a lot of ghost stories?"

"He loves stories, sir, but not reading. He don't even read the hymnal at church, but he loves when I tell him stories."

"Scary stories?"

"Yes, sir."

"Have you boys ever heard of a charnel house?"

The pronunciation was much different this time, heavier on the first syllable, to the point that Sonny didn't even recognize the comparison at first. And Mr. Stevens made the first two letters sound like a Ch-, not an Sh-.

"No, sir. I don't know that word. What's a charnel house?"

"It's a place where…remains are stored."

"Human remains? Like a cemetery?"

"Yes, very much like a cemetery. Anyway, I was figuring maybe your brother had picked up a story somewhere and was trying to scare you with talk of the Charnelle house."

"Nah, I don't think so, Mr. Stevens. Not Toby. He wouldn't have been able to fool me that long. He was convinced he found this house – he even said he rang the bell – but when he took me out to the woods the next morning, he couldn't find it again, only a clearing."

"Huh, that's mighty strange," John Stevens said, gripping the wheel with both hands.

Back home, Mama was waiting on the porch, arms crossed, when Stevens pulled up. Her face was blotched and puffy, her eyes red, tears shining on her cheeks when she pulled Sonny into an embrace.

"He's a good boy, a real good boy," Stevens called through the window before heading back down the driveway.

Ignoring him, Mama rasped, "How could you, Sonny Winters? I'm going through hell, and all you've done is fan the flames all day long." Her lips trembled, her voice becoming hauntingly small. "You rotten, horrible child."

"I'm sorry, Mama. I've been looking for Toby, I–"

"Go inside and stay out of my sight."

"Mama, please, we have to go back out and–"

"Drop your things. And go inside," she pointed, turning away and weeping into her hands.

Sonny set down the knapsack and dragged himself up to his room, exploding into tears at the sight of Toby's bed. When he woke, he was still collapsed on the cold floor, wearing the clothes of John Stevens's son, misty light drizzling through the window.

Panicked by the hemorrhage of minutes and hours, he launched downstairs and opened the front door, coming face to face with Chief Clark.

"Y'didn't heed my instructions, son," the Chief growled, letting himself into the foyer. "S'pose I would've done the same thing if it were my little brother." He rapped Sonny on the shoulder. "Go on into the dinin' room. I got some questions for ya."

"Where's Mama?" Sonny asked when the Chief settled into a chair.

"Down at the church. We got the search started back up – plenty more folks out there today." He cleared his throat noisily. "Meantime, I got some questions about this music I keep hearing about."

"Yes, sir, my grandfather and Toby both heard the music. And when I was in the woods yesterday, I heard it, too."

"Where was it coming from?"

"That's the thing, sir. It sounded like it came from all around."

THE NIGHTWOOD SONG

Sonny took some time to explain it better, Chief Clark nodding and jotting things down.

"They sent my grandfather up to Engelhard State Asylum," Sonny inferred.

"Yep. Your mama told me," the Chief grunted, sending cold spasms of confirmation through Sonny. "Sometimes people lose their way a bit," he murmured, glancing back to his notepad.

"I know Grandpa was acting odd, sir, but we all heard the music. He wasn't making it up."

Clark nodded at length and exhaled deeply. "You folks are hardly the first to hear music in them woods." He sighed again and crossed his arms.

"Who else has heard it, sir?"

"A few folks – it was a while back." His face seemed to darken a little, his scowl deepening. "You heed my words, boy, and stay out of them woods." Clark's eyes seared into him, Sonny averting his gaze. "I got more folks than I can count on two hands disappearing these last couple years. You best keep out of them woods."

Sonny knew far better than to start up with buts and questions.

"Now, what about this house your mama mentioned? The one your brother claimed to see."

"The Charnelle house. Or Charnel house. Do you know what a charnel house is, Chief? I just learned last night."

"Enlighten me."

Sonny carried on with explanations, stopping occasionally to swear to the veracity of his accounts. "I know how it sounds," he concluded, "but please, you have to believe me."

"I don't *not* believe ya…or your brother," he grunted.

"Thank you, sir. It means a lot, sir."

Clark nodded and rubbed his gnarled hands, which were so rough that they bled in spots. "Now, I might be old, but I sure ain't stupid. In spite of everything I told ya, I know you're gonna go running for them woods the second I leave this place."

"Yes, sir." Sonny risked meeting the Chief's icy stare. "I'm sorry, sir, but I can't sit here while my brother's out there alone."

"I get it. Thass why I want you joining my search group today."

"But we can cover more ground if we all split up."

"Yep, I s'pose we could do that. And then I'd have twenty more people to find 'morrow mornin'."

Sonny looked down, nodding.

"Son, this is the best offer you're gonna get from me. I won't see ya get torn apart by them woods." He nodded at Sonny's hands. "Look how poorly ya acquitted yourself in just one night."

"Yes, sir. I'm sorry, sir."

"You'll be truly sorry when I lock ya in the clinker till we find your brother." He reached into his belt and slapped his handcuffs onto the table, Sonny flinching. "Am I taking you to search with us, or the jailhouse?"

"I'll search with you, sir. I'm very sorry for all the trouble. I didn't mean it to be this way, I swear it."

"Enough, enough already! You're worse than a damn parrot."

"Sorry, sir."

"Let's get to work. Time's-a-wastin', kid."

Chapter 14

Chief Clark drove quickly through the fog, as if the navigation of these roads had become muscle memory.

"Tell Mrs. Winters her boy Sonny'll be searching with our group," Clark said over the radio, turning through the opened gates onto Route 31.

The road under construction had been transformed into a staging area for law enforcement and searchers.

"No updates," Clark growled upon stepping out of the car, immediately greeted by a pair of mustached newsmen with notepads and cigarettes.

"Chief, do you care to comment on–?" one of them started, but Clark dismissed him with a grunt, Sonny needing to jog to keep up with the Chief's pace.

"Reporters," Clark huffed when Sonny reached his side. "They're all vultures. Don't say a word to 'em if they come knockin'."

"Yes, sir. I won't, sir."

Farther along the road, past a row of tents, police cruisers, and school buses, dozens of searchers were placed in groups. Sonny recognized several faces – kids from school, teachers, a few waitresses from Huber's Roadhouse where Mama took them for burgers sometimes on Saturday nights – and all eyes washed over Sonny with sadness and pity. School had been called off district-wide, Sonny would later learn from Mr. Incobrasa, who hurried over and hugged Sonny.

"How bad were you hurt?" Incobrasa asked, Sonny made aware of his bandages yet again.

"It's no big deal, sir, just a few scrapes."

Sonny even recognized Roger Staley and his folks in the crowd, fresh twinges of guilt coiling through Sonny at the memory of beating up Roger at the Strawberry Festival and then threatening to burn down his house.

"Well, then, let's get to it, people!" Clark hollered. "Groups of ten, each one led by a man with a damn compass!"

Maps and compasses were properly distributed, and the groups broke off for the woods ten minutes later. Sonny's team was comprised of Chief Clark, Mr. Incobrasa, Principal Moffat, a blue-eyed family of four, a hunter named Richard Omya who said he'd hunted these woods for half a century, and a haggard looking vagrant whose name Sonny didn't catch.

Chief Clark and Mr. Incobrasa carried compasses and maps, Mr. Omya with a rifle slung over his shoulder. The blue-eyed family formed a cocoon around Sonny, the mother soothing and cooing, the father assuring him it wouldn't be long before Toby was found. With all these people trekking through the woods with him, Sonny knew by some uncanny intuition that the music wouldn't make itself known. He wouldn't see a lone coyote, and there was nothing baleful this time in the crows' caws.

Everybody called Toby's name, the discordance sharpening Sonny's headache. At one point, Mr. Incobrasa fell back in the group to ask Sonny how he'd come to meet his injuries; meanwhile, at the back of the line, the bearded, nameless man said nothing, carrying on with a face of stone.

An hour passed quickly, the fog beginning to lift. The blue-eyed boy and girl began to complain that their legs were aching, the blue-eyed woman barking about her knees, Mr. Incobrasa eventually steering them back to base. Sonny continued on with Chief Clark and the others, Mr. Omya giving him half a sandwich from his cooler, Principal Moffat offering his soda. Sonny tried not to cough too much and disturb the others, but a handful of times he was helpless to stop, turning away so nobody would see the blood.

They performed a lengthy square search, returning to base around noon. Sonny told himself there was still plenty of time left for Toby, but memories of the mud and the cold and the pain offered a strong argument. He knew that, without the good fortune of the passing train, he likely would have frozen to death out there – and how had Toby managed to endure the entire night and then the morning?

Sonny rubbed back his tears as meals were distributed. He tried to sit by himself, but folks kept coming over with tokens of hope to hand out, one old lady forcing him to sit still while she cleaned and re-dressed his wounds.

"Open your hands."

"I'm sure they'll be fine till later, ma'am."

"Go on, open 'em."

Sonny obeyed, wincing through the process, the woman kissing his forehead when it was done. "Lord, be with you and yours, child," she said before fading away.

A group prayer was offered, Chief Clark checking his watch, Mr. Omya yawning. The policeman with the search dog showed up a bit later, and the big shepherd sniffed off into the woods as far as his leash would allow.

In the woods, thin veils of stubborn mist remained. Sonny removed his soaked socks and banged out his muddy shoes, coughing the whole time. Murmurs sprang up about how he needed to rest before he caught pneumonia or his death, but Sonny was first in line when Clark reassembled a fresh group. The only other holdovers from the morning were Mr. Incobrasa and Mr. Omya, their voices booming into the woods as afternoon waved to evening in the distance.

Sonny spat several wads of bright blood, his throat burning each time. Dizziness overcame him when they crossed a creek, forcing him down to a knee. He lagged well behind the group on the second leg of the square, Mr. Incobrasa staying back with him. He tried to push forward and keep up, but his legs felt like they were made of sand, his head like a half-split log on the chopping stump.

He popped the aspirin he'd been hoping to save for later, washing it down with water from Mr. Incobrasa's canteen. For a while, the trees seemed to revolve around him – a silent, misty carousel.

"Did you hear that?" Sonny asked his teacher a while later.

"Hear what?"

"It sounded like drums, sort of. Have you ever heard music out here, Mr. Incobrasa?"

"No, but I don't spend much time in the woods. I'm usually buried in a book."

"I've heard–" Sonny declined into a bad coughing tilt, so intense that the others stopped to look back, their faces obscured by the freshly gathering mist.

Sonny went to both knees this time, and then he was floating in the fog, taking a moment to realize Mr. Incobrasa had scooped him up.

"Rest awhile, Sonny. Close your eyes."

"But I have to keep looking. I have to..."

When Sonny awakened, he was in Mr. Omya's arms, Route 31 appearing in the distance through the fog. Darkness was creeping steadily closer, precious minutes swirling down the drain. Sonny tried to follow Chief Clark back into the woods for his next search, but a policeman held him back.

"Take him to the Roadhouse," Clark instructed. "Get him a hot meal and take him home."

"No, please, sir, let me look! I have to keep looking!"

"Son, you can hardly move. You won't make it ten feet into them woods, and I need men searching, not carrying you."

Sonny brushed aside his tears. "Please, sir, please don't–"

"Rest up, son." Clark turned and waved his men after him. "And don't do nothin' foolish," he pointed, glancing back before disappearing into the fog.

At Huber's Roadhouse, the policeman ordered Sonny a burger, fries, and a Coke.

"Have you ever heard music in the woods, officer?" Sonny tried to meet the man's gaze, but it was a struggle to lift his eyes from the mesmerizing black-and-white checkered floor tiles. Conversations at the other booths sounded as if they were coming from underwater.

"Music? Nope. Never heard music out there. Why?"

"I've heard it," Sonny mumbled, hazy with pain and memories, feeling as if he'd briefly awakened from a dream, only to roll onto his side and re-enter the dreamscape. "Toby and Grandpa, too."

Sonny coughed into a napkin and stained it red, glancing down a few minutes later to find a burger and fries beneath him, the waitress's face blurry. The neon sign over the bar spelling **HUBER'S ROADHOUSE** looked like a nighttime city skyline glimpsed through squinting eyes.

"I've seen things in the woods," Sonny murmured, nibbling a fry and surprising himself with his appetite. Each swallow burned through him, but he managed a few bites of hamburger and washed them down with the solace of soda.

"Try to rest," the officer said. "You'll feel better. And don't worry – we're gonna find your brother."

"Not if *it* finds him first."

"What?"

"It."

The officer said nothing, a strangely echoey silence ensuing, Sonny groaning and nibbling, asking for ketchup even though the bottle was right in front of him, shaking salt onto his fries but tasting pepper instead.

"Excuse me, Sonny," the officer said after his meal arrived. "I'll just be a few minutes to wash my hands. You stay put, understand? Don't leave this seat."

"Yes, sir."

Sonny's appetite flew off like a night bird. It felt good to shut his eyes, but they wouldn't stay that way for long, not with the stranger settling into the seat opposite him.

"I believe what you said, kid," the old man growled, taking a sip of the officer's soda. "I've seen things, too – plenty of things in the woods."

Sonny was too sick and startled to register any details of the man's face beyond the hoary frost of age.

"The name's Durant," the man added. If thunder could have extended its hand and introduced itself, it might have resembled this stranger. "Donnie Durant."

Sonny held his hand out into space and let Durant do the rest.

"I'm Sonny Winters, sir. I apologize for my condition. I haven't been well."

"Don't apologize, kid. I've heard a great deal about your plight." His voice lowered considerably, almost a whisper now. "I can't stay long, but here's my address." He scribbled onto a napkin, folded it, and handed it to Sonny. "When you're better, find your way out there. I'll tell you everything then."

"Do you know where my brother could be?"

"Shh, say nothing of this to the police or anyone. Just drop by during the daytime, never at night. Never after dark."

"But–"

"Quiet! Eat your food…and keep that address out of sight."

The stranger whisked himself away with the subtlety of a warm breeze on a March evening. Pocketing the napkin before the officer returned, Sonny wondered if Durant's appearance had merely been a dream – a wishful dream that someone believed him. Anyone.

But when the officer paid the bill, Sonny stole a glance at the napkin and read the address three times for confirmation, hope warming through him.

Chapter 15

When Sonny awoke, he was slumped in a second-row pew at church, the sleepy-eyed Pastor Mahone watching him from the altar.

"Your mother's almost finished praying. She'll take you home soon."

"Yes, sir."

Adjusting his achy head, Sonny let his eyes slide shut again, and he would have drifted back to sleep if not for Pastor Mahone's hand in his. "You've been through so much, Sonny. We've all been praying for your family."

"Thank you, sir. You're all very good to us."

Mahone lightly squeezed his bandaged hand, even the thinnest pressure drawing pain and chasing sleep away. Slowly, the details of the dim, candlelit nave came into form, empty but for Sonny and Pastor Mahone.

Embarrassed, Sonny wiped a strand of blood-laced drool away. "I'm not well, sir. I'm sorry for my appearance."

"You must rest, Sonny."

"But I have to keep looking. This whole thing is my fault. It's–"

"Nothing is your fault, you hear? Nothing."

"Mama knows it's my fault, too." Sonny's valves broke and let loose a torrent of tears. "It was my job to watch him! He's out there because I didn't watch him!"

Mahone pulled him into an embrace until the tears thinned. Footsteps echoed down the aisle, and then Mama's voice.

"Let's go home, Sonny." She spoke softly, as if she, too, had just been sleeping. "We're both exhausted."

"We should keep looking, Mama."

"Son, I'm afraid there's nothin' more we can do right now." Chief Clark appeared at Mama's side. "With this fog, I can hardly see my own hand out there."

"But–"

"Go on, son – go home with your mother and get some rest. Come first light, we'll get back after it."

Sonny didn't trust himself to keep arguing, afraid that he'd crumble into tears again and make himself look incapable of continuing. Instead, he breathed deeply and nodded, following Mama out of the church to the wagon.

Fog had pressed in heavily, snapping over the woods like a glove. Mama drove slowly, with both hands on the wheel.

"I'm sorry for everything I've said and done," she said, staring straight ahead. "You didn't deserve what I put you through."

"Don't apologize, Mama. It's my fault. I failed."

She reached across and squeezed his arm. "You didn't fail, son – I failed. Since Papa's death, I've put too much on you. It wasn't fair."

"But I should've told you about what Toby saw. I was scared of the belt. I was weak, Mama."

"We all made mistakes." She spoke now with exceeding quiet. "All we can do is pray."

"No, we gotta keep looking, Mama. He won't last another night out there."

"Pray, my boy," Mama murmured. "The Lord will see us through. He'll keep Toby safe. He'll–"

"Mama, the driveway!"

She overshot it by a hundred feet and backed up. "Let us pray, Sonny Winters. Let us go home and pray."

Chapter 16

Sonny got some water and medicine into him, then prayed with Mama before the hearth. They began and ended with the Lord's Prayer, Sonny pulling a blanket over his mother once she fell asleep. He watched her for a while to make sure she was out for good, then scribbled out a note, switched off the lamp, and crept to the door.

In the foggy side yard, he stopped at the sight of his flannel jacket hanging on the line, Mama having washed the mud out of it. A trace of a smile came to his lips as he buttoned the still-damp jacket, but it was eradicated by the sight of the article hanging at the end of the line: his yellow raincoat.

The same raincoat he'd worn last night and tossed away on the rail line.

"What the–?"

He snatched it down and checked the tag to confirm it was his, gaping at the SW initials marked on the tag. But how could it have gotten here?

A twig snapped in the woods, then another. Sonny thought he saw a tiny glow deep in the woods, no bigger than a candle, and then it was gone, silence prevailing in the fog.

Listening a little longer, he heard a distant attack of coyotes and the clank of a freight train, perhaps even the warble of a police siren, and it all combined to cast a smothering pall.

THE NIGHTWOOD SONG

All that was missing from the nightmare was music, Sonny running to Grandpa's pickup truck, too afraid to cross the bridge into the woods and fire up Bertha. Plus, the old rig might wake Mama.

The cold air ripped him raw down Purgatory Road, whipping through the doorless truck and threatening to freeze his lips solid. He'd triple-checked the address on the napkin Durant had given him, and luckily he knew Walthers Lane from a recent delivery.

At least the freezing air kept him alert, to the point that he thought he heard calliope music cavorting along the wind. But it was only a memory, gone by the next bend, left for the fog and the miles of the past, quickly replaced by fresher memories.

How did my raincoat get home? Did Mr. Stevens find it? No, I chucked it before I even got on the train.

He remembered Grandpa's words and Toby's words, then Chief Clark's words and Mr. Durant's words. The memories festered like a septic wound, and now it was Sonny passing up the road he wanted, the sign for Walthers Lane flashing by. Reversing with the wobble of a drunk driver, he swung onto Walthers and followed the narrow road up a steep hill, past the house where he and Grandpa had delivered wood, creeping nearly all the way to a dead end. The road's penultimate property featured a rusty mailbox wearing 24 in white paint, looking like a worn-out football jersey.

The driveway would have been a tight squeeze for a bicycle, much less a pickup, Sonny scraping against branches and jolting over potholes, fog gliding lazily in the headlights, drawn as if by magnetism to a cloaked pond at the edge of the driveway.

In the distance, a mostly dark house appeared in the gloom, partially occluded by overgrown pine shrubs that threatened to blot out the windows.

Sonny shivered – and not from the cold. Something about this house dug down deep and triggered an atavistic, unexplainable dread.

Stepping through the exposed frame that had once been protected by the driver's door, Sonny stared up at the wooded skyscrapers encircling him. These trees were even taller than the ones back home, he figured, which made sense considering the Nightwood began about a mile north of here. For a few moments, Sonny's gaze remained fixed on the trees, his dread rivaling their height, and then he forced himself onto the rotted porch.

He rang the bell, suddenly remembering Durant's words: *Just drop by during the daytime, never at night. Never after dark.*

"I sure haven't been keen on following instructions lately," he muttered, ringing the bell again.

Durant didn't answer. After a few more minutes, Sonny hurried back to the truck, eager to get home, regretful over coming here, but then he heard Durant's voice to his left.

"Come quick, boy! Get to the gate!"

THE NIGHTWOOD SONG

Glancing left down the remainder of the driveway, Sonny noticed several pools of light that palely illuminated a gentle hill behind the house. Standing tall within one of those pools, Durant was maybe two hundred feet away, on a boardwalk at the hill's crest. His arms were crossed, a shotgun slung over his shoulder, a black dog sitting by his feet.

"Hurry up! What are you waiting for, boy?"

Sonny ran toward a chain-link fence separating the driveway from the hill, Durant rushing down from the boardwalk to meet him. He was an older man, but not nearly as old as Chief Clark or even Grandpa, probably in his sixties, his face glowing softly in the amber light supplied by an old lamp rigged to the fence.

"What are you doing here?" Durant waved Sonny over to an arched wooden trellis fronting a wrought iron gate, his fingers fumbling for the latch. "I told you not to come here at night."

"I'm sorry, sir, but I have nowhere else to go. I can't do this alone."

Durant snapped the gate shut behind them and latched it, taking a few extra seconds to search the fog, his right hand brought to his heavily wrinkled forehead as he scouted the driveway and woods.

"I think we're in luck, boy," he murmured, rubbing his thick white beard. "They're not here…not yet."

"Who's not here?"

"Up, up, up." He patted Sonny on the rump. "Up to the boardwalk – and stay in the light."

Sonny climbed the hill, tripping over a rock and falling sideways onto the boardwalk. Ignoring him, still sitting, the black border collie kept close watch of the driveway.

"Her name's Fast," Durant pointed. "Come here, Fast, ole girl."

With the obedience of a soldier, the dog lurched up and came to Durant, who joined Sonny on the boardwalk and scratched Fast behind the ears. "Good girl. Very good girl. This is Sonny Winters, girl – say hello."

Sitting and smiling, the collie held up her front right paw.

"Go on, boy, don't be afraid. Give her a shake."

Sonny hadn't heard of nobody shaking a dog's paw before, but Fast was less awkward about it than some humans. Following the introduction, she launched down from the boardwalk and sprinted toward a boulder within the enclosure, which she promptly conquered with an impressive vault. Standing atop the rock, she searched the foggy woods in all directions, making a complete circle before lying on her stomach, snout resting on her paws.

"That settles it," Durant nodded. "Coast is clear, for now."

"Clear of what, sir?"

"Don't know." He glanced behind them into the woods. "Something. My guess is it's been here a lot longer than you and me."

Durant wore a heavy wool coat over his long johns, a pair of brown boots rising almost to his knees. Leather gloves added to the repertoire, his breaths augmenting the fog.

At one end of the boardwalk, near the boulder, a gray tent was shadowed beneath the drizzle of a lamp mounted to a tree. At the opposite end, a staircase could bring you down to the dark house, but it didn't look like Durant had any plans of heading inside.

"Sir, you said before you've seen things in the woods. What did you mean by that?"

Durant eyed the woods again. "I only see 'em in flashes. Sometimes it's a shadow, other times a face, but I can never get a good look in the fog." He shook his head and spat. "They're always watching, and I think they're even taking people…or at least causing them to wander off."

"Have you ever heard music out there?"

"No, sir, but them woods are full of tricks. Don't ever let nobody tell you different."

Sonny quickly explained the last week-plus, concluding with, "They sent my Grandpa up to Engelhard Asylum. They think he's crazy."

Durant clapped Sonny on the shoulder. "He ain't crazy, son. He's got his eyes wide open now, but most people want you to go around blind."

Sonny didn't know what to say. A strong urge to pee throttled his insides, and he was taken by a coughing spell that squeezed a little urine into his johns. Shivering miserably, too afraid to spit on someone else's property even though Durant had just done so himself, Sonny swallowed it back down and tasted blood.

"Come on, kid, let's get a little warmer."

Durant led him to a fire pit behind the tent. Surrounded by stones and tall wooden benches, the flames were crackling in earnest before long, Sonny rubbing his hands over the fire.

"Go ahead, sit down and make a spot for yourself." Durant stooped and pulled a bottle of Wild Turkey from beneath a bench. Taking a seat and crossing his legs, he blew out a long breath and drank.

"Sir, if you don't mind me asking, why do you stay here if these…things are out here?"

"This is home," he said flatly. "I grew up here, and my daddy before me. I raised my own boy here." He brought the bottle to his lips. "He died in the war."

Sonny nodded and sat, the bench so tall that his feet barely scraped the deck. "I'm sorry, sir."

"He was a good boy. I told him to steer clear of the war, but that's precisely what my daddy told me before the First World War." He glanced up from the flames. "Boys were made to ignore their daddies' advisement. I'm sure your daddy told you to stay home tonight, am I correct?"

Now it was Sonny's eyes seeking the fire. "Papa died five years back. His truck wrecked south of Salt Lake City. He gave me this jacket just before he went."

If not for the pain in his bandaged palm, Sonny wouldn't have realized he was clutching the jacket by his heart.

Durant stood and handed off the bottle – *Distilled in Kentucky.*

"I probably shouldn't, sir. I'm not well. I might get you ill."

Durant waved away Sonny's concerns. "I haven't been well since the Great War, son."

Sonny nodded and drank, the liquor's bite not nearly as stunning as it had been in the boxcar. And unlike before, he had an urge to drink again this time. Somehow it tasted foul and fine at the same time, warming up his throat when he needed it most.

Fast, meanwhile, remained on the rock – but she wasn't sleeping, glancing this way and that way before resting her head on her paws again.

"Why'd you name her Fast, sir? That's a neat name."

Durant shrugged. "Everything that dog does – run, eat, crap – she gets it all done fast. I believe she's a foxhound-border collie mix, but who knows for sure. One day she just appeared from those woods over yonder, right about dusk, it was. I gave her my leftovers that night, and we've been together eight years strong."

"She's very disciplined, sir."

"Sure is. We used to call that rock House Rock, you know. We'd paint it different colors every summer when my boy was small. If you go up to it, you can probably still see some of the old paint on there, but now it's Fast's Rock. She made it hers from day one."

Sonny stood and passed back the whiskey. He had a thousand questions, but he didn't know which ones were proper and which might offend. Ultimately deciding on silence, he took his seat and watched the flames for a while.

"Fast knows when it comes around," Durant said at last, his voice lowered. "When the crickets go quiet in the summer, you know it's close. And whenever Fast jumps on her rock and growls, you know it's real close. And if she gets her hackles raised and barks herself into a circle, you know it's all around."

Durant's eyes blazed brighter than the flames, and he kept glancing into the woods.

"What do you think it is, sir?" Sonny could practically taste the desperation, but none of Durant's answers were bringing him any closer to Toby.

"Don't know." Durant shook his head, rubbed his beard. "Something, all right. Something evil. But I'll be damned if I let it commandeer my land, my *home*."

Sonny tried to cast away Durant's claims with assumptions of insanity, but there was already too much clutter in his head to allow for simple dismissals. He couldn't dismiss Grandpa's and Toby's claims about the music, nor could he dismiss Chief Clark's words. Above all else, he couldn't dismiss his own unanswered questions.

How did my raincoat get there? How? There's no way–

"Evil," Mr. Durant repeated, drinking, his eyes delving deep into the flames, so deep that they swirled with memories.

Sonny finally settled on his next question, but Fast began to bark, her gaze locked on the southern woods.

"Quick! To the tent!" Durant stumbled up and spilled his whiskey. Crossing the boardwalk to the tent, he scurried inside and readied the gun into position, Sonny wrinkling his nose at the stench of piss.

"Get in here, boy! What are you waiting for?"

Sonny ducked into the tent, Durant rushing up the zipper and switching off all but one battery-powered lantern, then pointing his gun at the sealed entrance.

"Mr. Durant, what–?"

"Quiet, soldier! Get in the corner and take cover!"

Durant went down to his stomach, concealing his gun among the blankets like a sniper, training it on the entrance. Outside the tent, Fast's barking became a fury, Sonny listening closely for footsteps or music or some other sign of a threat.

But he could only hear the dog, her barking so heavy and targeted that it sounded as if she'd come face to face with an intruder on the other side of the fence.

"Keep quiet," Durant whispered, Sonny shivering in the corner, his heart going like Grandpa's sledgehammer. "It usually moves on fairly quick if it sees it can't get to me."

His prediction was accurate, Fast's barks tapering off a few moments later. Then silence.

"We wait just a bit longer," Durant said, raising his voice negligibly.

Sonny ached with the need to pee. He was far less successful in suppressing a cough, Durant scowling at him.

Finally, when the silence stretched beyond a minute, Durant tore off a small patch covering a spyhole in the side of the tent. "Let's get a look," he whispered, peeping through the hole. "I'm pretty sure it was here, all right. Yes, yes indeed, those leaves weren't scattered that way before."

"Mr. Durant?"

THE NIGHTWOOD SONG

"What is it, son?"

"May I use your bathroom?"

Maybe it was the dim light, but Sonny thought he glimpsed a faint smile appear within Durant's beard.

"The latrine's closed from dusk till dawn, son. Do you need to piss, crap, or both?"

"Piss, sir. And mighty bad."

"Well, feel free to let loose off the boardwalk."

Sonny was loath to pee in the man's yard. "May I use the bathroom in your home?"

"Don't got one, not anymore. The pipes stuffed themselves up pretty thick one year, and my back is no good for prolonged bending no more." He unzipped the tent and stepped out, Sonny following. "Figured since I spend most days out here anyhow, I might as well just convert the bathroom into an armory. I get better use out of it that way."

"Why can't you use your latrine from dusk till dawn?"

"Haven't you been listening, kid? You can't go out there after dark. *It* lives in the dark!"

Sonny felt like he was going around in circles, no closer to finding Toby than he'd been before coming here. His heart was hot with panic; he needed to find a way out of this place, but where would he go? Where to search at night when hundreds of people, even a police dog, had come up empty in the daylight?

Sonny figured Durant wouldn't keep him here if he demanded to leave, yet he made no such demand, following the old man back to the fire pit, sitting opposite him again, drinking whiskey when it was offered.

Only when the urge became unstoppable did Sonny excuse himself to the boardwalk and unzip, embarrassed even by Fast's occasional glances. There was no place to wash his hands, and he didn't dare ask, instead returning to the fire.

"Last Sunday, I overheard Grandpa tell Mama the woods challenged him," Sonny said a while later. "Do you know what that could mean?"

Durant glanced up from the flames, his mind returning from a place much farther. "We're all at war with something."

"Do you think maybe the music was meant to draw my brother out there? Do you think it drew out all the people who've been disappearing?"

The more Durant offered Sonny the bottle, the stranger he began to feel, like his soul was no longer fully contained by his body. And his head didn't feel tight anymore, but exceedingly light.

"It knows us." Durant finished the bottle and fetched a new one. "Intimately."

"But how, sir?"

"No more of that *sir* business, you hear? We're just two boys drinking by the fire."

"Yes, Mr. Durant."

The old man laughed and drank. "No Mr. Durant, either."

"Yes, sir...I mean Mr. D...I mean..."

Durant didn't even bother to stand no more, tossing Sonny the bottle. He kept his sip small this time, and on the next toss he pretended to drink, his stomach souring. If he wasn't careful, he'd end up puking where he'd pissed.

Durant kicked his legs out, Sonny doing the same. A motor whispered in the distance; off to the southeast, a train horn wailed like a lost soul seeking even a semblance of companionship.

A while later, Durant was talking about how his son had been a great ball player, the best on his high school squad, not only playing infield but also pitching and catching. When it was Sonny's turn, he told Durant about rides with Papa down Route 66 and up to Portland, and how he'd never laughed harder than during those trips, so hard he'd cried sometimes.

"Certain times in your life, you'll never forget," Durant smiled, staring back into the flames. "You've got plenty more of those yet, son."

"Hopefully with Toby."

The old man nodded, Fast coming around for a quick appraisal, nudging against Sonny's legs and allowing for a brief scratch behind the ears, then sprinting back to the southwest, only to jump onto her rock immediately and lay with her snout on her forepaws, her sigh so loud that it could be heard above the fire.

Fog spread thickly in the predawn hours, threatening to diminish the flames, something unusually spectral about the layers of mist tonight. It was the spotty glows of the lamps scattered about the yard, Sonny concluded, which only served to accentuate the density of the gloom. Beyond the hilly clearing out front, the western slopes would have been visible from this elevation, but the fog rendered everything low and level, the surrounding trees like prison bars.

Sonny didn't want to drink anymore, but his burning throat demanded it as medication, each pop chasing the pain back. An hour later, he was pissing again, almost staggering off the boardwalk with his privates in hand, Fast glancing suspiciously at him from her rock.

Mr. Durant, meanwhile, didn't sleep or even come close to nodding off. "Have I explained the rules yet?" he said when Sonny returned to the fire.

"I don't think so, sir."

Durant shook his head. "Well, I've got a new rule tonight – and you keep botching it up. No *sir*. Call me Donnie, would ya?"

"Yes...Donnie." The name felt like a curse word. "Sorry."

"As for the other rules, number one is to keep the watch from dusk till dawn. If the sunlight ain't stronger than the yard lights, consider yourself vulnerable. Number two – never fall asleep after dark. Number three – keep the boardwalk clear. Number four – stay alert. Number five – keep the watch."

"What about during the daytime?"

"I ain't never seen it or heard it in the daytime. It comes out at night." He nodded at length. "You'll want to be particularly mindful of the west/northwest until midnight, and the east/southeast toward dawn. Like right now, can you hear it? Can ya, son?"

Durant was pointing to the east, but Sonny heard only a distant train wheeling slowly toward Sacramento.

"Is it music?"

"Nope. Footsteps. *It's* out there, but not close, probably watching from afar."

"Has it ever attacked you?"

"Nope, but only because I keep up the defenses. It tries to mess with the lights sometimes. Without those lights, I'd'a been devoured long ago, son. It thrives in the dark."

Sonny shivered and drank. He was quite sure he would puke, but he drank nonetheless. He drank so much that he forgot to pray.

Chapter 17

Coming groggily, nauseously awake, Sonny pulled aside the blankets and blinked his surroundings into recognition. Durant's tent. *Donnie's* tent, lanterns in every corner.

Unzipping the tent and stepping out, he glimpsed daylight breaking thinly through the eastern mist. Fast was curled up on the boardwalk beside Donnie's lounge chair, the shotgun in his lap.

"It's almost safe," Donnie murmured. "But not quite yet – still not light enough."

"I should get home and start searching again." Sonny's head felt like a heavy wooden door – and somebody kept rapping on it.

"Not yet. A little longer. Anyway, you should fetch yourself some water before hitting the road again."

Maybe it was the thought of water, or maybe it was his forward movement that caused Sonny to heave every drop of last night's whiskey onto the piss-stenched mud downhill of the boardwalk. Fast's expression was disturbed, but Donnie only laughed and clapped.

"What I'd give to be young again, eh, Fast, ole girl?"

Sonny was bent with his hands on his knees, teetering on the edge of the boardwalk, nearly falling face-first into his puke, but Donnie hauled him back. Unenthused, Fast chose the long way around the boardwalk and circled aback the tent en route to her rock.

"Go on inside for a bit, Sonny, and stir yourself up a mixture of saltwater and tree sap. You'll find the sap in the blue containers in the fridge."

Sonny heeded these words only so he could take shelter from the cold and the stenches, but the house was scarcely warmer than the outdoors. Guided only by the dim morning light and a single lamp glowing in the main hall, Sonny eventually found a light switch and gaped at the mess before him. The house was heaped with boxes and stacks of paperwork, the few patches of exposed floor covered with mud tracks. Dented and flattened beer cans poked out like weeds in a garden, most prevalent in the dining room.

Sonny flipped a few more switches, but only one of the four attempts resulted in a light going on. Further navigating the maze, he could only push the kitchen door open a quarter of the way before he was stopped by a stack of boxes, leaving barely enough space for him to slip inside.

The bare walls had been turned into a chalkboard of sorts, maps and ghoulish faces scrawled on every surface with blue, black, and red markers. Several exes represented locations known only by Donnie and God, the countertops covered with boxes and guns and ammo.

The sink basins overflowed with stinking dishes, the glasses filled with stagnant liquid that had developed filmy layers on the surface. When Sonny went to wash his hands, he dodged back from a gurgle and spout of brownish water that wouldn't clear for better than a minute.

Head pounding, stomach ready to revolt again, he stumbled back through the maze, his nausea worsened by the many stenches. He was sure he could smell dog crap hidden somewhere, and the miasma of piss wouldn't leave no matter where he went on this property.

"Did you find the sap okay?" Durant called from the boardwalk when Sonny staggered back outside.

"Sure did." The lie stung, but only a little. "Thanks."

Durant nodded. "I'd say it's safe to go now. It's always hardest to tell on the foggy mornings – it'll use every available drop of darkness against us. You'd do well to remember that, Sonny."

"I will. Thank you for the drinks and company."

"Not a problem, son. You be careful now. You and your family are known to it – that much is evident."

Sonny kept on walking, passing through the gate and beneath the trellis, Durant hurrying down to re-latch it.

"And once you're known to it, it won't ever stop hunting you."

Sonny shouldn't have turned back. Had he kept on going to the truck, he never would have seen the terror in Durant's bloodshot eyes.

"Hurry now, Sonny. Get back quick…and don't ever step foot in those woods after dark."

Chapter 18

Sonny drove slowly through the fog, his head a mess of aches and throbs and fears and memories. Other than the truck's headlights and the increments of road visible before them, it was hard to tell what was real anymore. He thought back to Mr. Omya and Mr. Stevens and the man in the boxcar, their faces blending in the mist of memory.

Sonny didn't think he was swerving, not until blue lights flashed behind him and Chief Clark appeared outside the doorless frame like a wraith. He had a thermos of coffee in one hand, a ticket book in the other.

"Sonny Winters," the Chief nodded. "Kid, would'ya mind explaining why I can't seem to drive two miles in this town without runnin' into ya?"

"I'm sorry, sir. I was just meeting a man who I thought could help find Toby."

"How much liquor did Durant ply you with?"

Sonny searched for a lie, but it was no use.

"Kid, I could've been blindfolded and kept that rig straighter. And your breath reeks of it."

"I'm sorry, sir. I'm just…I'm running out of options. Toby's probably freezing to death by now."

Sonny wasn't aware of his tears until they began to drip.

"Come, come. Step out," the Chief waved.

Exiting, Sonny faced the truck and put his hands behind his back like he'd seen on the road a few times. He began sobbing at the thought of his brother's helpless screams in some ditch or half-frozen swamp. "He's gonna die, he won't make it! I couldn't find him!"

"Come on, move, kid." Chief Clark took him by the wrist and led him to the car, Sonny expecting handcuffs, stunned when he was guided into the passenger seat.

"I'll radio for somebody to haul that junker back to your place," the Chief grumbled, settling behind the wheel. "That is, assuming ya don't wanna leave it out here for the vultures. I've seen carrion in better shape than that rig, son."

Sonny managed a smile through his tears, Clark handing him a napkin.

"As if you're not enough of a danger to yourself and others, you weren't even wearin' a safety belt."

"My grandfather took out the driver's side seatbelt years ago, sir. He said it was too big a hindrance when he was getting in and out all the time."

Clark shook his head. "What am I gonna do with ya, boy? If I didn't know any better, I'd say you're set on gettin' yourself killed."

"I'm sorry for making all this trouble, sir."

"Ya know what?" he chuckled. "I'd likely be doin' the same thing in your position."

"Mr. Durant says it lives in the dark…and it knows my family," Sonny blurted.

Clark slammed to a stop, Sonny's head jolting forward, the seatbelt digging into his chest.

"You stay away from that place, ya hear? That man ain't right in the head. He ain't been right since his son was killed at Midway."

"But you said yourself there's been other folks who heard the music. And people are always going missing in the woods. What if something's luring them–?"

"Enough! Stop with that nonsense right quick, and don't be spreadin' none-uh Durant's fires." He cracked the window and lit a cigarette. "Most of the people who've gone missing are runaways, the rest a bunch-a hikers and campers who come up here from the cities and start wanderin' around the woods unprepared, just like you did."

Chief Clark turned toward the driver's window and released a puff of smoke. "As for the music, people set up their campsites deep in the woods and get to drinkin' – next thing you know they're singin' and strummin'."

Sonny said nothing further about the music. He could see it plainly in Clark's eyes that the truth was as obscure as the road ahead – and this mention of campsites was nothing more than a guess offered into the gloom. Fear also resided in the Chief's eyes, hidden well but visible nonetheless.

And if the Chief of Police didn't have the answers, where would Sonny find them?

Chief Clark was quiet for a while, fog pooling against his cruiser, seeking a way inside. It was so thick that trees hugging the road were transformed into vague, distant forms, perfectly still, watchful, darkly anticipatory.

"School's back in today," the Chief announced at last, releasing the brake and continuing toward Purgatory Road. "I don't suspect you're plannin' to go, but do me a favor and make sure you bring an adult along for your next search. And not Durant."

Sonny nearly blurted the thoughts straight from his mind – thoughts about the raincoat and how it had gone from a wooded swamp beside the rails to Mama's clothesline, every last drop of mud removed.

Instead, he maintained his silence all the way home.

"Don't go back to Durant's place," the Chief warned before letting him out. "That man is in a bad way – has been for many years now. He'll poison your mind."

"Thank you for bringing me home, sir."

Clark nodded. "Run along. Go wash your mouth out before your mama catches a whiff."

"I will, sir. Thank you, sir."

Mama was up when he stepped into the living room, but she wasn't mad. Kneeling before a fire that had been whittled down to embers, hands clasped, she enjoined Sonny to pray, her voice barely exceeding a whisper.

"Kneel beside me, child."

"Yes, Mama. I'm sorry for going out, but–"

Mama started into prayer, her tone soft and dazed, as though someone had hypnotized her like Sonny had seen in a few movies during summer visits to Aunt Dana's in Los Angeles. And none of these strange prayers included an amen; Mama just went on murmuring and nodding, even after Sonny eventually stood.

"Mama, we should go out and search."

She ignored him. "Return my boy home, dear Lord. Return my boy, and guide his every step. Return my boy, Lord, I beg of You…"

"Ma–"

Sonny broke off when Mama started reciting the Good Book, her hands trembling. A heavy chill had spread through the house, Sonny deciding against relighting the hearth or wood stove. Mama was in no condition for tending the fire, and Sonny had a fresh course charted for the woods.

"I love you, Mama." He wrapped a blanket around his mother's shoulders, but she made no acknowledgement, murmuring the blessed words so quickly that Sonny couldn't understand them.

Watching Mama a moment longer, he shivered at the sight of her on the floor, broken by the same terror which had kicked Sonny around these last few days. The constant imagining was the very worst part, each scenario somehow more vividly gruesome than its predecessor, and Sonny could almost hear his brother screaming for help.

After collecting several items throughout the house, Sonny went to the garage and placed them in Grandpa's knapsack, now heavily caked in mud. He brushed off a few flakes and threw the sack over his shoulder, Grandpa's maps and Papa's compass ready for the next venture. The maps had been damaged by the mud, but they were still readable, only a few pieces torn away. Now that the mud was dry, Sonny could wipe away the dust until the words held meaning again.

He was sure to pack the flashlights again, just in case the search kept him after dark, but he prayed today would bring the miracle he'd hunted for miles, bleeding and crawling and puking, half-drowned and better than halfway frozen, and he would do it all again if it meant Toby slept in his bed tonight.

In the early misty light, Sonny set out for the east-central portion of Grandpa's map, where several ponds and streams were outlined. He figured maybe Toby had burrowed himself into a den around one of those ponds, eliminating dehydration from the equation. But keeping warm and nourished were another matter, not to mention eluding the predators whose wails sometimes poured in along the wind.

Sonny did his best to banish his questions and fears, but multiple voices competed in his head, Mr. Durant's the loudest among them. Farther along, Sonny kept coupling Toby's descriptions of the Charnelle/Charnel house with Durant's warnings about "It", whatever it was.

"They don't play carnival music at campsites," Sonny muttered, a response he should have given to Chief Clark, not the fog-festooned trees.

Pushing deeper, he wondered if he'd glimpsed a face briefly poke out from a stand of alders, their ash-white trunks blending with the mist. The crunch of footsteps quickly followed, surely not belonging to the family of turkeys crossing well behind him, too heavy, each step measured to match a person's gait.

Glancing back, Sonny half-expected to discover his raincoat hanging from a lone branch, but all he saw in the mist were the fading forms of turkeys waddling off to the northwest.

"How? *How?*" Sonny shook his head, remembering the exact moment he'd flung the raincoat away on the rail line.

But somehow it had gotten to Mama's clothesline, joining a preponderance of evidence that pointed in a direction not listed on Papa's compass.

Sonny whirled around. He hadn't heard a sound this time, reacting instead to a strong sensation of being watched, the strongest yet. Eyes flicking from tree to tree, branch to branch, he waited until the turkeys' footsteps gave way to silence, the fog curling around him.

His deep breaths sought composure, but they were mostly unavailing. He tried to imagine other searchers nearby, calling Toby's name and filling up the silence. But after ten minutes and twenty, when Sonny was back to his disturbed thoughts again, it was almost as if he were alone in the universe.

It made the music. It made Toby see that house. It made the others go missing, too.

Sonny began to feel faint after another hour of walking, his throat closed off to each attempt at swallowing. A throbbing burn was locked away, inaccessible to water, Sonny panicking as he gulped dryly, feeling as if a chestnut were lodged in his throat.

Bile blazed up his gullet and welled like a witch's brew. If he hadn't fallen to his knees, heaving and gasping, he wouldn't have glimpsed the cabin through the fog, nor would he have seen the countless forms surrounding it, rising by the dozen from the damp earth, every pair of eyeless sockets fixed on Sonny Winters.

THE NIGHTWOOD SONG

Awakening with a lurch, Sonny stumbled to his feet and searched the fog, desperate to trace back and determine where the nightmare had begun. Certainly not with the dilapidated cabin, for it was even more visible now, the fog having drawn back a few curtains since he'd passed out.

Massaging his throat with hopes of loosening the blockage, he tottered through a nest of briars, cutting his jacket. He surely would have injured his hands, but instead the bandages incurred the damages, torn into flaps and skeins.

The cabin's front door, already ajar, creaked open even further in a breeze so thin as to be nonexistent. The windows were smashed, the side walls ready to cave in, the roof riddled with holes.

Grabbing his flashlight, Sonny stepped cautiously inside, clinking over broken glass and crackling across leaves whose colors were long ago departed.

Deeper within the cabin, heaps of yesteryear's leaves lay in decaying mounds, the walls black with mold. The stench would have previously affronted Sonny's nose, but the last few days had toughened his tolerance for such assaults.

"Toby!" he called, his voice sounding very small and distant, as if it were being siphoned immediately through the rotted floorboards. "Toby, are you in here?"

He could say no more, wincing from the agony in his throat.

Stooping, he clutched his nauseous stomach and dropped a few tears, one of them falling upon a leaf that was different than the others, a faded yellow leaf someone had seen fit to paint with a single word.

"Woe," Sonny read, taking up the leaf and tracing his fingers along the flaky black paint.

Moving to the far corner, he discovered the same word painted on dozens of leaves. The countertops housed a handful of others, the closet empty but for a cluster of crunched beer cans and three more leaves reading WOE.

Shivering and shaking, feeling as if he'd dragged himself out of a freezing pond, Sonny left the cabin and pushed himself further, stopping only when he heard the whisper of traffic.

A trick. It has to be a–

But no, he could hear the rumbling engine of a truck now, the logging rig becoming visible two hundred feet through the woods.

Impossible. He figured he was at least half an hour's walk from the nearest road, yet, stepping out from the forest, he took in a familiar straightaway along Purgatory Road, not far from the Route 31 intersection.

A thicker swell of fog had tided in, obfuscating the horizons of the straightaway and making Sonny guess at what lurked beyond them. He thought he could see headlights burning brighter, but the next car didn't pass until a few minutes later.

Pawing the map into his bandaged hands, Sonny grappled for an answer.

I was here, roughly. I passed out about here. His pencil traced lightly across to Purgatory Road. *There's no way...unless I sleepwalked!*

Sonny's breaths wheezed icily. He tried not to inhale too deeply and worsen the stab that had grown sharper in his chest over the last day. Coughing up a wad at last, he spun away from the green-red poultice, its rot lingering in his mouth.

A dump truck blasted by him, sending up a muddy spray that kissed his cheek. Checking his watch, he discovered that it had stopped just after ten o'clock. In the extreme distance, so far as to be an imaginary creation, a howling coyote served as the introduction to a tune sung by a very old man.

Quickly, the man's voice grew louder, sweeping through the fog toward Sonny like the wind. His croaky croon barely carried the notes, but the song nonetheless prevailed, bringing a deep melancholy to match the gloom. After a while the music began to lull him, but he didn't realize how dangerously soporific it had been until a horn blared.

Turning around, Sonny lost his balance and collapsed.

"My God! Sonny!"

"Mr. Stevens, is that you?"

"It's me, Sonny. I've got you, buddy." Stevens scooped him up and settled him inside the warm car.

"You could've been killed, Sonny. You shouldn't go off on your own."

"But Mama won't" – he coughed lengthily, painfully – "she won't stop praying."

"You're gonna catch your death out here. Come on, let's get you some rest."

Sonny caught a delicious yet nauseating whiff, his eyes tracking to a styrofoam container on the center console.

Mr. Stevens put the car in motion. "Hungry, Sonny?" He grabbed up the container and opened it, the scents wafting brightly. "I've got a turkey club and plenty of fries – just picked it up from Huber's. It's all yours, if you want, kiddo."

"No, thanks."

"You sure? You should eat, Sonny. You look like death."

Sonny leaned back and closed his eyes, but a moment later Mr. Stevens was bumping him with a cup of soda.

"A nice Coke will feel awful good. Go on, take it."

Sonny obliged, and the iced Coke did bring marginal relief. "Thank you, sir."

"I'll call your mother when we get home. She's probably worried sick again with you out this close to dark."

"Dark? But it was morning."

"It sure was…six hours ago."

Sonny was half-awake as Stevens carried him up the stairs and helped him into bed.

How did I sleep that long? How did I get to the road? Was the cabin a dream?

"I'll draw you a bath and get you some fresh clothes and bandages. Then we'll get you back home. What do you say, Sonny?"

He nodded, hearing only a handful of the words, his delirious terror blotting out the others and threatening to strip the room of color.

Ten minutes later, Sonny sighed into the hot bath and peeled off his bandages, casting them away into the steam. His hands stung in the soapy water, two of the cuts oozing yellow, but these observations barely exceeded that of the wallpaper.

What's happening to me? Something's doing this.

It. It's doing this. Grandpa isn't crazy. Mr. Durant isn't crazy.

Sonny remembered the music heard from the side of the road, the man's soft croons soaking deeper than the bathwater. There'd been something else hidden in those notes, he thought, lurking just below the surface of sadness, threatening to announce itself.

A light knock on the door. "Everything okay, Sonny?"

"Yes, sir. Thank you, sir."

"I left some clothes on the bed for you. When you're ready, come on down and we'll get you bandaged up."

Sonny was so badly shocked with cold upon standing that he had to return to the tub, sliding everything but his head beneath the water. When he awoke, the water was lukewarm, Mr. Stevens seated beside the tub, a bowl of soup in hand.

"Here you are, Sonny. Have a few sips."

"Thank you, sir." Sonny's shivers rattled his teeth and made him slosh the soup. He tried to grip the spoon, but his fingers felt like they were frozen.

"Here, let's get you dried up." Stevens took the soup back and bundled Sonny in towels, wrapping one around his neck and whisking the other through his hair. He was gone a moment later, hurrying back with the clothes.

"That cough — I don't like the sound of it one bit. And you're running a fever, for certain," Stevens said in the kitchen, re-dressing Sonny's hands. "I believe you may have pneumonia."

Stevens's eyes were dark with worry, each wrap of the bandage made with exceeding care, Sonny barely feeling it. "You should leave the search to the authorities and rest."

Sonny tried to respond, but no words came out, only a lengthy cough that terminated with a lace of blood in his freshly bandaged hand.

"I know this is the last thing you want to hear, but you could die if you push this."

"But–"

"The next time you collapse in the woods or the road, you might be all alone. Then what?" Fear rose higher in his voice. "You're lucky I went to see Mom early tonight after class. If it had been someone driving faster – someone who didn't see you in the fog – you could have been killed, Sonny."

"I have to find my brother, sir."

Stevens held his shoulders. "Tell you what, if you rest tonight, I'll go out and look myself. I'll take your place."

"You will?"

"Yes, sir, and I haven't broken a promise in–" His words broke off suddenly, as though someone had chopped them. "Well, it's been years," he recovered, nodding.

"I'll rest for a bit," Sonny decided, his head feeling as if it had become detached, the fire poker stabbing even sharper in his chest. "Thank you for looking, sir. I'll join you in a bit."

Each word brought agony, relief to be found only in the depths of sleep, where not a single nightmare or hint of music disturbed him.

Chapter 19

Sonny awoke a few times to drink water or sip soup brought by Mr. Stevens. *Just a bit longer and then I'll search*, he kept telling himself each time he got up, knowing he should have ventured out the last time, knowing he should be looking for his brother – but he was repeatedly drawn to the warmth of the bed and the shelter from pain. If he kept perfectly still, arms at his sides, he could slip back into sweaty sleep without awakening the agony.

Please, God, save my brother. Let him come home.

Like half-remembered dreams, Sonny could recall Stevens helping him into fresh clothes and coaxing medicine and food into him. When he finally yawned fully awake, he was enraged by the bright light of Wednesday morning. He'd missed several hours – hours that could never be gotten back for searching.

"Did they find him?" he practically shouted when Mr. Stevens stepped into the room, another bowl of soup in hand.

"I'm afraid not, Sonny. I just got off the phone with the police department." He set down the soup on the nightstand. "They're calling off the search for your brother."

"What? Why? It's only been a few days." Sonny shot out of bed, grabbed and held by John Stevens.

"It's been almost a week, Sonny."

"But it's only Wednesday."

"It's Friday morning. You slept on and off for over two days."

Disbelieving tears forged their tracks, Sonny feeling like he would vomit. "Why didn't you tell me?"

"You needed rest. You still do."

"But–"

Stevens leveled a hand on Sonny's shoulder. "Hundreds of folks have been combing those woods for days, but with this much time going by" – his words gave way to headshakes – "I'm so sorry, Sonny."

Tearing free, Sonny stumbled dizzily down the stairs, clutching the handrail, John Stevens right behind him.

"Take me home! Please, I need to keep looking!"

"Sonny–"

"He's not dead! *It* has him – it took him!"

"*It?*"

"It lives in the woods. Ask Mr. Durant. He'll tell you everything!"

Stevens nodded, sighed. "Chief Clark told me you spent a night at Donnie's place."

THE NIGHTWOOD SONG

"He knows there's something out there!" Sonny frantically wiped his tears away. "He's seen things. There's something—"

Sonny was swallowed in John Stevens's embrace, the feel of his sweater reminding him of Grandpa but not the scent. "There-there," he kept saying, his big arms locking Sonny in place.

"Please, I have to keep looking. He's out there, Mr. Stevens, I just know it."

Nodding, Stevens released Sonny and pointed to the door. "Let's take a drive and see Pastor Mahone. What do you say, Sonny?"

"I wanna go home! Where's Mama?"

The darkness diffusing across Stevens's face knocked Sonny off balance. "Your mother, she's had some…struggles with grief. Lord knows she's handled things a lot better than I would have, but—"

"Where is she?"

"Pastor Mahone should be the one to explain."

"*Where is she?*" Sonny screamed, triggering a coughing rage.

"She went to stay with your aunt in L.A. for a few days," Stevens hastened, holding both palms up.

"Grief impacts us all in different ways," Pastor Mahone added half an hour later, sitting beside Sonny in a pew at St. John's Congregational Church, a small gold cross centered over his vestments. He stared sleepily at Sonny, nodding incessantly, a Bible in his lap. "For your mother, the lack of closure took a heavy toll...and you as well, Sonny."

"My brother's not dead."

"I admire the strength of your faith. You're a commendable young man." His hand went to Sonny's arm. "The strength of your family has been an inspiration to this community."

"Thank you, sir. I've been praying, and the Lord works miracles."

Pastor Mahone winced. "Yes, He certainly does."

Sonny turned away to cough, filling up the nave with echoes. "I know Chief Clark called off the search, but that don't mean we should stop looking. I understand the police have other responsibilities, but Toby's my responsibility."

The pastor's eyes shined a little. "You're very sick, Sonny. You should see a doctor."

"No!" Sonny's shout blanched Mahone's face. "No one believed Grandpa or Durant, and they don't believe me, neither!"

"Sonny, please–"

Sonny raced down the aisle, shoes thudding. "Pray for us, Pastor."

"But it was decided that Mr. Stevens and I will look after you. Please don't–"

"It's the Devil in those woods who's got Toby. He made him hear the music, just like the others. I heard it, too. I heard the song!"

In the entry, Sonny ran past John Stevens.

"Sonny, wait, please just wait!"

Sonny had hopes of running all the way home, but his body didn't sign off on those visions. Not even to the parking lot, he collapsed and clutched his chest, screaming from the radiating pain.

He coughed up blood, Stevens kneeling and holding him, Pastor Mahone limping out a minute later.

"Just hang on, Toby!" he shouted into the woods across the street. "I won't stop looking for you!"

Chapter 20

"We'll keep searching for him," Stevens promised on the way to the hospital. "You just focus on your recovery."

Sonny wanted to argue, but the light of realization began to spread through his bones. Even if he escaped and returned to the woods, his body would give out before he conquered another mile. He was no good to Toby in this condition, and by keeping up the arguments and refusals, he would only steal John Stevens's time to look for his brother.

"Take my maps. I marked all the places I searched," Sonny instructed from his hospital bed, John Stevens getting ready to leave.

"I will, Sonny. I promise."

"And talk with Mr. Durant. Please talk with him."

"Donnie and his family are good people," Stevens nodded. "Now, you rest up, Sonny. I'll be back to check on you later. I've canceled all of my classes for the day, and I'll be meeting Mr. Omya in an hour to search. You have my word."

"Thank you, sir." Sonny drove back his tears. "Thank you for everything."

Sonny was hospitalized until Sunday, released just after church began. John Stevens had visited frequently with reports of unsuccessful searches. Now, as he held Sonny's hand on their way out of the hospital, he promised to return to the wilderness.

"I'll go with you."

"No. You heard the doctor. Rest and hydration, Sonny – your recovery will take weeks."

"Can I see Grandpa? They sent him up to Engelhard Asylum."

"I'll make some calls for you."

Stevens helped him into the passenger seat, Sonny remaining quiet the whole way home. He'd had plenty of time to think in the hospital, desperation gradually yielding to depression; but like the carousel of the seasons, hope had come around again. Although he'd initially assumed his hypothesis to be a fever-induced, sleep-deprived contrivance, additional reflection had proven its plausibility.
Simply put, his hypothesis was this: the evil inhabiting the woods had taken Toby and driven Grandpa and Mama to madness. Why else would Mama have gone down to Aunt Dana's in Los Angeles? She didn't even like Aunt Dana (she didn't like anybody very much), and Sonny knew that no amount of grief could send her away from home.

Additionally, there were Durant's claims; Grandpa's reports; Toby's descriptions of the Charnelle/Charnel house; the music heard by three people, including Sonny; the multiple odd sights in and around the woods over the last week; the unexplainable return of

Sonny's raincoat; and the many unsolved disappearances throughout the region in recent years.

Perhaps Sonny, himself, was going insane for drawing hope from these circumstances. Yet he couldn't cast from his mind the belief that the menace in the woods was attempting to send him a message through the music and the fleeting appearances, even employing nightmares.

It wants something from me. It'll keep Toby alive until it gets what it wants. But what?

Sonny pressed the back of his hand against his forehead. He didn't seem to have a fever, but maybe his body was deceiving him. Maybe his faith had made him blind with hope, the woods having devoured Toby several days ago, the demons lurking only in his imagination.

But I heard it. It's real. Something's out there – and it has Toby.

Mr. Stevens had packed up all of Sonny's things – his clothes washed and folded, his knapsack organized – and set them in the trunk. Parking in Sonny's driveway and turning the car around, Stevens went to the trunk and readied his things.

"You go on inside and rest. I'm gonna head over to Pullman Motor Inn and meet Mr. Omya."

"Thank you, sir," Sonny brightened, pulling the knapsack over his shoulder and accepting a stack of folded clothes, his flannel jacket on top.

"Head on in, then. And get yourself right to bed…with plenty of water on the stand, you hear?"

"Yes, sir. Thank you, sir."

"And don't go running off nowhere. Pastor Mahone and I promised your mother we'd look after you, and that's precisely what we intend to do."

"I'll be right here, sir."

Stevens nodded, but his expression was empty of belief. "I'll fix you up some dinner when I get back. For now, you just rest up good…and let your mind rest, too."

"Yes, sir."

Ten minutes later, Sonny was about to fire up the pickup truck for Durant's place when, glancing down the driveway, he followed a pair of headlights as they neared the house – probably Pastor Mahone stopping by to check on him. But he didn't suppose Pastor Mahone drove a rusty Ford pickup with stacks of furniture, tires, and other junk heaped in the back.

Even before the truck reached the house, Fast's eyes were already locked on Sonny, who'd hidden by the footbridge to avoid Mahone. Head poking out through the passenger window, the border collie didn't simply wag her tail but instead wagged her entire back end.

"Fast!" Sonny celebrated. "Mr. Durant!"

Shirtless beneath a pair of badly stained overalls, Durant hauled himself out of the truck to greet Sonny. His beard seemed even longer than Sonny remembered it, his boots caked with mud.

"I had a vision, Sonny! It was wonderful!" Mr. Durant exulted, cackling like a marooned sailor whose rescuers are drawing nearer. He pulled Sonny into a stinking embrace. "You will reunite with your brother. I saw it clear as day."

"I sure hope so, sir. My prayers would be answered."

"Ahhh, you don't need no prayers, boy, just hard work."

"But…but don't you believe in–?"

"I took God with me to war, came back alone. Been doing just fine ever since, with Fast looking after me." He patted the rusty hood. "Let's get back to base – we've got a lot to discuss."

When Sonny opened the passenger door, Fast scooted into the middle, Durant scratching her behind the ears, Sonny picking up where he left off. For half a mile they went on that way, Fast smiling and then curling up in Sonny's lap.

"She sure does like you – and Fast don't take to nobody."

"I like you, too, Fast, ole girl." Sonny kissed the collie's head, Fast turning and giving Sonny a few kisses as well. He nearly cried, thinking of Durant's words and his hope, kissing Fast's soft black fur; maybe it was all insane, but he could stay awhile in this insanity. He could give himself to it because Toby was still alive here, with Durant behind the wheel and Fast in Sonny's lap. His brother wasn't presumed dead and given up on; he was only missing, soon to come home.

"Do you know Mr. Stevens? John Stevens?" Sonny asked as they climbed Walthers Lane.

"Me and his daddy were good friends – I've known John since he was a boy. Always had a feeling he might lean the way of education. Too smart for his own good, that boy."

"He's been taking care of me since Mama left. Him and Pastor Mahone."

"Where'd your mama go?"

"Down to Aunt Dana's in L.A. Chief Clark called off the search for Toby, and she didn't take it well."

Durant fetched a bottle of Wild Turkey from the side holder. "Parents aren't supposed to bury their kids. The thought of it was likely too much for your mama. She'll be back. I'm sure she loves you much."

"Yes, sir."

"Hey, now, let's not start up with that *sir* business this early. You'll ruin my mood."

"Sorry, Donnie. I forgot."

Durant chuckled and drank. "Can't say I'm surprised by Chief Clark calling off the search. Between you and me, Sonny, that man don't got the constitution for police work anymore. He oughta find himself a pasture somewhere and retire to it."

When Durant pulled into the driveway, Sonny barely recognized the house; it looked much bigger in the daylight – and realer somehow, as though it had only been a figment of the fog before.

The enclosure of chain-linked fences was equally real beneath the bright, cold sun, as was the trellis fronting the west gate. Durant's many lighting contraptions were switched off now, all but for one, which went on glowing from its rigging along a birch tree.

Leaping from Sonny's lap when he opened the door, Fast waited for Durant to open the gate and then sprinted to her rock.

"The way I figure it, Sonny, we're gonna have to go into the Nightwood and bring your brother back. They ain't just gonna hand him over."

"You think they've got him in the Nightwood?"

Halfway up the hill to the boardwalk, Durant turned back and crossed his arms. "When I was your age, this whole wilderness was known as the Nightwood. There was no Pullman State Forest or Nightwood State Forest, and certainly no Robinson Wildlife Preserve. They didn't have roads cutting this way and that through the woods, just one road in and out of town. To me, this region will always be the Nightwood."

He drank and nodded, scanning the woods and the hills to the west. Now that it was clear, Sonny could see for miles, all the way to the gray, distant hills rising from the wilderness. To the north and south, trees got to swaying in a nascent breeze that made Sonny shiver.

"You cold?" Durant said, rubbing his bare chest and taking another drink. "Here you go, boy, this'll warm you up."

Sonny kept his arm down. "Thank you, sir, but I probably shouldn't. They say I've got pneumonia. I was in the hospital for a bit – gave me plenty of time for thinking."

Durant continued to proffer the bottle. "Whiskey cures pneumonia. Don't you know it?"

"It does?"

"Sure does. Faster than anything else they'll jam down your throat."

Sonny accepted the bottle, and now that it was in his hands, he could already taste the whiskey warming through his blood and making him feel a little better, then a bit better still.

"That's a good boy. You're a quick study, all right."

"Yes, sir...I mean Donnie. Thank you."

Durant took him around the yard, which he called the compound, first showing him the generator that would automatically switch on if the power failed, then taking him up to the east gate. Beyond this slanted gate which jutted at an odd angle against slightly inclining terrain, a thin path knifed arrow-straight through the woods, resembling a railroad line with no tracks on it.

"Leads straight to the deepest wilderness – they call it Nightwood State Forest now," Durant pointed. "You'll find some of the tallest redwoods in the state out that way, and at night" – he shook his head and rubbed his hands against their opposite arms – "you can't see your hand in front of your face out there."

He let it sink into Sonny and incite a shiver, then nodded adamantly. "I do believe that's the path we'll have to take in order to find your little brother. It sure did look like that one in my vision."

Sonny nodded. "Should we go now?"

"Hell, no." Durant took a gulp. "I'll know when it's right. I believe you will, too."

"Do you think they – it – wants something from us?" Sonny blurted. "I got to thinking a lot in the hospital, and I figured it's probably keeping Toby alive for something. You think it could be true, Donnie? You think it's giving Toby food and water, keeping him strong till it's ready?"

"Perhaps so." Durant scratched his beard contemplatively. "Perhaps it was the same situation with all the others who went missing, but everybody gave up searching too soon."

"I'll never give up," Sonny declared. "If I can stand, I'll keep looking. Everybody thinks I should lay down and rest, but until he's found alive or…not alive, I gotta keep looking. It's my responsibility."

"Don't let nobody tell you different," Durant smiled. "You're a little soldier, you know that?" He patted Sonny's head and passed him the bottle. "I can die at peace knowing our country'll be left to boys like you."

They visited the Groaning Tree and the north gate, beyond which a rusty skidder was hooked up to a felled tree. Judging by the extent of the rot, the tree had likely come down sometime last decade.

"You do some logging out here?" Sonny said.

"Used to." Durant drank and waved Sonny along. "Older you get, the greater the number of things you *used* to do. Security's become my top priority around here, especially with everybody disturbing the woods and sending it closer to my fences."

"What do you think it is?" Sonny angled.

"Not a clue. Not even sure I want to know, but I've got a feeling I'm gonna find out real soon." He nodded repeatedly. "It's getting stronger, I believe – and it's definitely getting bolder, coming around here with that awful violin."

"A *violin?*"

Durant blinked with confusion. "Didn't I tell you about that already?"

Sonny shook his head.

"I told you about my vision, right?"

"Yes, sir."

"But not the violin?"

"No, sir."

"Are you sure?"

"Positive, sir."

Durant drank again and passed the bottle to Sonny. "None of that *sir* business, now, or I'll lose track of my thoughts. Well then, where to even begin." He nodded lengthily and finally settled on a course of recollection. "I heard the *music* you been talking about, Sonny. I can't believe I didn't tell you already. I got the vision just before I came out here last night, and somewhere around midnight Fast started snarling up on her rock. She took a while to pipe down, and when she did I heard the strangest music coming from the woods, nothing more than a lady and her violin going back and forth. It was faint at first, hard to hear over the wind, but then it crept closer and closer and closer, so close that Fast came into the tent with me, and still that lady was playing and singing, just outside the fence, but it wasn't a lady at all! I heard *it* whispering, Sonny, even with the music going."

He took Sonny by both shoulders, his eyes wide with memory, his voice lowering. "The music eventually faded, and I looked Fast square in the eyes and told her, 'don't you go hunting that music, girl! It's trying to lure us like it did to Sonny Winters's brother.' Did I tell you about my vision, Sonny?"

"Yes, sir, you did."

Finally he released Sonny, eyeing the storm-worn trellis for a long time. "It all happened right over there," he whispered, pointing. "Right over there around midnight, it came calling, but it couldn't get in here. It couldn't get in cuz I had my lights burning bright, and me and Fast hunkered down in the tent and wouldn't leave."

"I believe you, sir, every word. There's something horrible at work."

Durant was silent for a while, drinking and nodding and glancing about. "You boys are gonna reunite," he finally said. "It'll be one of the happiest days of my life, not a doubt in my mind, but we've got a lot of work ahead. I do believe we'll have to follow the song to the heart of the Nightwood. And we'll have to listen, Sonny – we'll have to listen good."

Chapter 21

After warming up by the fire pit, Donnie Durant took Sonny through the east gate and showed off the latrine. Nestled among a stand of young pines, the outhouse contained a pair of thrones covering holes six feet deep. Even in the depths of night, a man would require not a single light to guide him here, the stench carrying a great distance.

"Dug them out with my boy just before he went off to war." Durant smiled wistfully at the toilet seats fashioned out of unseasoned wood, probably a great many splinters having been collected from those thrones which were raised off the ground by rotted lumber frames. To the left of each seat, covered wooden bins hosted a variety of supplies, Durant lifting them open for review.

"If you've got business that needs tending to, be sure to come out in the daylight." Durant tipped back the bottle of Wild Turkey. From the other side of the east gate, Fast regarded them with dull curiosity, then retreated toward her rock.

"Well, I suppose that concludes the tour," Durant said, rubbing his hands together.

When the old man turned toward the gate, Sonny caught sight of a faded red stain on the rear of his overalls. Moving downhill to the boardwalk, Durant limped a little and grimaced, Fast watching him from atop her rock.

"When do we go into the woods to search?" Sonny walked alongside Durant, partly hoping the bottle wouldn't be passed back to him, partly craving the whiskey.

"Soon," Durant nodded. "I'll know it when the time is right. I always know where I belong."

It was uncanny that he should say that just then, for Sonny had been taken with an urge these last few steps.

"Donnie, would you mind driving me to the library?"

"The *library?*" He scrunched his face up and drank. "What for, boy?"

"I'd like to research the newspaper archives, if I could, maybe find out more about some of the disappearances."

Durant waved dismissively. "All you'll find is stories about the police wandering the woods and coming up empty. They couldn't find their own shadows in the Nightwood."

"Yes, but maybe I could speak with a family member of someone who went missing. Maybe they could give us a clue."

Durant patted Sonny's shoulder and, with a wince, settled into a lawn chair on the boardwalk. "I like your spunk, Sonny. You're a fighter." He took a while to get himself adjusted, Fast dashing down from the rock and leaping up to the boardwalk, whereupon she lied at Durant's side and watched the flight of a crow.

"So, you'll take me?" Sonny pressed.

"Sure, sure, but you're on your own in there, kid. Too many whisperers in that place – same for the grocery store. They're always watching."

On the way to the library, Sonny tried to sort out his thoughts and get a handle on what was real and what might be tainted by terror and desperation for answers. Independent of the other factors, Durant's words carried not a note of sanity – Sonny knew this well – but when combined with everything else, the man made perfect sense. It was everybody else who couldn't or wouldn't allow themselves to see it.

Fast whimpered a little when Sonny stepped out of the truck.

"Be careful in there, boy," Durant waved, then took up the next whiskey bottle, drawing disdainful scowls from an elderly couple walking out of the library with books in hand. Fast, poking her head out the window, expelled a vicious sounding eruption and even a head feint, as if she might lunge at the couple. Gasping and lurching, the woman stumbled down to the pavement and yelped, Sonny helping her up and gathering her books.

Meanwhile, as Durant's rig rolled away, Fast was wagging her tail and smiling at Sonny, Donnie Durant reaching across and scratching her behind the ears.

"That horrible man and his horrible dog!" The woman brushed herself off and accepted the books from Sonny. "Thank you, young man."

"Is that your grandfather, son?" the old man barked.

"No, sir. I only met him recently."

"You'd do well to stay away from him." The man shook his head in admonition. "That one's trouble. Combat exhaustion wore him out good. He won't never be the same."

"Donnie's a hero – his son, too," chirped a frail old man seated on a bench outside the building. Even after he spoke, Sonny took a moment to find him behind an outspread newspaper.

"He's a horrible man!" the old lady blustered. "Haven't you heard the things he's done? And his dog's vicious, to boot!"

The frail man folded up his paper and took hold of a cane. "He served his country proud! You oughta respect a veteran who–"

"I am a veteran!" the first man puffed.

A competition ensued, each man's years of military service measured, combat missions listed, Sonny hurrying into the building, the noise giving way to the silence of a mausoleum. It took his eyes a moment to adjust, and when they did he spotted a thin, bespectacled woman staring inexpressively at him from the circulation desk.

"May I help you?" she said blandly.

"Yes, ma'am, I'm looking for the local newspaper archives."

She nodded and led him past the card catalog, where a woman traced her finger along a card as she read, her glasses hanging from her nose.

In a dimly lit room toward the end of the hall, the librarian prepared a microfilm reader and asked Sonny about the years he sought from the paper.

"May I have the archives for the last five years?"

"I'm afraid we haven't received updated materials in two years. I believe our latest update for the *Sentinel* is the spring of '55."

"May I have 1950-55?"

Heels clacking, the librarian went to a large cabinet and reviewed several boxes with detailed labels attached to the ends. Crossing back to the reader with a box in hand, she threaded the first film along the spools.

"This is for 50-52," she said, flipping a switch and bringing old news back to the forefront. Now Sonny was peering into the illuminated pages of the past, the librarian briefly testing the dials and murmuring "Uh-hm, uh-hm."

"Thank you for helping me, ma'am."

"Not a problem." She showed him how to use the dials to move backward and forward in time. "Fetch me when you're ready to review the next few years. Don't try to mess with it yourself."

"Yes, ma'am. Thank you much."

For the next hour, Sonny pored over hundreds of headlines, his back hunched, his eyes strained and tired. He worked with the diligence of a grad student, scrawling out notes on a pad borrowed from the librarian. After a while, the snowy light and underexposed images began to conjure up tricks, making him see things that weren't there. A handful of times he turned the dial back, convinced he'd glimpsed ghoulish countenances, but they were nothing more than the faces of local politicians and featured residents and arrestees.

Eventually, after asking the librarian to set up the film covering the next few years, Sonny came across a headline and subhead from three years ago, April 1954:

MISSING BOY FOUND
Man goes missing while attempting to find him

ENGELHARD – Missing for nearly a week, 10-year-old Jonathan Penn was brought home safely by searchers last evening.

The Engelhard boy, who disappeared from his yard on the morning of April 12, was found uninjured in the woods off Ferromex Road. Police said the boy was in

*remarkably good condition despite having been
missing for six days, leading authorities to suspect a
possible abduction. Still in a state of shock, the boy
has not spoken to police, Engelhard Chief Burke
Bridges told reporters…*

*…The celebration was tempered by the
disappearance of search volunteer Randall Beach, of
Engelhard, who was last seen at the Westwood
Trailhead…*

Sonny took all the information down. Rubbing his
eyes, he read about a slew of hunters and hikers and
campers who went missing over the last five years,
their guns and tents and gear left behind. Many locals
had begun referring to Nightwood State Forest as
Deathwood. For a time, the Engelhard Police had
suspected a killer, but their investigation had faded
into the fog like everything else around these parts.

Gathering his notes, Sonny thanked the librarian on
his way out and hitchhiked home, catching a ride with
a dump truck driver who'd gone to school with Papa.

"I'm very sorry about your brother," the man said,
stopping outside Sonny's driveway.

"We're gonna find him soon," Sonny nodded. "Thank
you for the ride, sir, and for your kind words."

The man's features sagged into a sad heap. He went
to say something, but instead he just waved and
rolled up his window, Sonny starting along the
driveway and spitting a thin lace of blood into the
wind. It had picked up out of the west since morning,

THE NIGHTWOOD SONG

Sonny grateful for a hot soup and the sound of Mama's voice on the other end of the rotary. She didn't say much beyond a few questions and apologies, but it warmed Sonny's heart better than any fire ever could.

"You rest up, Mama. I'm getting everything taken care of."

"Good boy. Such a good boy, my Sonny."

"I love you, Mama."

"I love you, too, my son."

Aunt Dana came on the line a moment later, but she was full of condolences and talk of Sonny joining them in L.A.

"I'm gonna find Toby. Soon," Sonny answered.

She sighed laboriously. "It's been a week, Sonny. You need to start preparing for the possibility that–"

"Take care of Mama. Make sure she gets her rest."

"Sonny, please listen–"

"I'll call you when Toby's home. Mama will want to come on home then, and we've got much work to get things back in order."

Without waiting for a response, Sonny clicked the phone into place and moved automatically to the schedule and the books, his eyes passing over everything that had been of critical importance until a week ago…deliveries and payments and Mr. Singletary's name underlined with red marker because he was in arrears.

Now only one thing mattered. Just one thing in the entire world.

THE NIGHTWOOD SONG

Chapter 22

Bundled up in a coat topping his flannel jacket, Sonny gathered the notes he'd taken at the library and crossed the stream to Big Bertha. She offered an even lengthier growl, Sonny letting her warm up a bit while he spat some more blood and watched the wind take his piss. He searched the trees and swaying branches, listened for music, but there was only the howl of the wind to be heard, not even a train horn this time.

Fifteen minutes later, following Grandpa's map, Sonny arrived at the Penn residence he'd looked up in the phone book. The house was situated just inside the Engelhard town line, only a noisy brook separating them from the Nightwood.

"What in God's name?" a black-bearded man said when Sonny stepped down from Bertha. "Who are you, boy?"

"Sonny Winters, sir. Are you Jonathan Penn's father?"

The man blinked at him for a bit, then set down his axe and left a log to contemplate its imminent demise. "What do you want, boy?" he grunted, storming over like a defensive lineman. "If you're here for some kind of prank, I'll crack your skull."

"No, sir. I read about your son at the library, sir. My brother, Toby, he went missing last Sunday. He–"

"Come in, come in," the man waved, his expression softening. "I'm awful sorry for being rude, but some folks have given us trouble from time to time. Reporters. Kids looking for a laugh."

"I'm sorry, sir. Why are they bothering you?"

The man stopped just before the porch steps. "My son's still out there," he glared, eyeing the Nightwood.

"But...but the article said he was found."

"Technically, but that boy in there is just a body. That ain't my son. He's still lost, and he won't come home."

It looked like the man might cry, but then he was turning and leading Sonny into the house, where he was introduced to Barbara Penn.

"You poor boy. I'm so very sorry." Barbara glanced down to Sonny's bandaged hands. "You don't look well. Not a bit."

"I've been under the weather lately, ma'am. The searching's been hard, but I won't stop. Anyway, I was hoping I could speak with your son about what he saw out there while he was missing."

"I'm afraid that won't be possible." Barbara brushed a hand along the top of her bun, then straightened her apron. "Johnny hasn't spoken a word since they found him."

"We even took him to a specialist in San Francisco," the father lamented. "Nothing."

THE NIGHTWOOD SONG

"May I make acquaintances with him?" Sonny asked. "I won't disturb him none. I'd just like to tell him about my brother, if I could."

The Penns exchanged glances. "I suppose it can't do any harm," Mr. Penn shrugged.

"Yes, I suppose," his wife sighed, bringing Sonny into the living room, where a gaunt, pallid boy in a white button-down shirt and gray trousers stared out the window.

Impossibly, Jonathan Penn looked even more exhausted than he'd appeared in the newspaper photograph following his weeklong disappearance. And perhaps it was a trick of the underexposed image on the microfilm, but the boy didn't look a day older than his 1954 photo.

Turning only because of his mother's touch, not her words, Jonathan glowered at Sonny like an angered spirit, his face not merely pale but somewhat gray.

Sonny swallowed nervously, and the words he was planning got gulped down, too. "Hello. I'm Sonny. Sonny Winters."

The boy said nothing, only glared.

"My brother, Toby, he got lost in the woods like you. He's been missing for a week now." Sonny risked a few steps toward the boy and took a knee. "It's nice to meet you." He held out his hand but the boy wouldn't move, wouldn't even blink. He just went on glaring, arms at his sides.

"I was wondering if there's anything you remember from the woods that could help me find my brother."

"Moon," the boy blurted, his parents jumping back in shock, then hastening their child into an embrace.

"Do you remember the moon, baby? Could you see the moon out there?" Mrs. Penn dabbed her cheeks with a handkerchief, Mr. Penn placing his hands on Jonathan's shoulders. "Talk to us, buddy. Tell us about what you saw."

"Moon," the boy repeated, ignoring his parents, still watching Sonny.

"Was it a full moon, or a crescent?" Sonny said.

"Full. Bright. They took him."

"Took who?"

"Him. The man."

A dozen more questions were launched at Jonathan, but he ignored them, even when his parents beseeched and demanded he say more. Sonny wished the father wouldn't shake his shoulders like that, for now the boy was mewling deep in his throat, a horrible, tortured sound.

"Tell me!" Mr. Penn repeated. "What did the man look like?"

The boy whimpered and collapsed to his knees, the parents unleashing their frustrations on Sonny.

"Out! Get out!" the mother lashed, Sonny scrambling away, stopping at the threshold of the living room when Jonathan blurted, "Monnindizitwedezuda."

His parents coaxed and cajoled him, then shouted at him, but he only responded when Sonny asked from the doorway, "Would you mind repeating that just a little slower, Jonathan?"

The boy nodded, over and over, nodding so long that Sonny wondered if he might go on like that all day. Finally, when Sonny turned to leave, the boy said with perfect clarity, "Morning does not welcome those who die."

Chapter 23

"Don't come back here!" Mr. Penn shouted as Sonny climbed into Bertha's cab, Jonathan having declined into a sobbing paroxysm. "I'll call the police, you hear?"

Back home, Sonny checked Mama's Farmers' Almanac and discovered that the full moon was due this upcoming Friday. The realization surged electrically through his blood, galvanizing him.

Jonathan was rescued by the light of a full moon...and those are the first words he spoke since getting rescued...and he spoke them to me!

Sonny kicked off his shoes and went down to his knees before the hearth, clasping his hands and touching his face to the cold floor.

"Lord, please keep showing me the way and giving me strength. Most folks think my brother's gone, Lord, but only You know the truth. Only You." He sighed, kept his eyes closed. "If Toby's gone, Lord, please let it be known. One way or another, please let me find my brother. I will search the forest until my last day, if that is Your command, Lord, but please let that not be Your plan. And please protect everyone who goes out searching with me."

Perhaps the strongest gust of the day poured against the house, soughing along the eaves. Rising, Sonny hoped for continued strength but discovered only fear, cold and black and bristling, a fear to rival the force of the wind, a fear that made him feel completely alone, his father dead, Toby vanished, Mama and Grandpa gone away.

But then the phone rang, shattering the solitude.

"Winters residence."

"You doing okay?" Sonny never would have imagined that Donnie Durant's gruff voice could elicit such a smile.

"Yes, sir. Thanks for calling."

"None of that sir nonsense. I just wanted to make sure you made it out of the library all right and got away from those whisperers."

Sonny told him about his discoveries at the library and the exchange with Jonathan Penn.

"No doubt that boy saw something terrible in those woods," Durant said soberly. "Something that's kept him quiet for years."

"The full moon's this Friday. Do you think we can find Toby then, just like they found Jonathan when the moon was full?"

"I'll know when the time is right, but we can't risk it a minute too soon, understood?"

"Yes, Donnie."

"Good. Now, you make sure you keep your head up and your eyes open. I'll fetch you soon."

Barely a minute later, a pair of severe, reproachful raps sounded against the door, no surprise that Sonny found Chief Clark on the porch.

"My deputy just saw ya behind the wheel of that dumper, kid."

"Yes, sir. He did, sir. I had to speak with that boy who was found after going missing. Jonathan Penn."

The Chief let himself inside. "That boy don't speak to nobody, son. He's been mute since he got outta the woods."

"He spoke to me, sir. He told me about a full moon, and how morning don't welcome folks who die."

It was as if a cloud had passed over Chief Clark, his face heavy with shadows and disquiet. Waving Sonny into the dining room, he seated himself at the head of the table. "Go on, son, sit."

For a while, Clark sat with his hands folded on the table, his eyes carving into Sonny. Finally, with a deep sigh, he said, "There comes a time when every man's gotta face the deaths of his loved ones. You've had to do it far too soon with your father, and I'm sorry for that, son, I truly am. I know you're scared to face it again with Toby, but the facts are what they are."

"He's alive, sir. There's something in those woods that's got him."

THE NIGHTWOOD SONG

Now the shadows etching along Clark's face were comprised of sadness and pity. "What has Donnie Durant been fillin' your head with, son?"

"Nothing, sir. There's something in those woods – something evil. Please, you gotta speak with Jonathan."

"We've been tryin' to coax that boy's words for years. Bein' lost all that time drove him mad – pay him no mind."

Sonny put all his weight into convincing Clark, but he wouldn't be budged.

He ain't crazy, Sonny remembered Durant saying of Grandpa. *He's got his eyes wide open now, but most people want you to go around blind.*

Chief Clark was one of the blind ones. Sonny could see that clearly now, and so he made no further attempts at convincing him.

"What am I to do with you, son?"

Sonny kept quiet, his gaze lowered.

"Look at me, boy." Clark waited a moment, holding Sonny's stare. "My brother killed hisself in the Depression. I know how it is to bury a brother – I been there." He stretched his flaccid jaw and moved his tongue around in his mouth. "Make peace with it, or it'll tear you up, son."

Sonny wanted to argue. He wanted to tell Clark he would bury Toby proper if there was a body to bury, but until then he would never give up hope, especially with Jonathan Penn's story panging around in his head…and Durant's words ringing truer by the moment.

"I should be goin'," Clark said, requiring several wincing increments before reaching full height. "Take heed, son. A man's gotta be strong and keep moving forth."

After watching Clark's car slip off toward Purgatory Road, Sonny went back inside and happened a glance into the gilt-framed oval mirror in the foyer. He didn't recognize himself with all these bandages on, but even after he took them off, his reddened, exhausted eyes were foreign to him. The gash on his forehead would turn into a nasty scar, he figured, and the chin wound was starting to scab over. His hands weren't as far along, Sonny taking off the bandages and balling his fists in spite of the pain. It felt good in a way – a distraction from the agony roiling inside him.

Outside, branches waltzed in the wind, inspiring phantasms in Sonny's head. He kept seeing Toby out there in the shadowy woods, just beyond the stream, but closer inspections revealed only the movements of leaves and branches.

Returning to the cold black hearth, Sonny was again struck by the encumberment of a watchful presence. He'd felt the creeping sensation back at the library while examining the microfilm, a handful of photo subjects seeming to study him as they glided past, but now, remembering the horror in Jonathan Penn's eyes, Sonny twitched with a sharp pain in his head.

Morning does not welcome those who die.

He could hear Jonathan's voice so clearly that the boy might as well have spoken again.

Morning does not welcome those who die.

What did it mean? What did any of it mean?

"You're alive, Toby," he muttered into the hearth. "I know you're alive, and I won't stop looking."

Chapter 24

Pastor Mahone stopped over for a few hours, and then it was John Stevens's blue Plymouth Belvedere pulling in. Stepping out with a pizza box in hand, he waved to Sonny and Mahone on the porch, a deeply spiritual conversation recently completed.

The pastor had told Sonny about the strength God gives every woman, man, and child – a strength that can convey the heart and soul through all manners of tribulation. But although Mahone had intended these words to impel Sonny down the course of acceptance, they'd instead strengthened his resolve to keep searching. Unless Toby was discovered with life no longer beating through him, Sonny's faith would be wholly invested in the conviction that his brother still lived…somewhere out there in the Nightwood.

"Pepperoni pizza," John Stevens called. "Straight off the brick oven at Huber's."

Stevens and Mahone went inside, but Sonny stood staring into the woods, his wounds lashed by a cold gust which ushered in snow from the west. Long after the scent of pepperoni pizza was whisked away by the wind, Sonny stood with his arms draped over the porch railing.

Searching. Praying. Remembering.

Finally, a hand on his shoulder.

"Come in and grab a few bites," Stevens said.

Sonny nodded. Reflexes taking over, he prepared a fire for his guests and also freshened the dining room wood stove with a blaze. He was cranking the damper when he suddenly lurched back, thinking he'd heard Toby's voice down the hall, calling for help.

"Did you hear that?" He poked his head into the living room, where Mr. Stevens and Pastor Mahone were sitting before the hearth, the pizza box unopened on Mama's tea table, the chess set looking lonely in the corner.

"Hear what?" Stevens said.

Ignoring him, Sonny rushed to the porch and listened, no longer hearing Toby's voice but the faint, mellifluous soprano of an opera singer in the deep woods, her voice carried by the wind and scattered along with the fattening snowflakes. In a flash of memory, Sonny saw himself with Toby last winter, catching snowflakes in their mouths one evening just before Mama called them in for supper.

But now Toby was gone, and Sonny could still hear the music, a little fainter now, Mr. Stevens and Pastor Mahone joining him on the porch.

"Can you hear it?"

Mahone: "Hear what?"

Stevens: "The wind?"

"No, the music – a lady singing opera."

The volume increased a bit, the song becoming heavy with lament, as though the woman were pouring all of her grief into the music. And then it was gone, just the wind and the distant trickle of the stream.

Stevens and Mahone eyed each other worriedly, Sonny tilting an ear toward the woods but hearing nothing further. Inside, the pizza cooled, the fires blazing unsupervised.

"Come on, Sonny, let's eat and get you bandaged up again," Stevens said. "We'd be wise to keep ahead of the infection."

Back in the living room, Pastor Mahone dragged Grandpa's rocker over to the tea table, Sonny hating the sight of him in that chair, but he managed to maintain his manners and accept it. John Stevens settled onto the sofa, Sonny fetching plates and silverware from the kitchen, then pouring glasses of water.

Sonny cut his pizza slice into tiny squares that wouldn't give his throat too much trouble, Stevens and Mahone quickly devouring a pair of slices each.

"What do you teach?" Sonny finally asked Mr. Stevens, breaking a lengthy silence. "On Friday, you said you were canceling your classes."

"English," Stevens answered, dabbing his mouth with a napkin. "When I started at Engelhard Community College, I thought I'd leave after two years and maybe head down to Stanford or even USC." He smiled thinly and shook his head. "That was two decades ago."

"Why didn't you leave?"

Inhaling deeply, Stevens set his plate down on the table. "Family, mostly. My wife was happy at her job, and we'd just moved into our first home. I suppose I could've commuted, but that wouldn't have let me see Mom as much."

"Where's your wife now?" Sonny kept surprising himself with these questions, but they were a far better option than listening for music amid the silent patches.

"She passed on. Eight years now," Stevens said quietly, nearly whispering. "She was very sick. It's been just me and my boy ever since, but he's away at school now."

"I'm awful sorry, sir. At least you've got your mama to keep you company. Where's she live?"

"The southern part of town, a little past Huber's and the high school."

"At the nursing home?"

"Near there."

"Do you have any brothers or sisters?"

Stevens took up his plate but didn't eat. "Only child. Growing up, it was just me and Mom."

"I wish me and Mama were that close, but there's too much work 'round here. We don't see each other much, even in the same house."

Stevens nodded, Mahone eating quietly.

Giving up on his pizza after a few bites – his throat was flaring up a bit – Sonny tossed a napkin onto his plate and said with a measure of guilt, "Speaking of the work, I've gotten myself well behind. I'll need to make some calls apologizing, but I gotta keep up the search for Toby. No time for nothing else."

"You should return to school," Mahone said, his words sounding more like a question.

"No, sir. Can't sit in classes while Toby's lost in the cold. My brother needs me. Anyway, Mr. Durant's gonna get a plan worked out. I think we'll have a prayer when the moon's full. Donnie's seen me and Toby reunited, you know – he saw it in a vision."

The men eyed each other again, their stares seeming to urge the other man to speak. When Sonny returned from clearing his plate, John Stevens offered to take him back to his place for the night.

"Thank you, sir, but I should stay in case Toby finds his way home. He'll be mighty cold and hungry."

"Yes, you're right," Stevens murmured. "Tell you what, how about I stay here with you? Would you mind that?"

"No, sir, not at all. I'll fix up some blankets and a pillow for you, if you don't mind sleeping on the sofa. Or you can have my bed, if you like."

"No, no, the sofa will do just fine."

Sonny stoked the fire. "Tomorrow, I should be well enough to head back into the woods. I've been studying Grandpa's maps a lot – there's plenty of places nobody's looked, 'specially down by the swamps along the rail line. It sure is tough country down there."

The men said nothing, their expressions weary, Pastor Mahone repeatedly picking the skin around his fingernails.

"Sonny, I don't think it's such a good idea for you to be seeing Mr. Durant," Stevens finally said. "He's not well."

"I know, sir. Believe me, I do, but his not being well's got nothing to do with what's happening. Honestly, I think it helps him see things clearer. He knows things about the woods – and Fast, too."

"Did he tell you about his son?" Stevens said.

"Yes, sir. He died in the war – at the Midway. And Mr. Durant fought in the first World War. He's a hero like Papa."

"Yes," the men agreed, Stevens adding, "He's a great hero."

"Mr. Stevens, he told me he's known you since you were a boy."

"That's correct." Stevens straightened his sweater and cleared his throat. "He was a good friend of my father. I knew his son."

"What was he like?"

"Good boy. Smart as the day is long. Loved his country. Donnie was desperate to keep him out of the war, but he would've had better luck in convincing the fog not to come around than urging that boy not to enlist."

Pastor Mahone leaned back a little in the rocker, his eyes better than halfway shut. "The young Durant is with the Lord now, but Donnie turned from faith after his son's death. A tragedy."

"I can't say for certain I wouldn't have done the same thing," Stevens said. "There's only so much weight a man can carry."

"The Lord built us to endure." Mahone crossed his arms. "It is the only way. We all have our tribulations, but only those who *believe* will find salvation."

Now the pastor's eyes were wide, bright with the same fierce incandescence which often shone along the Sunday pews. "The Lord will guide us through all burdens. We need only to offer our hearts and hands to Him and *trust*."

"Yes, but our hearts sometimes aren't ours to control," Stevens pressed. "The wounds of war aren't just physical, my friend. Can a mind not be broken just as easily as a leg?"

"Yes, of course, but…I don't understand what you're getting at, John."

Stevens closed the pizza box and finished off his water, setting down the glass with a definitive clunk. "If one's leg is broken, he cannot walk, correct?"

"Of course not."

"Well, if one's mind is broken, how can it be expected to perform normally?"

"You can't break true faith." The pastor stood and hastened toward the door. "It can only be driven from those who are weak in their belief."

Stevens smiled, but there was no contempt in it, only acceptance. "Perhaps we're seeking answers only the Lord possesses."

"On that I suppose we can agree," Mahone nodded from the doorway. "Thank you for dinner, Mr. Stevens, and for your hospitality, Sonny. I better head over to the church and see how our alms ladies are getting along with their plans. We'll be hosting a number of feasts this holiday season, more than any year I can remember."

Even after he left the room, Pastor Mahone continued talking as he proceeded down the hall toward the front door, perhaps so disturbed by the conversation that he needed to expel it from his mind with the sound of his own voice.

"He's a great man – and an even greater member of this community." Stevens turned from the hearth in Sonny's favor. "But some men's minds will always be closed to certain ways of thinking."

"Is he blind to what others see?"

"Come again?"

"Donnie says some people are blind to what's right in front of 'em."

Stevens's face twitched in nodding rumination. "I suppose we're all blind, if you think about it. We go through this life acting like we've got all the answers, but none of us truly knows what comes before and after. There is no true proof, only the belief in each man's heart."

"Donnie says you don't need prayers, just hard work."

"He didn't always say that. He's been through so much, Sonny."

"His mind is broken."

"Now, don't go telling him I said that," Stevens pointed. "Just know that God is forgiving. I personally believe that even if we abandon Him for a time, He will never abandon us."

Now it was Sonny who was nodding.

"A lot of people just need time to heal," Stevens put in. "A broken leg doesn't heal in a day or even a month, and a broken mind is infinitely worse than any bone break."

Sonny recalled the months following Papa's death, life seeming to rush by in a fog far thicker than even the Nightwood's gloom. His grades had dropped off, church sermons unremembered; there'd been sleepless nights and plenty of nightmares that also eluded memory.

"Anyway, I don't think you should see Donnie for a little while," Stevens was saying. "You need to focus on *you*, Sonny, not all of these distractions."

"They're not distractions. I'm the first person Jonathan Penn has spoken to in years. That's no coincidence, Mr. Stevens, not with everything else going on."

"It is all very…strange, I'll admit. And there's no denying that several people have gone missing around these parts in recent years."

"Mr. Stevens, do you think it's possible Donnie's been right all along? Are we closing our eyes to the truth and making ourselves blind? And what if being blind made Grandpa's and Mama's minds break?"

"Now, I certainly wouldn't go that far. It's just–"

"Why would the Penn boy say morning don't welcome those who die? Where did he get that, if not from something in those woods? Something that kept him there. Something that's making the music!"

"All right, all right, let's just take it slow, Sonny. I'm sure there's an explanation for everything. We just need to sort through it, that's all."

Stevens's eyes flicked back and forth from Sonny to the hearth. Before long, he was standing and pacing, checking his watch often. They talked till the birth of a new hour, Sonny having added a few logs to the fire and checked in on the wood stove.

"What do you say we make some calls?" Stevens finally said. "You were mentioning earlier that you've got some folks you need to contact in regards to your business."

"I'll do that later. I should get to Donnie's house."

"Sonny, did you not hear what I said? Being there will do you no good."

"And staying here will be even worse. I appreciate everything you've done for me, Mr. Stevens, but you ain't my Papa."

Stevens held up his palms. "Of course not, I only want to help. Pastor Mahone and I promised your mother we'd look after you. That said, I wouldn't make you do anything against your will. If you're set on going to Donnie's place, I'll drive you there myself."

"You will?"

"Yes, but I would insist on staying the night with you. Your mother deserves at least that much."

"Fair enough. Let's get going. And tomorrow morning, no matter what anybody says, we need to go to Engelhard Asylum and ask for Grandpa."

Chapter 25

John Stevens was fraught with sighs and deep breaths during the drive to Donnie Durant's house. The sun was calling it quits for the day, ducking away beyond the western hills, sending out an amber glare as its death knell. The wind, meantime, was just blossoming into full strength, eager to make the night cold and mighty lonesome.

Smoke billowed from almost every chimney, the product of countless hours spent chopping and skidding and splitting and hauling by men just like Grandpa and boys whose hands bore the same grime and blood as Sonny's at day's end.

That life seemed like another life now, as did Sonny's trips with Papa down Route 66 – all of it fading along with the sun.

And soon it would be nighttime.

"I think this is a mistake," Stevens said. "It's not too late to turn around. You should rest."

"No time for rest, Mr. Stevens. Toby needs us."

Stevens bit down on his lip and blinked at the darkening road ahead. The rest of the way, he made an occasional groaning sigh but said nothing more in protest.

"Well, here we are," he finally said, stepping out of the Belvedere and getting a close look at the barrel of

Donnie's shotgun on the other side of the fence, Fast growling at his side.

"Get back in your car and be gone! It's after sundown, fool!"

"Donnie, it's me!" Sonny lurched out the passenger door. "I asked Mr. Stevens to bring me here."

"Stevens? Is that really you?"

"It's me, Donnie. Would you put the gun down already?"

Donnie unlatched the gate and let them in. "You damn near blinded me with those headlights, Stevens. What's the matter with you?"

Stevens had extended his hand, but Donnie didn't seem to notice. "It's good to see you as well, Donnie."

Ignoring him, Donnie put an arm around Sonny and guided him up the hill, Fast wagging her tail the whole way up to the boardwalk and then nuzzling Sonny's face when he took a knee. Her excitement was so intense that she rolled onto her back and squirmed around, accepting extensive belly rubs from Sonny and Donnie.

Stevens stood back and watched. "How have you been, Donnie? We don't see you much around town anymore."

"I've got little use for town. Just a bunch of whisperers taking their fill of gossip."

"People care about you, Donnie. They're worried."

Donnie spat off the boardwalk and rubbed his beard. "Tell 'em they don't got nothing to worry about. I'm doing just fine."

"Well, if you ever need anything, don't hesitate to ask."

"Sure thing, John." He turned to Sonny. "That's some awful good work you did today. I like your gumption, kid."

"Thanks, Donnie. But I can't get what that Penn boy said out of my mind."

Donnie's eyes narrowed. "He's seen horrible things, that boy. His clue about the moon will go a long way, I'm convinced of it."

"Now, let's not go making too much of this, Donnie," Stevens began, but his words once again went ignored.

"The more I think about it, the more your plan about Friday night makes perfect sense." Donnie was guiding Sonny toward the fire pit, Fast leading the way and leaping up to a tall bench. "We'll go searching 'neath the full moon, see what demands it makes."

It. Sonny shuddered with memories of Grandpa's words: *Fetch my damn gun! None of us are safe here. None–*

Grandpa had collapsed of a heart attack then, the ambulance taking him away, and Sonny hadn't seen or heard from him since.

Donnie opened a fresh bottle of whiskey. "Go on, sit. We've got a lot to discuss."

Sonny intended to sit beside Fast, but he noticed the collie was avidly sniffing a small stain of fresh blood on the wooden bench. Remembering the stain he'd seen in the back of Donnie's overalls, his eyes flashed across to the old man, who winced and groaned onto the opposite bench.

"Are you feeling all right, Mr. Durant?"

"Just fine," he managed through gritted teeth. "Although I might develop myself a headache if you keep on with that *mister* business."

Sonny smiled, Donnie Durant smiling back and holding out the whiskey bottle. "Care for a sip?"

"He's just a boy, Donnie," Stevens intervened, standing by the fire. "Have you been furnishing him with whiskey up here?"

Donnie waved him off. "Whiskey speeds the night along."

"Besides," Sonny added, "it sure can help with a case of pneumonia."

John Stevens shook his head at Donnie. "This isn't the old days anymore. It's against the law to supply alcohol to a minor."

"Stevens, you sound like a damn Prohibitionist. It was that kind of talk that had me and my uncle making moonshine for fifteen years in them woods."

"You oughta respect the law, Donnie, especially where the boy's concerned."

Donnie glanced into the southern woods, in the direction of a distant fisher's screech. "The only thing that matters up here is the law of the night."

As if to offer its assent, a shriek of wind rushed in and drowned the fisher's competing sounds. The sunset colors had departed the sky beyond the hills, leaving behind a soft blue palette striated with thin gray clouds. The earlier burst of snow had moved on, a fresh squall perhaps to replace it in a few hours. For now, only leaves and pine needles blew around in the feverish wind.

"What exactly is the purpose of this meeting, besides drinking?" Stevens asked after quashing Donnie's latest offer of whiskey to Sonny.

"We gotta keep the watch," Donnie answered.

"The *watch?*"

"It'll come for us if we don't keep our guard up."

"What will come for you?"

"It."

"It," Sonny repeated.

Fast, having launched up to her rock, barked intermittently at the family of fishers in the south, the fishers screaming back. Sonny endured a few coughing patches, turning away each time he spat so Stevens wouldn't catch sight of any blood.

"This is madness," John Stevens finally said. "You both know this, right? The only thing that's coming for you two is a hangover."

"Pipe down, Stevens, or you'll distract us."

"From what? Staring at the woods all night?"

The nearest light, affixed to a wood post beside the front gate and trellis, began to flicker, Fast noticing it first and chirping, Donnie following her gaze. Within ten seconds, the light was back to full strength, Fast going silent but keeping careful watch of the vicinity.

Sonny watched the trellis as well, imagining a great many fiends in the dark space between the top of the gate and the arch of the trellis. He briefly thought he heard music off to the south, but the wind took whatever hints he'd gathered and tore them to shreds.

"Mind if I use your restroom, Donnie?" Stevens said twenty minutes later. He'd paced around the fire for a while, hands stuffed into his coat pockets, Sonny wondering if he would pace all night.

"Latrine's closed after dark," Donnie grunted, bringing the bottle to his lips. "Feel free to piss from the boardwalk."

"You get used to it pretty quick," Sonny contributed, half-certain that the same bafflement on Stevens's face had limned his own expression not long ago.

"What about the house?" Stevens pointed.

"He took out the toilet a while back," Sonny answered while Donnie drank. "The bathroom's been converted into an armory, sir."

"My God," Stevens murmured, shaking his head as if a salesman had placed a contraption of rusted metal before him and advertised it as a time machine.

A far more private soul than Sonny, Mr. Stevens ventured northeast off the boardwalk and crunched his way through oceans of fallen leaves, his form fading away until it was swallowed by the woods.

Glancing west and then northeast again, Sonny shivered. In the strengthening wind, the trees were no longer individual creations but instead a black mass stabbed with spectral drabs of light. To the north, the naked, wishbone-shaped Groaning Tree delivered a baleful chorus; on the western boulder, meanwhile, Fast's silhouette stood out in vivid relief against the backdrop of a nearby lamp. Somehow detecting Sonny's gaze, her head lurched in his direction, her tail beginning to wag.

"Drink up, kid, before Lawman John gets back."
Donnie tossed the bottle to Sonny, but this one was
different than the others – no label. It tasted different,
too, potent and near toxic, as though he'd siphoned
diesel from Big Bertha and swallowed.

Sonny couldn't help but cough and spit. Standing,
doubling over with hands on knees, he smacked his
lips and tried to claim anything close to a normal
breath.

Donnie was hooting and clapping. "That's moonshine
right there, young fella – straight from my good friend
Atchison Holliday's still. How's it taste?"

"Like diesel, sir," Sonny coughed. "It burns."

"You'll learn to love it," the old man grinned. "I've got
plenty of great memories out there in the woods with
ole Atch Holliday. I was just back from the war when
we started moonshining, and we even took our boys
out there some nights. Of course, being the profiteer
he is, Atch eventually opened up his own still – but
don't go telling Chief Clark about none of this. I never
bothered to bring in any of the equipment once I shut
things down."

He went on nodding and drinking and staring into the
flames for a while. "Remind me, I'll show you the still
one day. Haven't made it out that way for a while." He
glanced to the northeast. "Say, you think John got
himself lost? It's a ways till you reach the fence back
there."

"He was probably holding it a long time. I feel bad for bringing him out here – I hope he didn't have plans to see his mama tonight."

"His mama?"

"Yes, sir, he visits her almost every night."

Donnie nodded and drank, then glanced in the direction of a flare-up from the fishers. Fast had grown bored with them, not even bothering to lift her head from her forepaws this time. Sonny coughed and warmed his hands over the fire (even if he happened to touch the flames, his hands wouldn't burn as thoroughly as his throat from the moonshine).

Stevens, rejoining the circle with a frown, caught Sonny during one of his coughs. "We should go inside where it's warmer. You don't want to push it out here, kid."

"First good idea you've had all night, Stevens." Donnie nodded toward the house. "You two go on upstairs and show yourselves to the guest room. Last door on the right – I freshened it up a bit this morning."

"But what if it comes for you while we're inside?"

Donnie took up his shotgun and pumped it. "I'm ready for the sonofabitch. War's back in my blood again, boy."

"Jesus, Donnie, be careful with that thing." Stevens stood between Sonny and the wild-eyed old man.

"You're fixing for disaster up here with all this drinking and spouting madness and arming yourself."

Donnie's answer featured four words and nothing more. "The night is long."

Shaking his head, Stevens took Sonny by the wrist and led him down the boardwalk toward the stairs, both of them glancing up when the Groaning Tree barked out a lengthy warning that sounded more like a slowly opened door than a wind-bothered branch.

The house was heavily candlelit this time, the flames like watchful eyes as they cautioned through the clutter.

"Dear Lord, the stench," Stevens muttered, stepping around stacks of boxes and eventually finding the stairs, which were lined on both sides with shadowy tools, trinkets, and paperwork.

Lingering at the base of the stairs, flipping a switch, Stevens recoiled when a stairwell sconce hissed to life as though its hibernation had been disturbed. The dim light showed the way upstairs, each tread groaning noisily beneath them.

The already narrow upper hall was further reduced by additional towers of boxes climbing nearly to the ceiling. In the guest room, a pair of thin, haphazardly made beds stood against opposite walls, heaps of dusty clothes, books, toys, and pet supplies having been stuffed into the closet.

"There's blood on this pillowcase," Stevens snorted, tossing it into the corner and checking beneath the blankets.

Sonny went to the lone window and drew back the curtains. At the rear of the house, the guest room overlooked the enclosed yard, Donnie still sitting by the fire, a bottle in hand and the shotgun in his lap, Fast still lying on her rock (and although Sonny couldn't be sure, he thought she appeared to be looking up at him).

"These beds won't do," Stevens said, Sonny still peering out the window, his eyes flicking expectantly from one light source to the next.

"Come on, Sonny, we're going home. This is ridiculous. The sheets are filled with dirt and dog hair – Lord knows the last time they were washed. Sonny, come on, boy. Sonny, what are you doing?"

"Can you hear it?"

"Hear what?"

Sonny hastened the window open, praying the song would still be audible. And it was.

Sonny waved John Stevens over. "It sounds like opera. I heard this same song earlier at my house."

Stevens stood beside him at the window and listened. "I don't hear anything besides that spooky damn tree."

THE NIGHTWOOD SONG

"You can't hear her singing?" Sonny pointed to the east, the music becoming even clearer now that a pesky gust abated and the Groaning Tree went silent. "She can't be more than two hundred feet into the woods. Look, Donnie hears it, too!"

Donnie Durant was following Fast down the boardwalk, his gun trained on the eastern woods. Sagaciously, the collie crept off the boardwalk and crouched along the brushy hill, ready to pounce as the soprano held a high, menacingly protracted note, silenced only by Donnie's gunshots.

"Good Lord!" Stevens flinched backward. "Come on, Sonny, we're leaving! This is madness!"

"No, I have to help! We're all in danger!"

Sonny rushed through the clutter and returned to the yard, Stevens calling after him.

"You heard it, too, didn't you? The opera singer?" Sonny panted upon reaching the boardwalk.

"You bet I heard it." Donnie was still pointing his gun toward the woods, but only the wind's music played therein. "It's getting stronger, bolder."

"It's challenging us, Mr. Durant – just like it did to Grandpa! Should we answer it? Should we confront it?"

Donnie gulped down whiskey and tossed away the bottle. "I will view the next song as a declaration of war!" he shouted into the windy woods. "I will enter your territory and free all prisoners!"

Stevens's attempts at placation were silenced by another series of gunshots into the southeastern woods, Sonny going briefly deaf as Stevens hauled him away.

Sonny tried to scramble back up to the boardwalk, but Stevens lifted him over a shoulder and started down the hill. He'd nearly reached the gate, Donnie Durant still shouting into the woods from the boardwalk, when Fast raced down the hill and stood between Stevens and the west gate, snarling.

"Go on! Git!" Stevens growled back, but this only drew a series of barks which stole Donnie's attention.

"Soldier, you will cease your insubordination or be shot on site!" Now the shotgun was fixed on Stevens. Staggering down the hill, white beard whipping in the wind, Donnie's eyes blazed brighter than the fire.

"Donnie, please don't do this. I can get you the help you need. There's plenty of resources available."

"You take orders, soldier – you don't give them." Donnie's voice was a little calmer, the blaze diminishing from his eyes. "Unhand the young sergeant and be gone. Leave us to our battle plans."

Stevens set Sonny down and shielded him. "You've been drinking, Donnie. You're not thinking straight."

"No, no, it's *you* who's blind. You're all blind to the danger!" Donnie's lips trembled, his eyes darting from Stevens to the woods. "The enemy is out there in great numbers tonight. You must not – and you absolutely will not – open that gate until daybreak. Am I understood?"

Donnie had inched steadily closer, still pointing the gun, Stevens holding up both arms. "He's just a child, Donnie. He's not a soldier. Please. Let us go."

"I can't do that. You know I can't do that. We must keep the watch."

"Donnie, will you listen to reason? This is–"

For a moment Sonny assumed John Stevens had been shot, but no, Donnie had only clapped him in the head with the gun and sent him down, blood spouting from the left side of his head.

"You are hereby found to be in defiance of your duties, soldier." Donnie hauled John Stevens up by the coat and shoved him along the back walkway. With the shotgun, he gestured toward the rusty bulkhead doors. "Go on, move! Open them! Down!"

Stevens wiped blood from his head, but still it dripped and spattered. "I'm going, I'm going, just don't hurt Sonny! Please don't hurt Sonny!"

With Fast sitting obediently beside him, Sonny stared agape as Donnie marched Stevens into the basement. A dull urge told him to run, but the thought of leaving the perimeter brought a far greater fear, the soprano's song still ricocheting through his head.

"Rest easy, Sonny," Durant growled upon emerging from the bulkhead and snapping the heavy doors shut. "The prisoner has been contained."

"Will he be all right?" Sonny's tears moved to the forefront, but he blinked them back. "He was bleeding pretty bad."

The old man waved and grunted, as though Stevens had suffered nothing more than a paper cut. "I'll fix him up, but he's not to be trusted, you hear?"

"Why not? He cared for me. He–"

"*It* got into him, just like it did to your mother and grandfather!" He moved in close, whispered in Sonny's ear. "It makes people blind...and weakens their minds. Did you see what he was fixing to do? He was about to leave the perimeter at night, Sonny, at *night!*"

Sonny lurched back from the hot, foul breaths in his ear. "He just wants to keep me safe, is all. You didn't need to hurt him."

Durant shook his head. "He can't hear the music, Sonny. He can't hear the *Nightwood Song!*"

"But there was a time when I couldn't hear it, neither."

Durant flinched back and glanced wildly about, searching each pool of light and targeting his gun in all directions, Sonny ducking when its track passed over him.

"Come on, boy," he said at last. "There's no time to waste. We've got battle plans to finalize."

Chapter 26

The wind eventually settled down, though Donnie Durant's storm required far longer. But with enough drinks in his belly – and no further music coming from the woods – he nodded away into a deep, brooding stare, Sonny wondering what he saw as he stared into the flames.

They hadn't done much battle planning, Durant mostly rambling about the woods and the enemy and the encrypted messages written among the bright stars. "We must crack the code," he'd kept murmuring, a fresh bottle of whiskey in hand.

Sonny hadn't offered many ideas, too afraid of disturbing Durant, but he was equally afraid of inaction. Whatever lurked in those woods was indeed getting bolder – and Sonny feared his name was next on its list.

Now it's me and Donnie who can hear the music while others can't, just like it was Grandpa and Toby who heard it when I couldn't.

But what did it mean? What did any of it mean?

Fast, back on her rock, renewed relations with the fishers. Chilled from the wind, throat sore, head aching, cough persistent, Sonny excused himself to the tent when it began to snow. Digging in beneath a piss-stenched blanket, he prayed through his shivers and murmured his brother's name. He never would have thought he'd be capable of sleep, not at this elevation of terror, but he nonetheless awoke with a gasp minutes or hours later.

Groggy, he unzipped the tent and staggered onto the boardwalk, but Durant wasn't sitting by the fire, the flames having dwindled down to embers. Morning's light greeted the sky, but only with a thin nudge of blue to encroach upon the blackness and mute the stars, not nearly enough for them to leave the compound.

"Donnie? Donnie, where are you?"

A low whine to his left, then a growl. Glancing down the hill, Sonny spotted Fast at Donnie's side by the fence, growling at something to the south.

"Donnie, what are you doing?"

Sonny took notice of the shotgun resting fifty feet away on the boardwalk, as well as Donnie's boots and socks. Checking back, he confirmed that Donnie was barefoot in the mud, and Fast's growls blossomed into barks as she tracked something from the southern woods. She followed it along the fence, snarling and leaping and snapping as though an intruder were taunting her from just beyond the fence.

Closer, closer still, and now Fast was at the main gate, launching herself against it in desperate warning. Donnie, apparently sleepwalking, moved lazily to the gate as well. "Go home, soldier!" he shouted, staring beyond the trellis with his arms at his sides. "The war's over, soldier – go home!"

A moment later, Fast's barks subsided a little. She ran back to the south along the fence, tracking the progress of an enemy invisible to Sonny, though he could hear its footsteps now, crunch-crunch-crunching back into the woods amid the earliest light.

"Donnie, wake up! You have to wake up!"

Sonny grabbed the man's arm and then slapped his shoulder. Durant murmured something about maps and trenches, his eyes distant and unblinking, his head turning slowly to the southern woods. "Go on, soldier. The war's over. We don't have to be enemies anymore."

Finally, with help from Fast, Sonny managed to wake Donnie Durant.

"He's gone now." The old man blinked repeatedly and rubbed his eyes.

"Gone where, sir?"

"Back to the grave."

"Was he one of...them?"

Durant shook his head. "He visits me from time to time," he whispered, staring past Sonny and the yard and even the woods, staring into another decade. "He's lonely. He don't understand why it's gotta be this way."

"What way?"

"With me here and him there," Donnie murmured. Moments later, as if a light had been switched on in his eyes, he took notice of Sonny and then Fast. "How long was I out?" he panicked.

"Not long, sir. Don't worry – I kept the watch."

"I've been having bad dreams, Sonny. *It*. It's giving me these dreams."

"Do you remember the music last night?"

"Course I do, son."

Relief swept through Sonny on a cold, nearly windless morning. As abject as this nightmare was, he was glad to not be alone in it.

"Where do we start with the plans?" Donnie said after restarting the fire.

"You've got Mr. Stevens held prisoner in your basement, sir," Sonny reminded. "Don't you think it's time to let him be with his family? His mama'll be worried about–"

"His mother's been dead five years." Donnie squinted into the flames, his face not merely pale but a decidedly sickly color inching toward yellow.

"But…but he said he visits her almost every night."

"At the cemetery, perhaps. Mrs. Stevens rests at Burlington Hill – I attended the funeral."

"But…I don't understand."

"She was very sick. Her suffering is over."

Sonny could only nod, Fast leaping onto the bench beside him for a scratch behind the ears, then alighting in favor of her rock.

Donnie glanced over his shoulder, checking the eastern sky. "Daybreak ain't far off. I suppose we'll be needing to deal with Mr. Stevens."

"Yes, sir…Donnie."

Durant crossed his arms. "That damn Stevens probably told people he was coming here, and I can't have nobody sticking their noses where they don't belong. I've got no choice but to turn him loose."

"That's a good idea, sir. He'll need to see the doctor and quick."

As the first tinges of pink and orange leaked into the sky, Donnie helped Mr. Stevens up the bulkhead stairs while Sonny and Fast kept watch. There was nothing suspicious to report in the short time while Donnie was in the basement freeing his prisoner.

"I'm releasing you on the condition that you don't run to the authorities…at least not yet," Donnie said.

"I won't press charges, but Sonny goes with me," Stevens glared, blood having crusted in his hair and down the side of his face.

"That's not possible, Stevens. Me and the boy must complete our mission."

"Sonny goes with me," Stevens repeated, "or my first stop is Chief Clark's office. They'll have you locked away at Engelhard Asylum by lunchtime."

Donnie grunted a concession. Minutes later, upon sighting the first edge of sun crest the eastern hills, he unlatched the gate and led Sonny and Stevens through the trellis.

"You know what to do," Donnie whispered to Sonny.

Chapter 27

"That man is completely insane. Never go there again," Stevens admonished on the way back down Walthers Lane.

Without responding, Sonny stared out the window and remembered the music, specifically the operatic tune he'd heard in two different locations.

It's calling me to the woods. It wants me to go.

"Sonny, did you hear a word I said?"

Sonny blinked slowly with memory. "Mr. Stevens, when you said you visit your mama almost every night, did you mean you visit her at Burlington Hill Cemetery?"

The only sound from Stevens's side of the Belvedere came from the left turn signal.

"Mr. Durant said your mama passed on. I shouldn't have said nothing just now – I'm awful sorry."

"You've got nothing to apologize for. Mr. Durant is correct."

"Sometimes I visit Papa at the cemetery, but not so much lately."

Stevens let out a groaning sigh, his speed dropping considerably. He stared at the road the way Donnie had stared into the flames. "I wasn't able to say goodbye to Mom the night she passed. There was a bad snowstorm that day, and I should've left earlier to give myself enough time." He shook his head and gritted his teeth. "My sister called that morning and said I should get there as quick as I could, but it was the last week of the semester and I had two final exams to administer that day."

Again he shook his head, the Belvedere remaining stopped even after the light switched to green. When Stevens glanced over at Sonny, tears shined in his eyes. "I didn't think the weather would decline so quickly. I thought I'd left enough time, but the police had Main Street shut down...and the detour up Hillside Road cost me half an hour. By the time I got to the hospital, Mom was already gone."

"She knew you loved her. She wouldn't be angry."

Stevens nodded, but there was no belief in his expression. "That's what everybody says, but I should've been there, Sonny. It was her last day on this earth, and I should've been there to kiss her and hold her hands and thank her for everything she did for us."

Behind them, the blast of a dump truck horn got Stevens moving again, both hands on the wheel as he inched along. "There's some wrongs that can't ever be put right, Sonny. I drive out to the cemetery every night and talk to Mom, but I wasn't there *that* night. My sister told Mom I would be there, and she died waiting for me to walk through that door."

"Just like Toby might die waiting for me."

Stevens pulled off the road and set a hand on Sonny's shoulder. "It's nothing like that, you hear? There's nothing more you could've done. You damn near killed yourself in those woods."

"It wasn't enough."

Stevens seemed inclined to say more, but he was held back, perhaps by his own demons or possibly just from fatigue. He didn't speak again until he entered Sonny's driveway, noticing several cars parked ahead of him, including Chief Clark's cruiser.

Clark stepped off the porch to meet them, Mama storming past him, her rosary beads in hand. "My boy! Sonny, my beautiful boy! I'm home now, child. I'm home."

"Are you feeling better, Mama?"

She sobbed into their embrace, the beads digging into the back of Sonny's shoulder. "We must take time to grieve, son. I've accepted Toby's passing – you must do the same."

Her words might as well have been knives plunging into Sonny's heart. "They found him?" he managed, robbed of breath.

"No–" she started, stepping back.

"Well, how can you be sure he's passed?"

"Son, it's been over a week," Chief Clark said behind her.

"It's not likely a boy his age could survive that long on his own out there," Pastor Mahone added from the doorway.

Sonny's anger built like storm clouds. "You can all quit searching, but I won't stop. I won't give up on him."

Clark removed his peaked cap and scratched his head. "Son, you can't spend the rest of your life searching."

"I'm not your son!" Sonny backed away, ready to bolt for the woods if someone came at him. "And I won't stop looking till I find Toby. Alive or dead, I'm gonna find my brother."

"Sonny, how dare you speak to Chief Clark that way!" Mama stormed toward him but stopped when Sonny outshouted her.

"How dare you send Grandpa away and lie to us about it! He's not at the hospital – you sent him up to Engelhard State cuz he knows the truth!"

Mama dropped her beads, her eyes shining like polished coals, her lips trembling.

"What truth?" Clark said. Behind him, Pastor Mahone yawned and checked his watch. Stevens, meanwhile, had retreated to his car and was presently rubbing his injured head.

Sonny pointed to the woods. "The truth is, there's something in those woods – something horrible that makes people disappear."

Clark snorted. "Boy, how many times do I gotta tell ya, there's nothin' in them woods takin' people."

"It doesn't need to take anyone," Sonny countered. "The music draws them...and the Charnel house. And once you go searching, *it* finds you."

The group eyed each other with a mixture of shock, fear, and anger.

"You stop this nonsense this instant, Sonny Winters," Mama finally warned, her entire face quaking. "Do you hear me? This family has already endured enough heartache – you're only making it worse."

"No, you're making it worse, Mama." Sonny was surprised by the calmness and confidence in his voice. "Every minute you waste with questions is another minute nobody's looking for Toby. Now, I'm gonna take Bertha back to Donnie's house, and none of you best follow me unless you're looking to join the war."

"*How dare you!*" Mama erupted, chasing after Sonny, but he was far too quick, already behind Bertha's wheel and ready to roll by the time the others caught up, John Stevens and Chief Clark holding Mama back.

Glancing in the mirror, Sonny caught sight of his sobbing mother collapsed on her knees in the driveway, the others simply staring at Bertha, probably wondering if this was the last time they would see Sonny alive.

THE NIGHTWOOD SONG

On Purgatory Road, Sonny expected a crush of blue lights to appear behind him, but no one pursued him.

Half an hour after he returned to Donnie's house and Fast greeted him with leaps and kisses, still no one had arrived to bring him home.

"I know the full moon ain't due till Friday, Mr. Durant, but we gotta fight today. We don't got any time left."

Donnie nodded, Sonny noticing for the first time that he was dressed in military fatigues. And he carried a second shotgun, this one offered to Sonny.

"Can you shoot, kid?"

Sonny nodded. "Grandpa used to take us hunting."

"Good. Next time the Nightwood Song calls us, we answer it."

Chapter 28

Sonny's aching throat craved whiskey – even moonshine, if that would put the hurt away for a bit – but Donnie was adamant about no alcohol.

"We gotta keep our heads clear for battle, kid. We'll need to be sharper than western lightning if we're to bring Toby out of there alive."

Sonny tried to expel guilty thoughts over leaving Mama sobbing in the driveway – and insulting everyone who'd committed so many hours to searching for Toby. But they didn't understand. None of them had heard the music.

After eating canned hams and stale potato chips for lunch – washed down by rust-tinged water – Durant brought Sonny through the east gate for a scouting mission. Just the sight of that long, straight track pressing into the woods as far as the eye could see brought a crawling sensation to Sonny's skin. It also made him grateful for the nearby latrine, and he held his breath as he sent liquid out the wrong tube, the cold wooden seat chilling his backside.

"I knew that ham smelled funny," he repined in the darkness.

The next round of diarrhea produced a godawful spatter that sounded like rainfall. The time it took for the waste to reach the pit unnerved him, suggesting a far larger drop than the one he'd seen in the light of day. Now that the door was closed and he was shut away in the darkness, maybe that pit was expanding by the second, and maybe, just maybe he would somehow slide through the too-wide rim and drown in his own excrement. Vividly, he remembered the muddy swamp near the rail line, and the feel of it from neck to toe.

Finally finished, staggering around with his johns at his ankles, gagging and praying not to vomit, he fumbled until he found the handle of the bin beside the toilet. Carefully, making sure to step fully around the throne, he pulled out a thin roll of toilet paper – but nobody had ever mentioned how difficult wiping was in the dark, when you couldn't even check to see if more paper was necessary.

Tugging his johns back into place, Sonny spun around and noticed a shadowy form crunching slowly over leaves and stopping just beyond the outhouse door, its tall outline visible in the slats of sunlight penetrating the rotted door.

Pressing his face to the wood, holding his breath, Sonny thought he could make out a glowering eye catch his gaze, but then the form was moving on, the footsteps whispering away toward the gate.

"Mr. Durant?"

When Sonny yanked open the creaky door, he discovered Durant and Fast walking two hundred feet ahead on the overgrown trail, both of them staring into the woods.

Sonny jogged to catch up. "Mr. Durant, does anybody else use this trail?"

"Nope, not unless they wanna be pulling buckshot out of their bee-hinds," the old man squinted. "Why do you ask?"

"Cuz I just saw somebody walking that way. He stopped outside the latrine."

"While you were in there? You get a look at his face?"

"No, I think he had a hood on or something. I thought I saw his eyes, but I couldn't get a good look through the boards. He was tall — I know that much."

Durant snorted and spat, then checked the branches above them. "There's a reason I don't come out this way anymore, but just wait till tonight. It's like a foreign land after dark."

They took a detour after another hundred feet, dodging tracks of mud and eventually arriving at a clearing that housed the remains of the moonshine still. A few barrels had been tipped and knocked off the platform, but the majority of the equipment remained intact, rusty but true, and you could still feel the work and laughter and joy hanging in the air like mist. It marked this land as much as any tree or stone, forever embedded in the soul of Donnie's property.

The old man closed his eyes and breathed deeply. "Can you smell it?" Sonny could. "Smells beautiful, don't it?"

"Yes, sir, it does."

"You see that burner there, just below the big pot? She used to fire up the whole operation."

"It sure is neat, sir."

"Hey, now. No more of that sir business," Donnie snapped, ruffling Sonny's hair. "It's your damn voice, kid. You sound like an echo of my boy."

"I...I'm sorry."

"Don't apologize. Having you up here has been good for me. If I didn't know any better, I'd say..." He shook his head, his words trailing off.

"You'd say what?"

"Never mind. Let's keep moving, what do you say? No time for reminiscing at length." He started away, but then he stooped and clutched his stomach with a tortured groan.

"Mr. Durant, are you all right?"

"Yep, just fine – only a cramp," he winced. "I should probably hit the latrine on the way back."

They angled across to an abandoned logging road, Fast staying close and sniffing a zigzagging path beside them. To the north and east, hunks of forest had been chopped down haphazardly, creating an odd series of muddy swaths, as though God had gone through the area blindfolded with a barber's buzzer.

"They stopped when it got too hilly and too wet," Donnie said, pointing like a tour guide. "This area is surrounded by wetlands, and any logger'll tell you the money's better where it's flat and dry."

"Yes, sir. Grandpa's always rerouting cuz of a pond that pops up and blocks his way. A lot of 'em weren't even there till the bad flood."

Donnie nodded grimly. "You know, all the trouble with…whatever's out here tormenting people – it didn't start till after the logging got heavy in the last decade. If I didn't know any better, I'd say all this tree-chopping awakened something that should've been left asleep."

Sonny flinched from a cawing raven. "This whole community sure has left a pretty big scar on the land. New roads going in, new neighborhoods going up, and everybody seems to be hacking into the woods one way or another."

"Damn right. Everybody and their grandpappy." Pointing past a bog, Donnie directed Sonny's attention to the scrapped frame of a rusty green pickup truck. "Funny story for ya right over there. About ten years back, I was hunting up here real early one morning and I heard somebody screaming like they were giving birth. Turns out, it was a couple high school kids who were looking for a quiet spot but ended up getting themselves stuck in the mud. The boy panicked and got his truck dug in even deeper." Donnie shook his head and cackled. "I brought 'em back to the house for breakfast and told 'em I'd hook up my winch and haul out the truck by lunch, but they must've been too embarrassed or something, because I never saw them two again."

"Does this road connect with Walthers Lane?"

"Sure does, about half a mile up. It's all a big maze out here." Durant spat, Sonny following his lead. "Anyway, I waited a few months for them two kids to come back, but they never did – probably too scared I'd tell their folks. When the Fourth of July came and went, I got to scrapping that rig, tires and everything, stuffed it all in my truck and brought it down to Chessie's Salvage Yard. Treated myself to a big dinner at Huber's that night, even an extra beer and a warm apple pie for dessert."

"Did you ever see the kids again?"

"Nope."

Sonny had figured the story might turn a slightly more humorous corner, but it was amusing enough to sustain Donnie's smiles and giggles. Yet there was something frighteningly spurious about that frequent smile, as though Donnie were forcing it onto his face as a mask to hide the fear.

Rounding the bog and then venturing off the road for a bit, Sonny's bowels burned with a deep, menacing intuition when they reached a clearing. Barely a few seconds later, Donnie murmured, "Here." He nodded sharply, as if Jesus Himself had confirmed something. "Yes, right about here, I believe, is where the music came from last night."

Sonny glanced up at the distant pines, which loomed with eerie similarity of height and spacing – a perfect grid of pines as far east as they could see.

"The Nightwood," Sonny murmured. "This is where it begins."

"To me, this whole area is the Nightwood, but yes, what they call the Nightwood State Forest starts here."

Sonny became oddly aware of a vacuum of sound. He couldn't hear the caw of crows anymore, or the rustle of squirrels, not even a distant car or train.

Pinpricks sprouted in his neck, then his shoulders and arms. Glancing over, he half-expected Donnie Durant to have vanished.

"Close your eyes. Take it in," Donnie instructed. "Picture the darkness and the fog. You know it will bring the fog."

Sonny kept his eyes open.

"Close them, boy. Be ready for the enemy. Be ready to *challenge* it."

Sonny shut his eyes but only for a moment, his ears ringing with terror. "Toby, can you hear me?" he shouted, but his voice sounded like a whisper against the block of pines.

Spinning around, Sonny took in a swamp of low trees to the west, and suddenly the sky was hard to find,

Sonny swallowing hard and wincing. "Take me back, Donnie. Please take me back."

Kneeling, Donnie grabbed his shoulders. "Are you afraid?"

Sonny nodded.

"Good! Any soldier who goes to war without fear won't ever come home alive, you hear? Do you hear me?"

Sonny began to murmur a prayer, but Durant knocked it out of him with a smack to the shoulder. "God won't help you. If I had a dime for every man I heard praying one day and screaming the next with his legs blown off or his guts spilled out, I'd be building hotels in Frisco, you hear me? Do you hear me, soldier?"

Sonny nodded weakly.

"I said, do you hear me? I prayed for my boy to come home, and you prayed for your brother to come home, and what became of those prayers? *What?*"

It looked like Donnie would cry, and Sonny felt his own tears on the precipice, but they didn't fall. "I won't send God away," he rasped.

"You don't gotta send nobody away, but you sure as hell better not rely on nobody but yourself in this world. You hear me?"

"Yes, sir."

Donnie's eyes bored deeply into him, until finally Sonny looked away. Glancing back, Donnie was still staring at him.

"Are you truly ready for this, boy? Are you ready to do whatever it takes to bring your brother home?" He shook his head thinly. "We always think we know what to expect from war, but when the world's shriveling up around you and the walls of hell itself are rising, you better be ready to act. If you freeze up, the enemy will swallow you whole. If you let fear in tonight, it'll flood you like the darkness."

Sonny was beginning to hyperventilate, and he had to clench his rear to keep from leaking where he stood. Eventually clutching his flannel jacket just above the heart, feeling its fabric, remembering the man who'd given it to him, he nodded his way into belief and then mild confidence, enough to convince Donnie.

"I'm ready," he glared, looking past Donnie toward the Nightwood.

Directly above him, a raven alighted from a high branch, making not a sound as it swooped down through the swamp, Fast growling at it until the small black form was lost from sight.

Chapter 29

Back at the house, they spent a few hours indoors, Donnie clearing off the dining room table – but only to clutter it up again with paperwork.

"When war is near, a man has got to get all of his affairs in order." Donnie lowered a pair of glasses over his nose and scratched his thick beard; in the soft lamplight, he looked decidedly like Santa Claus reviewing children's wish lists. "I've been remiss with quite a few items over the years, but I'll have it all taken care of by nightfall."

"Is there anything I should get taken care of, sir?"

Donnie chuckled. "No, these particular affairs are for tired old men."

Sonny caught notice of several hospital billing statements piled on the right side of the table. Donnie discreetly covered them with other documents, but when he took sudden, groaning leave for the latrine five minutes later, Sonny pored over the statements and traced a litany of activities dating back to 1951. Many of them were from the Valleyview Medical Center's oncology department, others from Mercy Community Hospital. Sonny didn't understand several terms – words like colorectal and adenocarcinoma. Though the word cancer didn't appear anywhere on these statements, there seemed to be fifty ominous synonyms, and after a while Mr. Durant's billing statements read past due by the dozen.

To Sonny's right, Fast watched with what appeared to be disappointment, or maybe it was only Sonny's guilt manifesting. He read with increasing panic through one letter after another threatening various actions if Durant didn't pay. There were also several letters and statements from the U.S. Veterans Administration, many of them regretfully declining Durant's requests for assistance. Several letters from 1953-55 had been scribbled with angry words from Durant: *Bureaucrats! Corruption! No gratitude!*

"They didn't start treating soldiers half-decent till after the Korean War was through," Durant said, appearing over Sonny's shoulder. Somehow he'd returned to the house and entered the dining room without drawing Sonny's attention.

"I'm awful sorry, sir. I just wanted to see who all these letters were from."

"No need to be sorry, boy." Durant rounded the table and grimaced into the seat opposite Sonny. "I suppose it ain't much of a secret that I haven't been well. The cancer's spreading, and the time for the veterans' agencies to give a damn has long passed." Groaning, he dragged the chair up to the table and folded his gnarled, scabbed hands – hands that had helped keep this country free.

"I always knew I'd die in battle, Sonny, but this wasn't the one I had in mind."

"I'm sorry, sir. I never knew you were this bad along."

"It eats you up slowly, drains the fight out of you. I'd be lying if I told you I don't think about ending it some days – but I've got responsibilities here. I gotta protect this land until my last breath."

"Is that why you stopped logging?" Sonny guessed. "Cuz you got sick?"

"Yes," Donnie grunted. "And also because of the evil in my woods. I started hearing whispers out there one day – the same whispers that were in my head. But all of a sudden they were outside my head, too, way up in the trees, as though something were stealing them from me and raining them back down on me."

Standing in creaky increments, Donnie said, "Would you like to help me out with something, young fella?"

"Sure. Anything."

Donnie nodded, a smile visible not on his lips but in his stare. "Grab all these papers and box 'em up. Here's a nice box for ya – go on and fill it up good."

"Are you sure, Donnie? Don't you want to look through these?"

"Not anymore. Anything you see from a hospital or a vets' agency, box it all up good. Just don't touch these papers over here – these are for my lawyer, the damn idiot. Hopefully he don't bungle it all up like everything else."

Before long, they were carrying two boxes of bills and letters outside, Fast leading the way to the fire pit.

Donnie got the fire going quickly and then took a gulp of moonshine. Handing the bottle to Sonny, he lifted the first box and held a pile of statements over the flames. "This is what I say to all the bureaucrats and money-grabbers!" he cackled, dropping one statement after another into the fire. "Take your money! Take it! Take your damn lies and empty promises and your suits and your sneers! Take it all, damn you!" He waved Sonny over. "Bring that other box, boy, bring it here!"

Sonny obeyed, too afraid to remind Donnie of his pledge not to drink before the war.

"Go on, feed the fire, boy!"

"Are you sure about this?"

"Feed the fire!"

Sonny let a single hospital statement fall into the flames. The final words he read were *Oncology Department* in the upper left corner, and then the sheet was curling and blackening in the fire.

"More!" Durant demanded. "Dump 'em all in, Sonny!"

When it was done, Donnie excused himself to the latrine and then returned to the house, emerging twenty minutes later with more boxes. But these ones weren't simply filled with papers – there were also books, magazines, family photographs, trinkets, clothes, and tools, some of it burning down to ashes right away, other items languishing in the fire. He even burned his flags and military dress.

Sonny began to feel queasy after a while, not only from all the wasted items but also the maniacal shine on Donnie's face. He drank and hooted and clapped, then fetched more victims.

"I should've done this a long time ago, boy!"

"But if you burn all your clothes, sir, what are you gonna wear?"

"I'll have no need for possessions much longer. War is surrounding me from all sides, boy. I'm long overdue for an endless sleep."

"You'll see your boy in Heaven," Sonny began, but Durant shut him off with shouting.

"No Heaven! Maybe for others but not me, boy, never me! Even if I still believed, I'd never get in, not after all the killing I've done."

"You should pray," Sonny said, gathering his bravery. "God will take you back."

"I don't want to be taken back!" he screamed, hurling the whiskey bottle against a distant rock and smashing it to pieces. "It's all a lie! Everything they ever told me was a lie!" He rushed over to Sonny and grabbed him by the shoulders, lifting him off the ground a few inches. "They put us all into the *machine*, boy, don't you know it? The machine's been grinding boys up and spitting out their chunks since the beginning of time, decade after decade, century after century." Spit flew from his mouth, his eyes so wide and bloodshot that Sonny feared they would pop.

Finally setting Sonny down, Durant circled the fire with clenched, raving fists. "Why do we do it? Why? Why do we protect the babies and the children with every strand of our beings, but eighteen years later we send those babies into the machine to get ground up like dog meat? Dog meat! Our babies are nothing more than dog meat strewn about France, Britain, Germany, Japan, Korea, the sea, the sky, everywhere! Slaughter, it was always just slaughter – and it always will be!"

"Mr. Durant–?"

Donnie Durant wouldn't stop circling. "And for what? What is it all for? Have we all sent our sons to the grave so the machine can move on to the next country, the next war? When does it end, boy? Tell me when! Will the babies born in 1970 be free of the machine? 1980? 1985? Will the babies born in the year 2000 be free of it, or are we condemned to forever watch our children burn?"

Fast barked once, twice, Durant torn free of his fury and set to immediate purpose, his gaze fixed on the southern woods where Fast looked. "Get your weapon, soldier," he said calmly but urgently, Sonny slipping into the tent to fetch the shotgun Durant had given him.

They waited a while, watching and training their guns, but nothing happened. Fast returned to her rock,

Donnie and Sonny sitting opposite each other on the too-tall benches, the fire between them.

"Are you sure you're ready for the machine, kid? There are no winners in war – everybody loses something." Donnie tossed a few remaining items into the fire, including an old photo album. "You've been bruised and bloodied and damn near killed a time or two already, but that's only the beginning. Once we go out there seeking war, you're gonna see things that'll forever change you – things that will haunt your dreams until your dying day. Steel yourself for it, Sonny. Be ready for the darkest of dark, the purest of evil. Whatever's in those woods is of the strongest order, something ancient and all-knowing, I fear. It's in our minds, even as we speak right now, so we'll have to improvise at the spur of the moment."

Sonny nodded over and over and over, until Donnie said, "You may even need to kill me."

"What? Why?"

"If it consumes me, you must be prepared to end my life, Sonny…and that goes for anyone else who comes between you and your brother."

"But how will I know if it consumes you?"

"Very easily. My eyes won't be mine anymore."

Sonny might have gone on questioning for an hour, but a convoy of vehicles entered the driveway, Mama's station wagon and John Stevens's Belvedere among them. Chief Clark's cruiser led the way, Pastor

Mahone in the passenger seat, and several other community members were present as well, including Mr. Omya and even Mr. Incobrasa on a school day.

Fast sprinted along the fence line, barking at every face, snarling especially viciously when Clark approached the trellis.

"Don't take another step closer, Chief!" Durant warned, steadying his shotgun from the boardwalk.

Though the others backed away and hid behind their cars, Clark didn't move or even reach for his gun. "Thass damn well enough of this madness, Donnie! Put your gun down and let the boy go!"

Donnie racked the shotgun. "Get off my property! I won't tell ya again!"

"You keep goin' down this road, it won't end well, boy."

"Every road ends the same way, Chief. Death!"

"Come on down, Sonny!" Stevens called. "Nobody's gonna hurt you."

"None of you believe!" Sonny shouted. "You all just wanna send me to Engelhard State like Grandpa."

"No, that ain't true, not a word of it." Clark glared at Donnie. "Look what you've gone and put in this boy's head."

"It's the evil that's turning our heads around, not me," Donnie growled. "I ain't done a thing but protect my land."

"Let my boy go!" Mama wailed, held back by Stevens, Incobrasa, and Omya.

Donnie shook his head. "Ma'am, you best return to Los Angeles…or wherever you went while Sonny was damn near killing himself looking for his brother."

"You horrible man! You horrible, evil man!"

"You don't have to tell me, ma'am," Donnie snorted. "There comes a time when we've all gotta take stock of our shortcomings. I did it a long time ago."

"It's all right, Mama. We're gonna find Toby. We're gonna bring him home!"

"Nobody's goin' nowhere!" Now the Chief had his gun out, and it was pointed straight at Donnie. "Let's not make a scene out of this, Durant. Nobody's gotta get hurt."

"Then I suggest you leave my property peaceably, sir. Any breach of this compound will be viewed as an act of war, you hear? Don't make me have to put you down like a filthy Kraut!"

"You have a child in your custody!" Clark shouted above Mama's sobs and Fast's barks. "That poor boy's been through enough. Just let him go, please! Let the boy begin to heal."

"Please, Chief," Sonny begged. "I have to stay and look. We aren't hurting nobody – we just want to keep looking for Toby."

"He's gone, Sonny. Your brother's gone."

"You're probably right, Chief, but I won't give up. Not yet."

"We'll take ya to your grandfather," Clark offered. "How does that sound?"

"You sure will," Donnie laughed. "And you'll lock 'em both up in the same padded room, won't you?"

"Just let him go, Donnie," Stevens said, joining Clark.

"The jig's up, Durant." Clark holstered his pistol but took a few steps closer. "Do I hafta bring reinforcements out here? We're not leavin' without the boy."

Durant kept his weapon fixed on the Chief. "Oh, you'll be leaving, all right. You breach my gates, and they'll take you out of here in the coroner's car."

"I don't got time for this, Durant."

"Nor do I, sir. I'm due for a long walk in those woods tonight."

"Quiet!" Stevens shouted. "Everyone, quiet!"

Mama got her sobs under control, and even Fast stopped barking, her head now tilted toward the

THE NIGHTWOOD SONG

southern woods where John Stevens pointed. "Can you hear it?"

"Music," Incobrasa said.

Omya: "Yes, I hear it, too."

"The opera singer," Sonny murmured, his relief that the others could hear it matched by his terror.

"What in the hell?" Chief Clark said. "Some lady's singing out there."

"No, not a lady," Incobrasa shook his head. "It sounds just like a theremin."

"A what?"

"A theremin. It's quite the strange and complicated instrument – my mother occasionally dabbles with one. Listen closely, it sounds like a lady's voice, but it's actually the instrument."

"Cut the gas and let us hear it!" Stevens barked.

The music quickly began to fade, sounding especially ghoulish in the absence of wind.

"Can't hear it no more," Omya said.

Mahone (zipping up his coat): "Me neither."

Donnie and the Chief appeared ready to renew their standoff, but then a horribly strident guitar screeched off to the north, followed by an equally ghastly guitar in the east. It sounded as if someone were trying to play with half the strings broken, the noise so insufferable that it caused birds to take flight.

"Whoever's makin' that godawful racket – come out with your hands up!" Clark shouted, pulling his gun again, but the hideous guitars amplified, another one igniting in the southern woods.

When the guitars simultaneously went silent, a single voice was heard in the southern woods: Toby's voice.

"Help! Somebody help!" he screamed.

"Toby?" Mama dashed for the woods, Clark and Stevens right behind her.

Sonny would have gone, too, but Durant held him back. "It's a trick. That's not your brother – you know it's not your brother."

Sonny stopped trying to pull away. Even as the others entered the woods, Sonny stayed with Donnie Durant – the only other person who knew the truth.

War was afoot.

Chapter 30

Search teams promptly scoured the woods, Donnie's driveway converted into a makeshift staging area. He even allowed two officers to enter the compound and pass through the east gate, as long as they promised not to approach Sonny or make any sudden movements.

Fast followed the officers the whole way, trailing them as though they were sheep being funneled into a pen. After Donnie latched the gate behind them, he and Fast returned to Sonny at the fire pit.

"We'll slip away after dark," Donnie whispered. "These people will be hunting shadows all night, I'm afraid. The darkness is only concerned with us."

Sonny nodded. "I'm ready, sir. I'm awful glad you're with me."

Donnie leveled a hand on his shoulder. "One way or another, tonight will likely be the last time we see each other. I want you to know how much your friendship has meant." He rubbed his eyes and took a deep, shuddery breath. "It's been good having you up here, kid."

"I'll pray for you, sir. I want you to be with your son again."

The old man smiled, nodded, bit his lip. "Rest up, kid. Darkness ain't far off."

After the searchers trailed off, Donnie retreated to his tent to catch a few hours of sleep. He advised Sonny to do the same, but there was no rest to be had, not with the toxic questions poisoning his mind. He wondered whether these latest appearances of music in the woods had been meant to draw new victims or simply to taunt the searchers.

Sitting on one of the too-tall benches, Sonny watched and waited. As daylight became longer and redder, he closed his eyes and tilted his head toward the southwestern sun, catching the thinnest warmth between the trees. Gradually, searchers returned in duos and trios, though Mr. Incobrasa came in alone just before dark.

Sonny unzipped the tent to check on Donnie. He was still asleep, but there was great turbulence in his rest; he kept tossing about and groaning and murmuring about trenches and maps and places that sounded decidedly French.

Sonny gathered an extra blanket from the corner of the tent and spread it across Donnie Durant. Pulling the zipper again and stepping out, Sonny descended the hill and unlatched the gate. With a stab of guilt, he relatched the gate behind him and passed beneath the trellis, Fast watching him with disapprobation from her rock.

Mr. Incobrasa was smoking by his car – smoking and staring into the woods. He jumped when Sonny called his name.

THE NIGHTWOOD SONG

Incobrasa crushed the cigarette underfoot. "The music started up again in the woods. We followed it for over a mile, but then it just…stopped."

"It's making you go 'round in circles, sir."

Incobrasa nodded. "I'm still convinced it was a theremin. Strangest instrument, you know – it can be played without even touching it. A pair of antennas and oscillators control and amplify the sound, and I suppose it could travel great distances."

"Mr. Incobrasa–"

"My mother bought one about ten years back. It can sound like many different instruments, even a woman's voice."

"Mr. Incobrasa, I know you're looking for rational answers, but there ain't nothing rational about those woods."

Incobrasa nodded, smiling thinly. "Look at you, Sonny – you've been out of school only a few days and your speech is already reverting. You must return to the fold, young man."

Sonny stepped back. "You know there's something in them woods that can't be explained. You and me know it both."

Incobrasa turned to face the amber-streaked forest. He and the other searchers had walked deep into those southern woods, well past the fishers' den, but all they'd brought back were more questions.

"Did you see my Mama out there?"

Incobrasa kept his eyes on the woods. "She's with the Chief. Still searching."

"Thank you for searching again, sir, but you'll want to get on home now. These woods ain't safe after dark."

"The theremin is an electronic instrument," Incobrasa muttered to himself, raising an invisible piece of chalk to an invisible chalkboard and scribbling along the chilly evening air. "I'm unsure how it could be operated effectively deep in the forest. Amplification would be impossible without the proper equipment..."

A hand on Sonny's shoulder. He spun around to find Pastor Mahone's pale face and sleepy eyes.

"Are you aware of the Book of Job in the Bible, Sonny?"

"No, sir."

"Well, let me take a moment to explain. You see, Job was a virtuous, pious man whose faith the Lord saw fit to test." Sonny tried to back away, but he was held in place by Mahone's passionate, well-enunciated storytelling which filled up the nave on Sunday mornings.

"The Lord afflicted Job with a great many torments, including the loss of his home, wealth, and even his children. But no matter what was taken from him, Job never lost his faith, just as you will never lose yours amid great tribulations."

THE NIGHTWOOD SONG

The hope brimming in Mahone's eyes emptied a little when Sonny said, "Will you pray for me, Pastor? I'll be heading for the woods soon to fight the evil."

Mahone shook his head. "You must accept the Lord's plan, Sonny. Your brother is with the Lord now, and kept safe from any harm. The darkness lurks as much in your heart as it does in those woods – and it will eventually consume you if you don't accept the plan."

"I will accept it, sir, but only after I find Toby one way or the other."

Mahone's expression twisted sourly. "You must accept the plan, my boy. Do not venture astray!"

Returning to the west gate, Sonny expected the pastor to follow him with additional urges against searching the woods. But Mahone only stood watching, arms at his sides, and he was gone by the time the sun slid away behind the hills.

Sonny had expected Donnie to be up by now. Fast shared his expectation, whimpering outside the tent and scratching the fabric.

Sonny unzipped the flaps and let the collie in. "Wake him up, girl. There's much work to be done."

Donnie groaned and cursed when Fast licked his cheeks, Sonny wondering if the rictus stretched across his face would be permanent.

"It's almost dark, Mr. Durant."

"Donnie," he growled, scratching Fast's belly as she rolled beside him.

"Sorry, sir...Donnie. It'll be dark soon, and I figured we should get a head start."

Donnie nodded. "Take your gun and go to the east gate. Give me a few minutes to get my thoughts straight and my feet under me."

"Yes, sir."

"And stay on this side of the fence," Donnie called as Sonny passed through the flaps. "Don't go out there without me, you hear?"

"Yes, Donnie. I'll wait right there for you."

Sonny climbed the shadowy hill toward the gate. Risking a glance up the long track beyond the east gate, his body temperature plunged and his bowels roiled. In the dying light, he thought he briefly espied all manner of faces peeking out from the woods, but the narrow, overgrown path was empty, backlit by a low moon perfectly centered between the horizon trees.

Sonny gulped and winced, the gun feeling like a toy slung over his shoulder. To the north, the Groaning Tree sounded despite the absence of wind. In the driveway, more searchers returned from the southern and western woods. Sonny could hear the voices of Mama and Chief Clark now, but they couldn't see him up here at the edge of the woods.

"They're in the tent," Clark told a pair of officers. "Fetch the boy."

"What about Donnie?"

"I'll deal with him."

The officers approached the west gate and unlatched it, Sonny forced to pass beyond the east gate and hide behind a tree to stay out of sight.

Grunting and grimacing up the hill, gun in hand, Clark led his officers toward the tent and positioned them with hand signals, three others joining them from the driveway.

"Durant, this is the police department! We've got you surrounded, so come on out nice and slow with your hands up!"

Sonny's fists were frozen blocks, his throat dried out and tasting of blood.

"Durant, this is your last warning! You are in unlawful possession of the minor child Sonny Winters! Now come out with your hands up, or we will enter!"

The wait couldn't have exceeded half a minute, but it felt like five, Clark finally rushing open the zipper and storming inside with the others. They were bunched so tightly together that it looked like a bunch of football players piling onto a fumble recovery, one officer stumbling onto the back of another like a fallen domino.

Tears were ready in Sonny's eyes, but then he became aware of the lack of commotion. No gunshots. No scuffle. Not even any barking. But Fast should have been furious, perhaps even attacking the officers.

A series of snaps sounded to Sonny's left, followed by crunching footsteps. Glancing left up the trail, Sonny saw Durant with a wry smile in the dawning moonlight, Fast grinning at his side.

Durant had brought flashlights and an extra coat for Sonny. Shotgun slung over his shoulder, he led the way slowly but with great determination, the moon becoming a little bigger with each step.

"How did you get out?" Sonny asked. "I thought they had you for sure."

"A soldier is always prepared," he answered, glancing left and right into the woods.

Sonny stopped cold. While Donnie had been checking the woods, Sonny's gaze had lifted higher, eventually tracking to a gently flapping item hanging from a branch up ahead – Sonny's yellow raincoat, every last button fastened.

Before Sonny could dredge up a frozen word, he turned left toward the northern woods, where a maddened piano tune seemed to tumble through its notes like whitewater approaching the falls, culminating with a chime of high notes and then a low, foreboding finish that was as much a harbinger as it was a musical rendering.

Donnie and Fast were turning in a circle, trying to seek the source of the piano, but yet again the music seemed to emanate simultaneously from within the woods and their souls alike.

"Keep moving," Donnie finally ordered. "We must ignore these distractions."

Farther down the path. Closer to the brightening moon. Behind them, the east gate faded like a memory, little more than a shadowy shape backlit by the burgeoning colors of twilight.

Are you truly ready for this, boy? Sonny remembered from earlier, when the sun had been bright and several hours had stood between then and now. *Are you ready to do whatever it takes to bring your brother home?*

"That's my raincoat," Sonny pointed as they passed beneath it. "The evil's been moving it around, using it to scare me."

"That's good," Durant nodded. "Men fight better when they're scared."

Glancing back at the raincoat, it seemed not merely to flap in the wind but inflate, as if some invisible force had donned it and made it puff out. A stronger gust made it crackle and lean toward them, finally slipping free and rushing like a ghoul into Sonny's face, bowling him over.

"Woe, woe, woe, woe," something whispered as he struggled and flailed in the entanglement, Donnie and Fast combining to tear the thing away.

Only Fast heard the rapid crunch of footsteps from the west, barking long before the large approaching form became a face.

"John, what in the hell are you doing out here?"

"I couldn't let you go it alone," John Stevens panted as Sonny unbuttoned the raincoat and felt around inside it, discovering a handful of leaves painted in black: WOE.

"I didn't get there in time for Mom. I was too late, but I won't let it happen again," Stevens said. "I'm here now. Whatever happens, I'm here."

"We don't need you," Donnie snorted. "We've already got our battle plans laid out."

Stevens crossed his arms. "Donnie, the police are saying *you're* the one who took Toby. They think you're holding him captive in the woods, for God's sake. You need as many folks on your side as you can get."

Donnie nodded, Fast gazing suspiciously at Stevens and then the raincoat in Sonny's hands.

"The police are fools, all of them," Donnie glared. "They could be buried alive, and they still wouldn't understand what darkness is."

THE NIGHTWOOD SONG

They were interrupted by a cold gust freighted with music.

An old woman sang with great melancholy, Sonny immediately recognizing the tune as "Winter Wonderland" – except the words were all different:

...The price that we pay
For goin' astray,
Walkin' in a wooded wonderland.

"Move!" Donnie ordered. "Cover your ears and move!"

Somehow the song became louder when Sonny covered his ears, but it was gone altogether when he lowered his hands, Stevens reporting the same experience.

"What in God's name *is* this?" Stevens's face was exceedingly wan in the moonlight. "This is unholy, I say! We should go back before–"

"There's no going back now," Durant said softly, pressing further down the narrow trail, his boots squishing through a patch of mud. "The war's on, boys. Fight or die."

Sonny glanced over his shoulder, the gate now fully concealed in darkness, barely a few tinges of twilight still visible beyond the trees. The wind stirred up afresh, bringing a little snow to the woods but no further music.

They walked for many minutes, embarking on a slight declivity that lifted the moon higher. It was nearly full but still a thin shave away from totality, Sonny remembering the words of ten-year-old Jonathan Penn: *Morning does not welcome those who die.*

"Toby, can you hear me? Toby!"

Sonny shouted up through his burning throat, deciding after a while that he better conserve his voice so he would have it for midnight and beyond. He was sure there were at least a few wars over time that had lasted just a few hours, but he figured this wouldn't be one of them.

"Careful on these rocks. Watch your step," Donnie warned, leading the way down a muddy, rocky stretch barbed with bramble.

Fast alternated between guarding the rear and going ahead a short distance; presently, she stood watch behind Sonny and Stevens, scanning the woods with unnervingly minor darts of the head, as though she were zeroing in on a threat.

The terrain flattened out after a while, but there was no further trail to speak of, the moon obscured by megalithic oak trees. Donnie and Sonny directed their flashlights this way and that, Stevens following the tracks of light.

"What's the plan?" Stevens eventually said. "We really oughta fetch Chief Clark and–"

"No time for that." Donnie shined his light into a sea of underbrush, seeking different angles as though he knew something were hidden just out of sight.

"But we can't wander around the woods all night, just the three of us."

"We'll know what to do when the time is right."

"What the hell does that mean?"

"Trust your instincts, Stevens."

Sonny had thought he was ready for this, but the surrounding walls of blackness had a way of suffocating you. All these trees and oxygen, yet somehow Sonny was short of breath as they weaved and wended through the forest.

The passing minutes were marked by an owl, a distant coyote attack in the east, and, half an hour later, the eerie screams of fishers in the north. Sonny would have been afraid of the myriad night predators, but instead he brushed these noises aside; the return of the music, however, threatened to topple him.

It was the same old lady singing as before, her voice crackly and distant, as if coming over the radio. This time she sang "Dream a Little Dream of Me", the lyrics slow and dulcet like a lullaby.

"Let's stop until it stops," Donnie said, checking his compass. "It's trying to lead us around in circles."

"But isn't that what we're doing, anyway?" Stevens said. "We have no specific destination. We're just…searching."

"The path will be known to us," Donnie nodded. "Soon."

Still the old lady crooned, her words both near and far, seeping in from the branches and the fallen leaves and the tree trunks and the wind; from the white alders and the pine needles and the mud and the stones. Seamlessly, she progressed to a different song and then another, Fast barking by the time she sang:

Mr. Siiingleta-ry, Siiingleta-ry, crossed the sea and went to-war.

Mr. Siiingleta-ry, Siiingleta-ry, broke his leg and works no-more.

Unlike the others, this very brief song came from a specific direction, perhaps two hundred feet to the north, followed swiftly by a wave of low, windy, barely audible laughter.

Then silence.

"Jesus, are they talking about *Lionel* Singletary?" Stevens said.

"I believe so, sir." Sonny's light united with Donnie's in the north woods, spraying up shadows but nothing more beyond the closely spaced trees. "I delivered wood to Mr. Singletary just before Toby went missing. He told me he busted up his leg in the war and couldn't find work."

THE NIGHTWOOD SONG

"It knows us," Donnie said flatly. "It knows all of us even better than we know ourselves."

"It's been watching us a long time," Sonny added.

"Jesus Christ. Christ Almighty, protect us." Stevens crowded in between them, Fast prowling among the trees pooled in their lights. For a moment, Sonny thought he saw movement behind Fast, something creeping after her, but it was gone before he could confirm it.

"Ain't nothing but our own wit'll protect us in these woods," Donnie murmured.

"No!" Sonny refused to hear it any longer, falling to his knees and praying, Stevens doing the same, Donnie Durant keeping his light on the woods.

"...Fear no evil," Stevens finished, the wind heard but not felt, not yet. For now it was elsewhere in the woods, creeping toward them, no doubt, but it couldn't be everywhere.

Silence. Stillness. Even their breaths were silent, though Sonny's thoughts were getting loud.

"Maybe we have to challenge it," he blurted.

"How so?" Donnie said.

"Whenever the song comes, we always listen and try to figure out where it's coming from, but maybe we need to challenge it next time."

"Challenge it openly," Donnie nodded. "A formal declaration of war."

"And then what?" Stevens crossed his arms and shivered. "We start shooting at shadows?"

Had Fast not erupted with barks, then a low snarl, they wouldn't have spun around and seen, one by one, the lights of a house switch on in the distance, not more than a football field away. It started on the ground floor, but before long the attic lights were glowing softly, beckoning them like a lighthouse.

"The house," Sonny Winters murmured, his skin creeping. "The Charnel house."

THE NIGHTWOOD SONG

Chapter 31

"Impossible," Stevens said as they carefully neared the house, ducking out from the last tree and stepping into a clearing.

Their flashlights shined out along the foggy waters of a pond downhill from the house. Just ahead, a curving gravel driveway swung up to meet the house.

But even though Sonny had just witnessed the lights of a second floor and attic, the structure now boasted only one floor. And it seemed to keep slipping a little farther away, receding incrementally into the night.

To their left, nailed to a dead tree, a slanted sign proclaimed in red paint: CHARNEL.

"It's just like Toby described it," Sonny whispered, but he dared not raise his voice.

Even Fast tiptoed toward the house, her head kept low as she sniffed the gravel.

There was no need to ring the bell as Toby had done, the front door creaking open when they neared it. Soft, indistinct music oozed out from the depths of the house, but they couldn't hear the words, only the hint of a melody.

When Donnie climbed the porch steps, his shotgun fixed on the lighted doorway, the music abruptly stopped. The front door inched open a little more, as though somebody were standing just behind it.

Despite the horror flooding Sonny's heart, there was still room for confusion. Toby had seen this house just beyond the woodyard on their property – so how could it be here as well, the same exact house? How could it have uprooted itself and moved across the wilderness, plopping down in the Nightwood?

"Give us the boy and we'll call a truce!" Donnie shouted, butting the door fully open with his barrel.

Fingers of cool fog slipped out at them, followed by misty snakes and vines. Sonny couldn't see much in the hazy orange light, only a bare foyer.

"Give us the boy!" Donnie repeated.

"Toby, are you in there?" Sonny shouted, thinking he'd heard his brother faintly call his name. "Toby, can you hear me?"

The fog became instantly heavy and frigid when they ventured inside, as though they'd triggered some kind of hideous machine from a sci-fi comic that could produce plumes of icy vapor.

Hands held out in front of him, seeking the way through the amber-clouded obfuscation, Sonny felt as if he'd pressed one of Mama's opaque fruit bowls against his face.

"This way. Stay close behind me," Donnie called, their footsteps trooping over creaking floorboards, Fast's paws clicking along beside Donnie.

THE NIGHTWOOD SONG

In the distance, Sonny heard a door very slowly groan open, causing Fast to erupt with barks. Donnie had her by the collar, Sonny noticed when the fog momentarily thinned. Standing on her hind legs, Fast leaped and snapped at the gloom, choked back by Donnie's grip.

Stevens, meanwhile, closed a hand around Sonny's wrist. "Don't leave my side, kid. And be ready to run."

Stevens's words were hollowed out by fear, Sonny's gut made nauseous. Within the depths of the gloom, he could hear the heartbeats of time pronounced by a grandfather clock.

"What is this place?" Stevens finally said.

"Hunting lodge," Donnie grunted. "But this time, *men* are the game."

"We shouldn't be here. We never should have come here! For God's sake, it said *charnel* on the sign!" Stevens turned toward the foyer, but Sonny pulled free of his grip and moved toward the sound of his brother's voice.

It was much stronger now, coming from somewhere below them.

"Toby, I'm coming for you! Keep yelling!"

His brother's pleas strengthened, louder, louder, louder, Sonny moving the right way through the fog, the others thudding behind him.

"Sonny, help! Get me out! Please get me out!"

"I'm coming, Toby, just keep yelling! Don't stop yelling!"

Toby's voice was drowned by the others' shouts: "Sonny, where are you? Stay with us!"

Although they were close behind Sonny, they shouted his name as if they couldn't see him anymore.

"I'm right here! Keep quiet so I can hear my brother!"

"Right where?" Donnie said.

Added Stevens: "Sonny, slow down. You're too far ahead."

"Just keep coming. I'm right here."

"Sonny, stop moving."

"I'm not. I'm standing still."

"Where?"

"Sonny, where are you?"

"You're going past me! Stop!" Sonny extended his arms, but he couldn't make contact with their forms in the fog. "Follow my flashlight!" He danced the light along the floor. "Can you see it?"

"No, nothing," Donnie growled.

THE NIGHTWOOD SONG

Deep, rolling laughter preceded a chaotic piano rendition that sounded as if it were coming from above and beneath them. It even seemed to emanate from within the walls.

"Sonny, stop moving!" Donnie and Mr. Stevens were jogging now, drifting away amid the heaviest fog yet, Fast barking fiercely.

"I'm not moving, I'm right here! You went past me!"

They didn't respond, Sonny giving up and forging his own route, for he could hear his brother again now.

"Sonny, help! Get me out!"

The piano rambled on, but Toby's shouts were much louder, Sonny following them through the fog until he reached a black rectangle beyond a fully opened door.

As though his body and the door were rigged with same-poled magnets, he recoiled and stumbled backward, his mouth agape. Toby's shouts were coming from the perfect darkness within that room, but so, too, were other sounds...impossible sounds. Voices from Sonny's past. Sermons from Sundays long gone. The fading horn of Papa's Kenworth.

Blinking in disbelief, Sonny moved to the threshold and discovered not a room but a staircase, only five steps visible before darkness ruled.

"Toby, can you hear me?"

"Yes, come get me! I'm in the basement!"

Sonny shined his light down the stairs. The imagined fiends looming in his head were so detailed that he briefly saw them congregating on the lowest steps, but for the moment there was nothing requiring the gun, only stone walls and a stone floor laden with cobwebs.

Yet Sonny could hear Papa's words and Mama's words as though they stood at the base of the stairs. "Get out! Get out now!" they warned. "Morning does not welcome those who die, Sonny Winters!"

"No, it sure don't," Chief Clark put in.

"I'm afraid not," added Pastor Mahone.

Toby's voice prevailed over the others. "Sonny, please! It's coming! It's here!"

Sonny burst through his terror and descended into darkness, taking hold of the thin, cold metal handrail. Flakes of ancient paint peeled away and clung to his bandaged palms, cobwebs brushing against his face. Treads groaned beneath him, each one louder than its predecessor.

The fog tapered off, gobbled up by the darkness. Even Sonny's light thinned as he progressed, becoming weak and yellowish before flickering. He clapped the flashlight with enough force to match the clouts of his heart, but the light refused to return steady, and now Sonny was convinced that the faces in the distance were not imaginary products.

THE NIGHTWOOD SONG

"Sonny, *help!*" Toby wailed with a gurgling gasp, sounding as if he were being choked.

Sonny ran down a slightly curving corridor, no longer needing the flashlight because a group of flames brightened in the distance. Torches. They were spaced unevenly on the walls, affixed by rusty sconces, and the flames swayed as if bothered by a changing wind.

Sonny tried a pair of opposing wooden doors that were deeply inset into the walls. Locked. So, too, was the next door, but then Sonny arrived in a small room that would have been empty if not for three items: a dusty mahogany writing desk situated against the far wall, a wooden stool before it, and a glowing microfilm reader atop it.

No sooner had Sonny stepped into the room than the door snapped shut behind him and locked. He tugged and kicked and shouldered it unavailingly, even rammed it with the gun, screaming for his brother the whole time, but he couldn't hear Toby anymore, only his own panting and the boil of blood through his veins.

The room was lit solely by the faint glow of the microfilm reader. Kicking the stool aside, Sonny stood before the device and gaped with the need to understand. But as he read the headlines and stared at the photos and then turned the dial to the next page of the newspaper, there was no comprehension to be had, no possible explanations for why every story focused on his quest to find his brother.

LOCAL BOY REMAINS STEADFAST IN SEARCH FOR BROTHER

BOY SEEKS HELP FROM WITHERED OLD MAN

OUTLOOK GRIM FOR MISSING BOY

POLICE CALL OFF SEARCH FOR MISSING BOY

MORNING DOES NOT WELCOME THOSE WHO DIE, SONNY

DON'T LOOK UP, SONNY

IT'S ABOVE YOU

Sonny jolted away from the device and pointed the gun upward, but the greatest threats lurking in the cobwebs above him had eight legs and could be crushed in Sonny's palm.

Glancing back to the microfilm reader and past it, Sonny noticed several messages scrawled on the wall in red paint – messages he was nearly certain hadn't been there before. Centered among them was:

DON'T LOOK ↑

IT'S ABOVE YOU

Again Sonny was compelled to look up. And yet again he found nothing but cobwebs.

The microfilm reader began to flicker and rattle, headlines and images whizzing past, even though

THE NIGHTWOOD SONG

Sonny stood ten feet from the dial. As if the device doubled as a record player, drizzly music emitted from it – the same old woman's voice they'd heard in the woods, but this time the lyrics to "Dream a Little Dream of Me" were much different:

Night rising dark ab-ove you
Dead leaves whisper, Woe will find you
Crows staring from the white alder tree
Dream of being home, Son-ny

Leaves rained down from the webs, each one painted black: WOE, WOE, WOE, WOE. One leaf read MORNING, another featuring DOES NOT, and Sonny didn't have to scoop up the others to glean the rest.

"Let my brother go!" he screamed.

The music went silent. The microfilm reader faded to a blank, milky white screen. Sonny expected to see a photo of himself plastered on it – a photo taken from this very room – but blank it remained.

On the wall behind the desk, the upward arrow had been replaced by a downward arrow, Sonny's eyes angling to the floorboards and the black nest of hair poking up slightly from the far right corner, followed by a fleshless skull and eyeless sockets.

The faint glow failed, Sonny reeling backward and falling as the scrape of fingernails and the bony, dragging thuds of knees and elbows approached in the blackness.

"It. Will. Find. You. It. Finds. Every. One," came a dry rasp that gritted in Sonny's veins.

Thudding closer, closer, Sonny pressing himself against the wall, desperate for breath, but there were no more inches to be had between himself and it.

"Morning. Didn't. Welcome. Me. And. Not. Your. Brother. And. Not. You."

The remaining space between them was covered by a rapid series of thuds, Sonny gasping when two icy fists closed around his neck – but then the door snapped open. For a moment Sonny thought he would be shredded apart by a charging coyote, but these roars and snarls held a note of familiarity.

"Good dog! Get it!" Donnie bellowed from the doorway as Fast did battle in a hail of screams and screeches. "Tear it apart!"

A pair of yelps preceded a lengthy banshee wail, Donnie's flashlight revealing the scratching, scrabbling, rapid retreat of the shadow-form to its trapdoor, the door scraping shut just before Fast reached it.

"Sonny, are ya all right, boy?" Donnie's hands were around Sonny's cheeks, pawing him, clutching his shoulders, blinding him with the light. "Are ya hurt? Did it get to ya?"

Fast ran to Sonny's side, kissing his cheek and chin, jumping on his left shoulder, Sonny's hands coming away slick and warm with blood.

"Fast, she's hurt, Donnie! She's bleeding!"

Donnie secured her by the collar and put the light on her, the collie beginning to quiver as Donnie patted her thick fur. "You'll be all right, won't ya, ole girl? Where ya hurt, Fast, ya brave girl?"

Donnie's fingers were streaked with blood, but there was no time to determine the source.

"Sonny, help! Help me, Sonny!"

Toby's voice came from the hallway, but this time it sounded a little less like Toby than before…and a little more like the old lady whose sorrowful voice conveyed the Nightwood Songs.

Donnie started toward the hall, shotgun ready, but Sonny shouted, "Don't go, I think it's a trick!"

"But–"

"Where's Mr. Stevens?"

"We got separated. We were looking for you, and the fog, it got so heavy I couldn't see two feet ahead." He took hold of Sonny's arm. "Come on, we have to get out."

"But my brother, he's–"

Donnie shook his head. "He's not down here, Sonny. It's like you said, a trick – a horrible trick."

Stepping back into the basement hall, Fast leading the way, they were guided not by torches this time but buzzing, sickly yellowish overhead lamps. They swung gently, creakily, and all the doors to their left and right stood open now.

"Give up, Sonny," Chief Clark's voice crackled from one of the empty rooms. "Time only moves in one direction. Don't waste another second searching for shadows."

Added Mr. Incobrasa's voice: "You won't see it till it wants to be seen. And once you see it, you won't ever leave."

Mr. Omya's voice: "Don't go searching *around*. Just get out quick, and you might not be *found*."

Mama's voice came from another room, Papa's voice from another, accompanied by the faint horn of his Kenworth...and an eruption of crushed metal and smashed glass.

"It's been watching me all my life," Sonny murmured.

"Just keep moving, boy. There ain't nothing for us to find here but traps."

Sonny followed Donnie and Fast back toward the staircase, but the curving hall went too long, terminating not at the base of the stairs but a wide space with a furnace in the corner and a half-built workbench along the far wall. To the left of the workbench, a black, arched iron door clanked slowly open and banged shut, making a similar sound to the wood stove back home.

Sonny was paralyzed with dread at the sight of this thin arched door, which belonged in a castle dungeon. The darkness beyond it, though briefly seen, had delivered even greater terror – and now Sonny could hear his brother's voice behind the door.

"Help, please help," he murmured, barely audible, his voice a ghost.

"It's just a trick. Come on, Sonny."

"No, it's him. That's my brother!"

Fast sniffed frenetically around the door, springing back when Toby called again. "Help me, please."

"Toby, it's me! I'm gonna get you out!"

"Sonny?"

Tears stung his eyes. "It's me, brother, I'm here! I'm gonna get you out!"

"Hurry, it's coming! It knows you're here!"

Fast barked and leaped at the door, then stood on her hind legs and used her front paws to repeatedly scratch the black iron.

The door featured a small square window at its center, Sonny discovered. Pulling aside a wooden casing and tossing it away, Sonny stood on his tiptoes and peered through the glassless window.

A dimly lit hall. Pools of gray light scattered here and there, as if created by streetlamps. Brighter lights in the distance, perhaps one hundred feet away, where a tall, hooded form held its bony hands above an instrument of some kind. Twitching and trembling, kept about a foot apart, the hands engendered strident music as they hovered over the instrument, never contacting it.

At first, the music sounded vaguely like the opera singer Sonny had heard in the woods, but then, with a wider spacing of the hands and a faster series of twitches, it was reminiscent of a coyote's howl. Much slower now with the movements, It delivered the carnival music, Its face changing as well, no longer hooded but hatted: Chief Clark's peaked cap; Chief Clark's worn, tired eyes; Chief Clark's saggy jowls and heavily wrinkled neck.

The fiend moved closer, the instrument sliding out ahead of it as if fixed to a rolling platform, the song ranging from a piano to a harmonica to a violin, the faces shifting from Chief Clark to Pastor Mahone to Mr. Incobrasa to a pair of ravens staring at Sonny with yellow and red jewels for eyes.

Twenty feet away. Fifteen and ten and five feet away, and now the only music came in the form of whispers: "Morning does not welcome those who die," it repeated briskly, the face transforming within seconds from Mama to Papa to Toby, and finally Sonny.

THE NIGHTWOOD SONG

The face was just inches from his own now, pressed up against the small, glassless window slot, watching him, and he might as well have been staring into a mirror. When he adjusted slightly, it matched his movements. When he blinked, it blinked, but those eyes were not his own, too dark and dead.

"Sonny," it whispered icily, stealing whatever words might have slipped across his tongue. "You can go, Sonny. We will let you leave, and trouble you no longer."

"No. My brother."

A slight smile, barely perceptible. "Stay at your own peril."

"I won't leave without Toby."

The smile widened a little, accompanied by a faint violin and the Kenworth's horn and the sound of distant sirens. It went on staring at Sonny a while longer, without nodding or blinking or moving whatsoever, just staring with the visage of Sonny Winters.

It even mirrored the tears in his eyes, but then Donnie was at his side, asking questions about what he saw. When Sonny glanced back through the small opening, there was only darkness beyond the door…and the distant hum of "Dream a Little Dream of Me."

"Sonny, what's in there? Who are you talking to?"

"It," Sonny murmured, feeling as if he'd been awakened from a long sleep devoid of rest. "It's behind that door."

Fast roared and attacked the door, jumping higher than Sonny's head, her eyes maddened with the need to protect.

"You can't hurt us!" Sonny reacted, pounding the door. "We have the Lord in our hearts! He protects us from all evil!"

Wind stirred in the corners of the room, whipping dead leaves off the workbench and nudging tools hanging from hooks on the pegboard. Sonny didn't need to scoop up the leaves to know the single word painted on each one, nor did he require a closer look at the folded yellow raincoat on the bench to know it was his.

Sonny began the Lord's Prayer. Closing his eyes, he pretended he was in church, with Mama and Papa and Toby surrounding him and Pastor Mahone behind the pulpit.

Sonny did not complete his prayer, for the arched door flew open and Toby tumbled out, his clothes torn, his hands and face bloodied, his skin dangerously sallow.

A pair of rusty chains angled out from the darkness like vipers, but they weren't meant for Toby, instead winding around Donnie's ankles and hauling him down, then dragging him toward the door, his shotgun trailing behind him from its sling. Sonny and Fast tried to pull him back, Sonny taking hold of his wrist, Fast tugging his coat, but the chains wrested him away and stole him through the door, gun and all.

Before Sonny or Fast could reach the door, the arched menace clanked shut with the finality of the first crow's caw following a funeral.

"*Donnie!*" Peering through the small frame, Sonny saw only darkness.

"He took God with him to war," hissed an ancient malice from the other side. "Came back alone, came back alone, came back alone, came back alone."

The whispers and shuffling footsteps and clinking chains faded down the darkened hall, yielding to weighty silence – strong enough to stop a heart.

"Sonny!" Finding his feet, Toby launched into his arms, Sonny wondering if it was real.

"Is it you, Toby? Is it really you?"

His brother sobbed, Sonny touching his blood-crusted, dirt-smeared cheeks, squeezing his shoulders, pulling him back into an embrace.

Fast whimpered at the door and scratched it repeatedly, then stretched out on her stomach, head resting on her forepaws, waiting.

"Sonny, run!" Mr. Stevens shouted, appearing at the base of the original staircase, the room having changed again, the workbench and arched door vanished.

With a series of jostling groans, beams turned themselves loose from the ceiling and collapsed on John Stevens, knocking him flat. Blood ran from his head, Sonny helping to free him from the wreckage, but more beams fell around them, shadowy hands reaching up through the debris…grasping, clawing, enlarging, clarifying into full forms and then faces, dozens of voracious faces.

"Run, Sonny! Get your brother out of here!"

The nearest beast, a wolfish face of shadows and mist, snapped its jaws at Sonny and Toby, but John Stevens dove toward its ever-expanding maw, drawing the other fiends like piranhas.

Sonny reached for Stevens but could no longer see him amid a thickening swirl of shadows and screams – not just those of a single man, legions of screams spiraling in trapped, perpetual agony.

A hand on Sonny's arm, tugging. Toby's hand. His next yank jolted Sonny just far enough to elude a falling beam ticketed for his skull.

"Come on, Sonny! Run!"

Discarding the gun, trailing his brother and Fast up the stairs, Sonny glanced back and saw a cast of grinning faces around a collapsed, lifeless John Stevens. One of the faces, blood ringed around its mouth, belonged to Roger Staley, who Sonny had beaten up at the Fourth of July Strawberry Festival four months back, in an altogether different world.

"Run, Sonny!" Roger chirped with a singsong giggle. "Run, Toby! Run, Fast! All of you best run *fast!*"

The serenade pursued them through the Charnel house, but Toby's exhausted legs wouldn't take him far. When he fell in the hall leading to the foyer, Sonny carried him and followed Fast through the fog, ignoring the clash of music all around them – violin and piano and soprano and even accordion – not even daring to turn around when icy breaths kissed his nape.

Approaching the front door, the music fell abruptly silent. Now, all Sonny heard was his name whispered in his ear – "Sonny, Sonny, please stay, Sonny, we want to play, Sonny" – everything else fading off, even his own footsteps, and then he was stumbling onto the porch and leaping off the steps, stopping only when he reached the edge of the woods.

Above them, the moon was high and bright, penetrating the night wilderness but only a little. Risking a backward glance, Sonny did not see a house or a sign announcing CHARNEL. He didn't even see the ruins of a house or the hint of a foundation, only a moonlit clearing fronted by a foggy pond.

Fast barked tepidly into the woods, then eyed the clearing.

"Come on, girl," Sonny called, carrying his brother into the woods.

But Fast wouldn't budge. Lying flat again at the base of a tree, she studied the place where the house had been, her whimpers still heard several minutes later, when it was only Sonny, Toby, and the Nightwood.

Chapter 32

"Where are we, Sonny? What happened?"

Still carrying his brother, Sonny panted and grimaced and tripped over a fallen branch, collapsing and spilling Toby into the brush.

The moon peeked down at them with pity, but its light wasn't sufficient to show the way. Sonny's flashlight was dead, his compass equally useless, for he had no orientation out here in the wilderness, clueless as to whether Durant's place was north or south of here. And after everything he'd seen, he barely trusted his own senses anymore, half-expecting to blink and find himself alone.

"It's really you, Toby, right? You're my little brother?"

"Uh-course," Toby murmured, closing his eyes as Sonny held him.

"What do we do on Sunday mornings, Toby?"

"Go to church with Mama."

"And who's my chem teacher, you know, the really tough one who gives us piles of homework?"

"Mr. Incobrasa."

Smiling with tears, Sonny slid a hand through his brother's hair and pulled him close.

"Pray with me, Toby." Sonny began the Lord's Prayer, his tears flowing stronger when Toby joined him, and together they prayed and shivered and held firm to each other in the brush.

"What do you remember?" Sonny said a while later.

Their eyes having slowly adjusted to the moonlit wilderness, they'd followed the sounds of a stream and quenched their thirst, Toby drinking too much and puking, Sonny settling with his back against an oak tree and pulling his brother against him.

"It's okay. I'm here now. You can tell me." Sonny removed his flannel jacket and hat, giving them to Toby to stay warm.

"I don't remember much," Toby murmured. "The house."

"What did you eat this whole time?"

"Dunno."

"How were you hurt?"

"Dunno," he shivered. "When can we go home?"

"Soon. Real soon."

"I'm cold."

"I know. Me too."

"We won't last the night out here. Too cold."

Toby's words worsened the numbness in Sonny's nose and cheeks. It had begun as an itch and throbbed into a dull pain, but now even a slap to his face might go unfelt.

Thin rustling in the woods to their left, across the stream. Louder, closer. Sonny stood, ready to engage an attacker and tell Toby to run.

Closer, a shadowy form splashing across the stream, heading straight for them, tackling Sonny, but he wasn't greeted by fangs but licks. Kisses.

"Fast! You found us, ole girl!"

The collie danced around him and then licked Toby, who curled up and protected his face with his arms.

"It's okay, Toby. This is Fast – she's a great ole girl. She knows when it's coming. She'll keep us safe."

Fast yipped and snorted as if in agreement, then made a series of starts and stops, seeming to beckon the Winters brothers. Sonny scooped Toby into his arms once more, Fast barking often as she set off slowly into the deeper woods, looking back frequently to make sure the boys were following her.

"Show us the way home, ole girl. That's it. You know where it's at."

Each time Sonny got himself twisted up in a thicket or bogged down on a slippery hill, Fast stopped and waited patiently. Occasionally her barks were replaced with furious snarls, Sonny glimpsing shadows of myriad shapes and sizes receding into dark hollows carved out of the moonlit woods like caves. A distant crunch of footsteps followed them indefatigably, but Sonny kept his gaze mostly on Fast, his arms burning and trembling.

"I can walk," Toby said when Sonny went at last to his knees. "I can do it, Sonny. It'll be faster."

"Are you sure?"

He nodded feverishly, his eyes dilated beneath the bright November moon. Up ahead, Fast barked and wended, Sonny checking the compass often and noticing that she maintained a southwesterly pace.

Toby moved sluggishly, though far quicker than Sonny had been while carrying him. They crested a steeper hill and angled more sharply to the west on the downside, the stately trees thinning, the moonlight brightening as they stepped onto a path.

"You did it, Fast! You found it!"

They were on the old logging road Donnie had shown him, the scrapped frame of the pickup truck waiting just up ahead like a crouched gargoyle. It shimmered softly in the moonlight, Fast picking up speed but then stopping with a sharp snarl. She turned back, staring past them, Sonny becoming aware of the thin music prevailing over the wind.

Well down the road, easily over two hundred feet back, a large hunched form was barely visible. Staggering toward them, it produced an instrument from its cloak and spaced its hands into a similar hover as before, all while Fast stood with her chest puffed out and her teeth bared.

"The carnival music," Toby murmured once the fresh tune ensued along the wind.

They stood briefly mesmerized by the music, Fast nudging Sonny's leg and then jumping against his hip, knocking him off balance. By the time he shook himself free of the trance, the composer stood fifty feet away, its instrument set atop a stand.

The instrument looked like a wooden box with a bunch of dials on it, no bigger than Mama's jewelry box, and when the fiend's twigs-for-hands hovered over it, the result was a whining thrum followed by Mr. Incobrasa's voice: "A theremin. It's quite the strange and complicated instrument."

"Run!" Sonny spun his brother and shoved him into motion, Fast racing out ahead of them, the theremin warbling and twanging behind them like a radio seeking a signal.

Opposing gusts encroached on the path, warm and cold, and each time Sonny glanced back the demon was a little closer, its cloak comprised of black leaves, its arms bristled with branches and thorns.

All around them, wooden javelins began to rain down, every tree sounding like the Groaning Tree. To Sonny's right, a vine lashed out and twisted itself into a noose, but he ducked away from its lasso.

Up ahead, Fast angled through the woods toward the track that would lead to Donnie Durant's east gate, still too far to go, much too far.

It'll catch us! We won't make it!

But Sonny was impelled by a sudden memory that silenced the Nightwood Song. Perhaps it wasn't a memory at all, for he could hear Papa's words as clearly as their footsteps and Fast's barks.

"Son, there's gonna come a time when you have to push through the pain. The measure of a man is how hard he's willing to push when it hurts. Does he quit when the pain comes, or does he keep pushing for what he wants?"

Sonny couldn't be sure of which road had seen Papa speak these words – perhaps Route 66, perhaps the long road up to Portland, perhaps even Purgatory Road – but they'd managed to stay with him all these years and now opened themselves anew like pearls. He could hear Donnie Durant's words as well, steeling him for war – but he didn't know how to fight this enemy. All he could do was run.

Just keep going! Don't look back!

The taste of blood boiled into his throat, his knees feeling like they might splinter. Toby went down ahead of him, Sonny lifting him into his arms and somehow returning to his previous speed, faster, faster, leaping over a log and hurtling through saplings, almost catching up to Fast.

THE NIGHTWOOD SONG

Soon, they were back on the long track. Much earlier, when they'd taken this path into the woods, the moon had been on the rise. Sonny and Fast had been with Donnie then, Toby still trapped, but now the moon hung high and bright above them. It must've been nearing midnight, but this thought wouldn't pass Sonny's mind until several minutes later, long after they reached the gate, Sonny struggling to unlatch it, struggling and fumbling so badly that the demon caught up, its theremin keening shrilly, its arms reaching, its jaws snapping like castanets.

Finally, Sonny popped the latch and shoved open the gate. Fast and Toby spilled through, then Sonny, who swung the gate nearly shut, its progress stopped by a mass of black mist.

The nearest light was extinguished with a hiss, two more lights exploding into sparks and then darkness.

"Run, Toby! Get to the tent!"

Sonny strained to oppose the immense weight pressing against the gate, throngs of black-rotted tendrils and hands scraping his face, clutching his arms.

Breaking free, staggering backward, he noticed in a blur of recognition that the demon wore his yellow raincoat…but then the other lamps scattered about Donnie's property began to fail, one by one, night closing over the yard like a coffin lid.

Sonny dashed for the tent, a stampede thundering after him along the boardwalk.

He dove through the unzipped flaps, finding Toby and Fast huddled inside, Toby's face poking out from blankets.

The pursuers did not enter behind him, instead swarming multitudinously around the tent, this time in the form of bats.

"What do we do, Sonny? We're trapped!"

Rushing the zipper up, Sonny expected a massive hand to plunge through the flaps and haul him into the screeching-whispering-chittering night grave, but he managed to seal the tent and spring back toward Toby.

Donnie had left two of the battery-powered lanterns on, Sonny activating two others, and they waited there for many minutes, listening to the hungry shriek of bats and wind and fishers and coyotes, predators of all forms congregating just beyond the tent, surrounding their prey.

Kneeling, Sonny kept one arm around Toby, the other around Fast. He watched the collie closely, her head darting from one corner to another, but she stayed perfectly silent.

Not a single glow burned beyond the tent, nothing to reveal the besieging silhouettes. Perhaps the darkness had even snuffed out the moon.

"What's out there?" Toby finally whispered.

"It. Evil."

THE NIGHTWOOD SONG

"What is it?"

"Just keep quiet. I don't think it can come in here. Maybe it'll pass."

Fast began to growl deeply. Moving toward the zipped entrance, she crouched off to the side and let out a series of savage barks.

Despite Fast's fury, Sonny could hear the approaching footsteps down the boardwalk, perfectly measured in sets of three before reaching the next landing – clack, clack, clack, THUD; clack, clack, clack, THUD – and then Sonny could hear fresh whispers. They came from just beyond the entrance, but also to Sonny's immediate left and right, hot, reeking breaths in his ears, the lanterns doused all at once.

"Morning. Does. Not. Welcome. Those. Who. *Die!*"

This last word was uttered in a low, menacing voice – Donnie Durant's voice – and Toby yelped as something began to drag him out from under the blankets.

Fast attacked, setting off a vicious war that sounded like two coyotes sinking fangs into each other, but still Toby was dragged toward the entrance, the zipper coming open, the flaps forming a threshold between darkness and absolute darkness.

With one hand, Sonny blindly latched onto his brother's ankle. With the other, he strained for

Donnie's pillow, pushed it aside, groped for the flashlight Donnie had said he always kept there.

But he found nothing, nothing, swiping and grasping but there was nothing, only his brother's screams and Fast's roars cannoning through the darkness.

A trace of cold metal caught the edge of Sonny's fingertips, but he wouldn't reach it if he held firm to Toby. Letting go of his brother's leg, he dove for the flashlight and struggled to find the switch, finally engaging it and lashing the light toward the entrance, where *it* held Toby in a coil of vines and briars at the gateway to inescapable darkness. It had Papa's eyes, Donnie's beard, Chief Clark's peaked cap, a raven's beak, and features from countless others, perhaps every soul to be sighted in the Nightwood.

But when the light struck its eyes, it shrieked maniacally and released Toby, his face cut open in multiple places.

Trailing chains of bramble behind it, the fiend fled into darkness, Fast chasing it. But after a few moments her barks died away and laughter rose.

"You won't have the light for-*ever*, Son-*ny*," the old woman crooned with low melancholy, her voice encircling the tent but also echoing distantly. "Tiiiime moves in one die-*rection*, and morning welcomes not the dead." The tune took on a cheery mood, the woman's voice lifting and quickening: "Darkness will find, darkness will find, darkness will fiiiind your heart. Darkness will kill, darkness will kill, darkness will killlll your God."

THE NIGHTWOOD SONG

"Cover your ears, Toby! Don't listen to it!"

Sonny pulled his brother against his chest, the music slowly wilting away. Returning to the tent, Fast licked her wounds and let out an intermittent growl.

For a while they prayed, and then they simply stared and listened to the rise and fade of the wind, Sonny wondering if his heart would hammer his bones down to splinters.

The lanterns still refused to work, but the flashlight stayed true for several hours, finally weakening and dying as the wind resurged.

Beyond Donnie's piss-stenched tent, the blackness was no longer absolute, but Sonny knew there wasn't nearly enough light in the sky to venture out. He could picture the blue predawn sky, lightest in the east, darkest in the west. Now that Donnie's lights had been extinguished and the moon had set, the brightest light would be provided by the open sky stretching across to the wooded hills, everything else a gloomy maze, trees spearing up all around them. Watching.

"Sonny, I hafta pee."

"You can go in the corner."

"But–"

"We wait for sunup. We can't go out."

Toby spattered in the corner, Fast frowning. A while later, voices flared up in the distance, belonging to Chief Clark and other searchers.

"Quiet! It's a trick!" Sonny urged after Toby called for help. "*It* wants us to go out there."

But the voices were getting louder, closer, and Fast wasn't barking, instead sitting bolt straight and wagging her tail.

In a moment, the blue flash of police lights penetrated the west side of the tent.

"I'll go," Sonny said. "Stay here. Don't move until I come back, got it?"

"Uh-huh," Toby nodded.

Armed only with his dead flashlight, Sonny unzipped the tent and poked his head out. The western sky was a mottled canvas of gray and early blue, the mountain slumbering in low sheets of fog. To the north, the Groaning Tree creaked a little louder than usual, perhaps offering a warning.

Searching the near-blinding police lights in the driveway, Sonny spotted Chief Clark and another officer approaching the trellised gate. But there was a third face among them, a bloody soldier whose helmet was pulled down low, turning his eyes into slits. He spoke something in German that the others couldn't hear, his glare fixed on Sonny.

THE NIGHTWOOD SONG

The wind lashed with its greatest force yet, knocking Clark and the other officer off balance as they passed beneath the trellis and climbed the muddy hill.

The soldier did not cross the threshold of the gate. Still eyeing Sonny, arms at his sides, he murmured, "Morning does not welcome those who die," his words somehow audible above the wind.

Nodding solemnly, the soldier turned and slumped toward the southern woods, his gray eyes never leaving Sonny. When he reached the trees, he was received by a thin mist that rendered his crunching footsteps silent, Sonny no longer afraid because morning was deepening and would not welcome this specter or any other.

Chief Clark finally reached Sonny and launched plenty of questions, but he ignored them, watching the woods.

"Sonny, what're ya lookin' at, boy? Pay attention!"

"He's in shock," the other officer said.

Clark held Sonny's shoulders. "It's time to go home, boy. Time to–Jesus Lord! It can't be!"

Sonny glanced back to find Toby emerging from the tent.

"How…how did ya find him?" Clark managed.

"Took him from the Devil," Sonny whispered. "The Devil's in them woods, Chief."

Chapter 33

Both boys spent the day and night in the hospital, Sonny insisting that Mama stay with Toby.

"Don't let him be alone. It'll come back, Mama – he can't be alone."

Mama nodded, her face pale. "The Lord will keep us safe, all of us."

"He will, Mama, but He also gives us the strength to keep ourselves safe. Go now. Be with Toby."

Chief Clark returned after dinner, bringing word that John Stevens had been found dead in the woods.

"Terrible thing," Clark grunted. "A branch fell and got him in the head."

"*It*," Sonny whispered.

"What was that, boy? Speak up."

"*It* got him. He died to protect me and Toby."

Clark nodded blandly, either failing to hear Sonny's words or ignoring them altogether. "Damn unluckiest thing you'd ever see, boy. He was a good man, John Stevens. He must've figured out what Durant was up to and came lookin' for you boys."

"Donnie wasn't up to anything, sir. He helped us get out."

"Sonny, he abducted your brother and kept him in those woods – it's plain to see. Don't you worry, though, we're gonna find that bastard and hold him accountable. He might have even caused John's death and made it *look* like an accident."

Clark and another officer asked Sonny about when he'd last seen Durant, but there was no use in answering honestly. After a while, Sonny took to claiming he couldn't remember things, Clark nodding skeptically and promising a thorough investigation.

"Ya don't need to protect him, Sonny. That man can't hurt you boys no more." "How's Fast doing?" Sonny said. "Who?" Arms crossed, Clark squinted with confusion. "Fast. Mr. Durant's dog. How is she?"

He shrugged. "They took that mongrel to the pound. S'pose they'll hafta put her down, with those injuries."

Sonny cried and prayed after Clark left. He prayed for Donnie, prayed for John Stevens, prayed for Fast, but his words felt like a single flashlight in the dark, windy woods.

And all he could see when he closed his eyes was John's ruined body and Donnie being dragged through that hellish arched door in the Charnel house. All he could hear were the Devil's whispers: *Came back alone, came back alone, came back alone...Morning does not welcome those who die...* Each time Sonny slid a little closer to sleep, the dial of memory would turn again and flash the horrors across his eyelids like microfilm images.

Chapter 34

Over a month later, on Christmas Day, Sonny fired up Big Bertha and lifted Fast into the passenger seat. Mama had allowed him to adopt the collie, with strict conditions, including an order that Sonny pay for Fast's care and tend to her daily constitutional. He'd already exhausted his funds and borrowed from Mama to cover Fast's veterinary bills, and she would need continued treatment for several months, Pastor Mahone and others having alleviated some of the burden with donations.

Last week, Toby bought a pair of bowls and a red bandana for the collie at Sal's General – an early Christmas gift – and Fast sure did look sharp with the checkered pattern resembling Sonny's beat-up flannel jacket.

They were partners, forevermore. They would look after each other now that Donnie Durant had gone off to war in the dark.

"Look, ole girl. We match."

Sonny smiled thinly, Fast smiling back and then nuzzling Sonny's face.

"Oops, how could I forget?" Sonny said when the collie brushed a paw against the passenger window.

Cranking down the window but only halfway, Sonny's smile widened when Fast poked her head out, her gums flapping in the breeze when they set out on Purgatory Road. They passed the Route 31 entrance and moved north through a thin fog, the ground piled with over a foot of snow from last week's blizzard.

Even Bertha couldn't chug through the snow all the way up Donnie's driveway, the rink of white disturbed only by a few ribbons of footprints from Sonny's previous visits.

Stepping out of the truck, Sonny set Fast down and they bounded through the snow together, Fast following in the prints cleared by Sonny's boots.

Panting and rubbing his ruddy cheeks, Sonny hauled the west gate open just far enough for them to slip through. Now it was Fast leading the way, launching up to the boardwalk; all around them, snow-caked trees climbed toward a softly blue sky.

By the time Donnie's lawyer arrived an hour later, parking his car in the road and carefully venturing up the treacherous slope, Sonny and Fast were sitting around the fire pit, Sonny drinking whiskey, Fast racing off to her rock to bark at the slowly ascending visitor.

Grimacing and struggling and cursing as he neared the top of the driveway, the lawyer must have felt like he was carrying cinderblocks in his briefcase.

"Goddamn it! Jesus Christ!" he raged after slipping to a knee, Sonny hurrying down the hill to help him, Fast approving the visitor and falling silent.

"Hi there, Mister. I'm Sonny Winters."

"Lloyd Laithwaite," the thin, mustached man panted.

"Pleasure to meet you, Mr. Laithwaite." Sonny took up a shovel and got to work on a path. "Follow me to the front – I'll clear the way a bit."

Inside, Laithwaite eyed the clutter nervously, as though something might pop out and attack him.

"Donnie was a very busy man," Sonny explained. "He didn't have much time for indoor work."

"Evidently not," Laithwaite nodded, Sonny guiding him to the dining room table, where Donnie Durant's hospital bills and other documents had been scattered about, just before they'd found their way to the flames.

Sonny breathed back tears and sat before the table, Laithwaite removing his coat and wrapping it around a chair. He wore a gray jacket and vest above a blue tie, his pocket watch shining in the dim light.

"I apologize for conducting business on the holiday, Mr. Laithwaite."

The attorney waved a hand. "No bother. It's just another day to me."

"I would offer you water, sir, but it comes out a little rusty and doesn't sit great with the stomach."

"We best steer clear of it, then," Laithwaite chuckled. "Now, as I explained over the phone, Donald Durant named you the sole beneficiary of his entire estate."

The attorney laid out a series of documents whose words would keep Sonny flipping through the dictionary for hours. "Because of your status as a minor, Mr. Durant listed your mother as the custodian of all specified assets until you come of age, whereupon the entire estate will become yours to manage."

"Yes, sir."

"You must bring each of these forms to your mother to sign."

"I will, sir."

"Of course, this bequeathal is contingent upon Mr. Durant officially being declared as *presumed dead* in five years' time under California State Law."

Sonny wiped his eyes. "Yes, sir. I understand, sir."

"The house is fully paid off, and Mr. Durant's debts will be covered by his estate."

"Even his hospital bills?"

"Among others."

"If you don't mind me asking, Mr. Laithwaite, why was he in debt if he had so much money saved up?"

The attorney twirled his gold pen. "As I'm sure you came to discover, Mr. Durant's penchants for both the battle and the bottle caused him to do some…peculiar things. The Veterans Administration was one of his many foes."

"Yes, sir, it certainly was."

Sonny drifted away for a time, hearing Donnie's words, not his lawyer's words. The memories gave him a smile as he lifted the whiskey bottle to his lips and fended off an urge to feed all of these papers to the fire pit.

"Sonny? Are you listening, young man?"

"Yes, sir. I'm sorry, sir."

Laithwaite frowned at the bottle, his reading glasses set over his nose. "You shouldn't be drinking at your age."

Sonny nodded. "It keeps the pneumonia away, sir."

Laithwaite lifted his eyebrows, then returned to the documents. "Anyway, I'll need you to sign here, here, and here," he muttered, making little exes with his gold pen.

When the pen was in Sonny's hand, he felt like a pharaoh, but it had nothing to do with the wealth Mr. Laithwaite kept mentioning. Donnie had trusted him with his family's home – the only home he'd ever known – and soon it would be in Sonny's care…Fast's Rock and the Groaning Tree and the east gate, the rusty skidder off to the north and the ramshackle shed to the south, even the nasty latrine. It would all be

Sonny's responsibility, Donnie trusting him to keep the darkness away.

"Congratulations, young man. You're going to be a very affluent boy, Mr. Winters. Use your assets well."

"I will, sir. Thank you for your help."

Sonny showed his guest out and helped him down the driveway, his head already a blur of thoughts. Grandpa had returned from Engelhard Asylum in time for Thanksgiving, and he'd been whooping Sonny at chess ever since. Toby was healed up and well of spirit, though he couldn't remember much about his disappearance (and sometimes he woke up screaming and sweating). Sonny would need to take a good deal of time with him, nurture him back, but they would do it. They were the Winters brothers and they could do anything.

Meanwhile, returning to Donnie's dinner table and scratching Fast behind the ears, Sonny slid his other hand beneath his shirt and took hold of the cross pendant Pastor Mahone had given him during the Sunday service following Toby's return. At first, the pendant had hung weightily from Sonny's neck, but now the physical weight was unfelt; its weight of significance, however, guided his every thought and decision.

"We gotta do this just right, Fast, ole girl."

Fast eyed the front door, then the basement door, her gaze fixing on the latter, her mouth closing, her features darkening into a scowl.

"Fast, we gotta bless this place and protect it forever from the evil. The Nightwood Song'll play again real soon, I bet, and we gotta be safe from it."

It was Christmas morning, the town abuzz with merriment and celebration, but the only carol sounding along Donnie Durant's property was that of the north wind. For a moment, opening the dining room window and letting in the cold, Sonny thought he could hear another song rising over the wind.

But it was quickly gone, if it had ever been there to begin with, and Fast was at his side now, ready for lunch.

"Let's go home, ole girl." Sonny gathered the stack of documents that had been left for him. "We'll get this all figured out, and we'll make Donnie proud."

THE NIGHTWOOD SONG

Thanks for reading, everyone! Be sure to check out the sequel to The Nightwood Song, Never Let It Out, followed by Burn, Do Not Read!